NOSTALGIC RAIN

A.S. ALTABTABAI

To my mom

Chapter One

Voices

The ceiling, barely visible in the dark room, greeted Leland. He didn't know how long he'd slept, but that didn't matter much. It was summer. A thump resounded in the atmosphere, and it mixed with the squawking of birds and the chirping of grasshoppers. Leland rose from the sweat-soaked sheets of his bed and went to the window overlooking their small house garden. The sky was a mixture of red, orange, and yellow on one side, where the egg-yolk sun rose, and black on the other. In between the two, various degrees of blue adorned the horizon. *It's dawn.*

Be it summer, spring, winter, or autumn, all dawns in Temblewood City were cold. Leland put on his red hoodie, the one he got last year on his sixteenth birthday from Jennifer, his best friend, and stomped down the wooden abode's creaky stairs. Leland's heavy-lidded brown eyes skimmed the familiar dilapidated furniture of the living room, but he didn't dare complain. It was his grandfather's house, and he had lived here with his mother and two little siblings for ten years now since his father had died.

Today, he didn't want to drink coffee. Drinking coffee meant staying awake and alert for a long period, and he didn't want any of that. He wished he could sleep for the rest of this summer. Instead of coffee, Leland headed to Jaime's Café, a place more popular than Starbucks in Temblewood City, and bought a cup of hot chocolate. The cup was so hot he had to wrap it with two layers of napkins.

This summer was different from the last. Last year, he'd seen Jennifer and Dylan almost every day. He'd gone hiking and horse riding and fishing, and he'd camped on Mount Lamen, which wasn't a good idea—they had ended up lost for two days with cops searching for them. But now he was running from everyone and everything. Jennifer and Dylan were calling every day, and he'd been creating excuses to be alone. But he missed them. A lot. The most awful thing in life is changing into someone worse but not realizing it.

Leland sat on a wooden bench not so far from Jaime's Café and gazed at the road, which was gradually getting more crowded with cars and people. A young man wearing a black suit and a red tie sat beside him. The man, who genuinely smelled good, scrolled down his phone's screen, checking his Twitter timeline. *Yeah. That's what normal people do. They work and they socialize and they live.* Leland missed that. Fear can paralyze one's mind and create thousands of fake barriers.

A raindrop fell on Leland's cup. He stared at the gray clouds in the sky, and an army of a million other drops flooded the ground. That's why he hated Temblewood. It would rain any time of year, and Leland despised rain. He knew it was going to be a bad day. *All rainy days are bad.* The day his father died had been a day of heavy rain and dark memories he wished he could forget. But that was impossible because it was impossible not to have rain throughout the year. And every time it rained, a powerful resurrection of that day occurred.

Leland realized the suited man beside him had left at some point during his deep and useless thinking session. It seemed Leland was the only one on the street now. He put the hoodie cap on and walked underneath shop awnings on his way back home. Now that he thought about it, Leland hadn't learned much from his absent father.

But there was one sentence that kept ringing in his head. Leland wasn't even sure how or when or why his father had told it to him: "*The more you feed your fear, the more you become imprisoned by it.*"

***

Karla and Fred giggled and ran in the corridor. *They've grown up really fast. I can't believe they're starting to write and read already.* Karla opened the door wide and nestled between Leland's arms. She curled and made herself comfortable in his hands.

"You can't touch me now!" she told Fred, sticking her tongue out.

"You're cheating!" Fred replied, his palm on his waist.

"Hey, you two," Leland said. "You're supposed to be in your beds now, aren't you?"

"We're waiting for Aunt Abbey!" Karla said. "Mom said we can stay up late tonight."

Leland had totally forgotten that. His aunt, Abbey, was coming back to Temblewood from Todland, a city five hours away by plane. She worked as a nurse there. The last time he'd seen her was a year ago when she came for New Year's Eve. She'd brought them two bags of Made-In-Todland-Only candies. Leland hoped she'd bring them again this time.

Leland's room was the smallest in the house. In one corner was his bed and in the other was a desk and a bookshelf with many Xbox games and a few novels. The only good thing about the room was the window that overlooked the street.

Fred toured Leland's room. He flipped the pages of a book he could barely carry and then dropped it when the doorbell rang. It was more of a noisy croak rather than a musical sound.

Abbey had arrived.

***

Leland's grandma, glued to her usual spot on the worn rocking chair she'd bought right after Leland's birth, glimpsed him for a moment and then rolled her eyes back to the TV.

"Where have you been all day?" she complained, switching channels. "Your aunt is here, for God's sake."

On the table in the living room sat a cake with 'Welcome Home' written on it. The living room was lit by an old, handcrafted chandelier, but it did its job quite well. Leland hugged his aunt. She hadn't changed much.

"How's everything?" Leland asked.

"Perfect!" She replied, taking a bite of her cake. "Everything is too perfect!"

"Great. I'm glad." He took a seat beside her. Fred and Karla were on the ground playing rock, paper, scissors. His grandfather, Richard, was listening to the news, his ears touching the radio's speaker.

"What about you?" Abbey asked.

"I'm fine," Leland replied, faking a smile.

"No, he's not," Leland's mother said, cutting cake for Fred and Karla, pretending not to care much about the issue. "Something's wrong with him. He hardly leaves his room."

Leland's face flushed. He felt stupid for not realizing his mother must have felt something was wrong with him. This meant Dylan and Jennifer, his friends, likely also noticed.

"No, it's just—" Leland said, attempting to fake an excuse.

"Is he always alone?" Abbey asked.

"Almost," Maria, Leland's mother, replied.

"And he's not eating a lot?"

"Yes."

Leland's heart raced. There's no way Abbey would know what he'd been through lately. She'd been away, and he made sure no one knew.

"And he doesn't talk much?" Abbey asked.

"Yeah. Only a little," Maria answered.

Abbey clapped her hands and cried, "He's in love!"

All eyes turned toward Leland. But he was relieved. She knew nothing after all. Leland pretended her assumptions were correct. He gazed down and said nothing in reply.

"There's nothing to be ashamed of, Leland. We've all been through this before," Aunt Abbey said, and then her voice dropped to a whisper. "And don't chicken out. Women hate that."

Leland didn't know how to reply, so, rather awkwardly and loudly enough that everyone stared at him again, he said, "I like her."

Okay. That's enough for today. Leland had paid his social dues and now he had to leave. Embarrassed, Leland said, "I gotta go."

And he went back to his room.

***

Leland collapsed into his bed with *Les Miserables* in his hand. He'd bought it a month ago from Harry's Bookstore, a local shop at the end of the street. Leland read a book or two per year, but he wished he could dedicate more time to reading. He read some pages then put the book on the bedside table. With the lights on and the window opened, Leland dozed off without realizing it. Deep in his sleep, Leland woke up, sweating and trembling in fear. His breath quickened and his heart hammered against his chest. It had happened for the fifth time this week.

Voices—hundreds of thousands of throats— whispered in Leland's ears and mumbled words he couldn't understand. And it seemed he was the only one hearing them.

For God's sake, what the hell is going on?

Chapter Two

Midnight Journey

To everyone else, it was just another day. To Leland, it was hell. Haunted by dreadful, creepy voices for days, Leland wondered if they were real or if he was on a bullet train on his way to psychosis. The latter seemed more convincing. He sluggishly went to the bathroom and let hot water stream down his body.

Leland had established a rule to himself a while ago: If you have a secret, then keep it to yourself. If it's hard for you to keep it to yourself, then it's harder for others to keep the secret too.

But rules are created to be broken.

Leland decided he *must* tell someone about his secret. *Jennifer.* When his father died, Leland told only Jennifer. And he didn't regret it.

Leland made himself tea, still continuing his rebellion against coffee, and then collapsed into his desk chair. Strongly doubting the usefulness of this method in his case, Leland began googling. The Internet had many relevant topics (though not really): a psychotic man heard his dead daughter's voice every day, a serial killer whispered words into his victims' ears before killing them, and an old woman claimed she was haunted by ghosts. *Well.* That wasn't what Leland searched for. But there it was, ironically on the second page of search results, the page no one cares about:

30-year-old employee quits job, claims he 'hears voices no one else could hear.'

But it was only a title with no text. Reading the comments wasn't a good idea, though. Most people said he should have had mental therapy and that he must be arrested for being "too dangerous for the people around him." Few felt sorry for the man. This made Leland sure he must not speak publically about his secret. People need a hot topic to babble about, no matter how much it hurts others. And Leland didn't want to give them what they wanted.

The day went by as another day without him telling anyone. He was so close to telling Jennifer, but then what he'd read on the Internet had turned him off. If he was questioning his sanity, what would Jennifer think?

Nothing exciting happened that day, except that Aunt Abbey had taken Fred and Karla out, and the house had become too quiet for the first time in weeks. In fact, nothing exciting or new had happened in his life since his father's death, except the second marriage of his mom to a man named Jason—which ended traumatically for Leland's mom after Jason dumped them the same year Fred had been born.

Leland put his head on his cold pillow. He hated this part of the day the most. The voices haunted him, particularly at night. Not necessarily while he slept, but always in the night.

School would start two days from now, and the only thing Leland was sure about was that he wasn't ready at all. Being a senior meant he had to fight so hard to reserve a seat in a proper college. With all the mess in his mind, Leland could only hope for a job in McDonald's or Starbucks. And that's not the career he pictured himself in. He imagined himself wearing a white coat and roaming a hospital, or, when he didn't want to be too optimistic, wearing a red tie and lying to people about how good the company he worked for was. Leland wouldn't mind working for Harry's Bookstore though. That was free access to a countless number of books, if the owner was nice.

Moonlight sneaked into his room through holes in an old curtain. Wishing it could be another night without terror, Leland hid under a thick blanket and closed his eyes. He dreamed of a dragon carrying thousands of people on its back heading to Earth. And then there was a period of nothingness. But that didn't last too long before the voices crept in on him, muttering and shouting and giggling all at once. He closed his ears and pushed his head against the pillow. A cold wave enclosed him as every hair on his body stood erect. His heart pounded fast and his mouth ran dry. This time something was different: the voices came from somewhere within the house. Leland could only tell that.

***

Leland swayed on his way to the bathroom, one eye open and the other closed. The thick red carpets were the best thing in the house according to Leland—or so he told himself when his legs were like blocks of ice every morning. He reached the bathroom and turned on the shower. Steam floated to the ceiling. Today was the first day of school. Walking to school was the greatest advantage of their house's location.

Leland realized he needed something to take his mind off what he'd been thinking about. High school, and all the drama that comes with it, seemed like a good escape—hopefully. He put on his school uniform, styled his hair, and then went downstairs.

"Good morning." His mother greeted him while preparing cereal for Fred and Karla. "Are you ready?"

"Yeah," Leland replied, "I guess."

"Alright, then. Remember, this is your final year." His mother moved closer to him. "Give it all you've got."

"Of course I will," Leland replied. Leland's mother worked as an accountant at TW City Bank. They don't pay a lot for accountants in Temblewood. That's why she didn't want him to be one.

"I was wondering," Leland eyed his mom for a second and then asked, hesitantly, "Did you hear something last night?"

"Something like what? I hear all sort of things at night starting from—"

"I meant something unusual."

"A new neighbor just moved in, and he has four children. They're noisy, and everyone in the neighborhood complains about them. Is this what you're asking for?"

"Oh. That explains it then."

A negative test result. Leland left the house. Sniffing fresh morning air was one reason Leland preferred walking over driving.

Ford NewGate High hadn't changed a bit. With a principal like Mr. Kerry, who secretly paid the teachers extra to ensure his son Barn got the highest marks, you can't really expect much change. But his arrangement wasn't too secret. Everyone knew about it.

"Over here!" Jennifer called for Leland. She stood by the gate, wearing a gray skirt and a white polo shirt. A red ribbon shone through her silky blonde hair.

"Hey," Leland replied, waving.

She smiled. "Where have you been all this time?"

"Been kind of busy. What about you?"

Jennifer paused and eyed Leland like a detective questioning a criminal. She knew him too well to accept a vague excuse. "Is there something I need to know?"

Leland knew he wasn't a good liar. But he didn't know he was an *awful* one. *Why can't I keep something to myself without others noticing?*

"No. Really. Don't worry," Leland denied.

"Alright, then. Let's get inside."

***

Mrs. Dina, Head of the Psychology Department, walked into the classroom. Leland loved Mrs. Dina. Her classes were always exciting, and she knew psychology very well.

"How are you all?" Mrs. Dina asked. "Glad to see you again."

Dylan walked in sporting dark circles under his eyes from playing too much Halo, messy blonde hair, and Harry-Potter-style glasses. Last year, Dylan had received a warning from Mr. Kerry for being absent the whole first week. But everyone knew the school couldn't kick Dylan out. He'd won the Temblewood Olympics for Physics for two consecutive years. And Mr. Kerry loved trophies.

"Sorry for being late," Dylan told Mrs. Dina.

"Better than last year at least," she said. Everyone laughed.

"All right, let's start," Mrs. Dina announced. "Our topic for today is very interesting."

She scanned the class, cleared her throat, and then asked, "Who knows what OCD stands for?"

"Obsessive-Compulsive Disorder," Dylan answered.

"Good," Mrs. Dina said. "This is a common disease in which the person experiences episodes of obsessive thoughts. The thoughts often lead to compulsive behavior. OCD manifests in many forms. Some patients feel the urge to repeat sentences and/or actions several times. Others experience a perpetual chain of repetitive thoughts, or, as they report, 'voices in their heads.'"

Alright. School wasn't quite a distraction as Leland had hoped. But this was relevant. Maybe he had OCD after all.

"I have a question," Leland said, raising his hand. "Is there any specific age for this disease?"

"There's no specific age for OCD, but it usually starts before the age of twenty-five."

"This is the first day," a student complained. "We just got here for God's sake. Save all of that for later." That was Frank. He's known for his bad attitude, but that wasn't why Leland hated him. Frank's name was also his father's. And Leland hated his father. *He left when we needed him the most.*

***

The school day ended. Leland went home and placed his backpack right next to the door. He would pick it up from there next morning. Excluding his grandparents, who were somewhere in the house solving crosswords, no one was home. He went back to his room, changed into cotton shorts and a comfortable yellow shirt and then lay on his bed.

Maybe Leland needed to socialize earlier instead of focusing on problems that might not exist aside from only in his head. Leland's stomach growled. The bad thing was that eating dinner before everyone arrived home was taboo in his house. The good thing? If everyone arrives early, it's more of a lunch than a dinner.

***

The family gathered around the dining table. Abbey carried a grilled turkey from the oven and put it carefully on the table. Leland salivated. If it weren't socially unacceptable to grab the turkey and dive into it, Leland would've done it. *Hunger is lame.*

"It's ready," his aunt announced, placing dishes for everyone. The turkey tasted good. Genuinely good. *Just how many nurses were out there who could cook like this?*

"This is good," Maria praised.

"I know it is," Abbey replied. "And no. I won't cook every day."

Fred struggled to speak with food in his mouth. "This isn't fair, mom. Karla has more food than me."

"Finish yours and I'll put more for you," Maria told him.

Leland's head suddenly became heavy. Everything around him moved in slow motion. He could hear his family talk, but he couldn't understand what they were saying. His vision blurred, and a white flash that gradually brightened was all he could see.

And then they whispered again.

All of them.

The millions of throats, they all talked to him. And they were saying something. For the first time, they said something.

His heart skipped a beat.

"Are you okay?" his mother asked.

With a tied tongue, he glanced at her, then inconvincibly answered, "I'm fine."

"Are you sure?" she said, with a slight degree of dissatisfaction.

"I need to rest," Leland said, maintaining no eye contact. "Excuse me."

I need to get to the basement.

***

Sweat poured down Leland's back. He turned the lights off and threw himself on the bed. The voices said one word but in different tunes and pitches: *basement.*

But what does that mean? The basement of the house had been deserted for years. That was one thing Leland was sure about. Thoughts spun in his head like a tornado. He went to the window and opened it. The wind howled. The street was empty except for a man walking his dog. Temblewood was a dying city of many old people and few youngsters. And when you have too many old people and few youngsters, you don't expect the streets to be active. In fact, most shops closed at 6 p.m. except for a few restaurants and coffee shops.

Leland plugged in the Nespresso coffee machine. He hadn't used it for a long time, but he had to now because he didn't want to go downstairs. He craved coffee. *A small cup of decaf won't harm me, will it?*

Leland went back to the window and stared at the gleaming moon. He didn't know what was in the basement, but he was sure it was one hell of a scary place to be. *All deserted things are scary.* Leland sat on his desk, the cup of coffee beside him. He googled "OCD." The threads were terrifyingly relevant to what he'd experienced. People complained of repetitive thoughts or things that would frequently happen without any satisfactory explanation. Some swore there was a voice in the back of their heads that was impossible to get rid of. Leland sipped his coffee and regretted withdrawing it. The warmth and richness were indescribable.

Then, the door behind him opened. Leland's mother walked in.

"What's wrong?" she asked.

"Nothing," Leland replied. Maria shook her head in disbelief. Her eyes caught the PC's screen. She looked straight into his eyes and said, "Don't lie to me. Tell me. What's bothering you, sweetie?"

"Believe me. I'm telling the truth." *People sometimes try to help you, but they don't realize the only way they could help is by pretending not to notice something's wrong.*

"So, you're not in love as your aunt says?" Maria asked, grinning. "Because that's something you shouldn't really stress about."

"Eh." Leland sighed. "I don't know. Really." He shrugged.

"I know how you feel, but we're always here for you."

"Thanks, mom."

Maria turned around and was about to leave when Leland called, "Mom?"

"Yes?"

"How did my dad die?"

Knowing how you lost your father must not be, under any condition, a mysterious topic. Doubts had tormented Leland for years, and that was all because Maria was always too vague about it. Every time he'd asked her, she'd say something like, "When the time is right, I'm going to tell you," or she'd simply change the topic. And it pissed Leland off.

"An accident," she said. "He died in an accident."

"An accident?" Leland wondered. "Why didn't you tell me earlier?"

"Because you wouldn't understand," she said. "No reason in the world is enough to convince a kid desperately waiting for his father."

"What kind of an accident?"

"Car."

Leland remembered his last day with his father very well. But when his father had left the house that day, Leland didn't know he wouldn't see him again.

"Alright," Leland said. "Thanks for telling me."

Tears welled up in Maria's eyes and rolled over her cheeks. She inched closer, and then she hugged Leland. It had been years since they'd hugged. But it was the same feeling every time, no matter how old: warmth.

"I love you, son," she told him.

"I love you too, mom," he replied, wiping tears off her face.

Maria was about to leave, but Leland stopped her again.

"One more thing," he said. "When was the last time someone got into the basement?"

"Why are you asking?"

"I'm thinking of making a small office down there," Leland explained. "I want a quiet place to study, away from Karla and Fred and all the noise."

He lied and hoped it was convincing enough.

"Ten years, maybe more."

"You didn't even check it out or clean it?"

"No. No one has been in there for years."

Maria left the room. Leland couldn't enjoy his coffee. It was too cold now. He made a decision and hoped he wouldn't regret it later: *I'm going to the basement tonight. What could be down there anyway?*

But he had to wait until everyone was asleep. Leland grabbed a book, *Step Toward Your Fears*, and sat beside the window. He read:

We all face situations where we should realize our limits and step back, but we keep pushing and pushing out of curiosity. Knowing what's behind all the confusion is sometimes worth the trouble, but we might reach a point where nothingness is all that exists, and previous naive actions are then strongly regretted. The pyramid of achievements you were trying to build might be collapsing before you even notice, and there is nothing but this dark path, whether you fall, or you keep rising until you reach a point where nothing fits you anymore.

***

Leland's body was heavy. He opened his eyes, and the first thing he saw was an open book between his thighs. It was midnight. Jumping into the clutches of the unknown demanded courage, and courage was the only substance running through Leland's blood.

Carefully, slowly, and stealthily, he exited his room. Leland walked on eggshells down the stairs. Each step brought him closer to the basement. He didn't hear anything coming from downstairs. *Perfect. Everyone's sleeping.*

He reached the ground floor. No one was in the living room, and the stairs leading down to the basement were right in front of him. But his tank of courage was leaking the closer he got. *Why am I holding back? It might be nothing.* He tried to keep his courage levels steady.

Cautiously, he went down the spiral stairs leading to the basement door, turning his back now and then to see if someone was following.

Leland was at the bottom of the stairs now. The door of the basement stood an inch away. It was very dark down there.

Leland's hand trembled as it reached for the doorknob. He took a deep breath and struggled for another. He tightened his fingers around the cold knob and plucked up his courage to open the door. The basement was even darker than the stairs. He desperately attempted to switch the lights on.

Freakin' dusty.

Leland turned the lights on. He scanned the basement while standing with his back against the door. It was filled with old boxes, books, papers and, naturally, dust. Leland wondered what kind of books these were. But he didn't dare take a step forward.

I knew nothing was here.

He turned his back and almost switched the lights off, but he thought he'd detected an outline of a person. Leland turned his back once again and did a double take. Shock abruptly soaked his body. His skin crawled.

"What?" He stuttered, breathless, as he fell on his back.

His mouth gaped and he cried, "What the hell are you doing here, Jennifer?"

She didn't answer but simply stared at him. She was on both knees, gazing at him with blank eyes. *The basement's been shut for years, right?*

"What are you doing here Jennifer?" Leland roared again. The lights went out in a spray of sparks. It was pitch black again. Sitting there and shaking in his boots wouldn't help him.

"Answer me, Jennifer!"

Leland stuck his body on the walls and tried to turn the lights on again. He succeeded, but Jennifer wasn't there. Leland jumped out of his skin. He looked everywhere, but she wasn't there. There were no signs of a living creature having ever been in the basement.

Apprehensively, Leland barked, "I don't get it!" He placed his hands on his head and then wailed, "I need help!"

He hurried to his room. He picked his phone and dialed Jennifer's number. She didn't answer. He sat on the floor with his back against the wall. *What's going on? Am I crazy or what?* Leland repressed the urge to vomit. His face was pale.

Then the phone rang.

It was Jennifer.

Chapter Three

The Truth Lies Beneath the Skin

Leland's vision blurred. He found himself on the ground in his dark room. He was still holding the phone in his hand. It was three in the morning. *What the hell happened?* he asked himself, standing up. The last thing he remembered was seeing Jennifer in the basement, then he hurried back to his room, then she had called. He remembered nothing after that. It seemed he'd slept for a couple of hours. He checked his phone and saw a missed call at 12:45. Then, at 2:33 a.m., there was another missed call, also from Jennifer.

Leland went to the bathroom, stared at his weary face in the mirror, washed it with cold water, and then returned to his room. He checked his phone again. Jennifer had texted him at 1:45 a.m.

What do you think you're doing, Leland?

He went to the window, opened it, and fresh air entered the room. *What the hell was she doing in the basement, and how did she disappear suddenly?* He tried calling her a few times. She wasn't answering.

***

Leland stood by the gate, his back against the walls and his eyes staring at the ground beneath him. His first class started at eight, but he was there at 6:30 a.m. for another reason. He waited for Mrs. Dina. He had to talk to someone, and she was the first person who had come to mind. His hair was messy and his eyes were as red as chili peppers. At seven, her car parked close to the gate. He waited until she got out and then went to her.

"Who is it?" she asked loudly, moving toward him. "Leland? Is that you?" she wondered, uncertain.

Leland nodded. Something about her always made him comfortable. He knew she didn't have any children although she'd been married for years. *Maybe that's why she's so kind.*

"Oh, son," she said, smiling. "What are you doing here this early?" Leland knew she always came very early to school. She once told her students so.

"I have to tell you something," Leland revealed.

"Let me guess," she said as she entered the school. "You had a fight with Dylan."

"I wish it was that."

She turned around. She wore a red pencil skirt with a white long-sleeve shirt on top. "Hmm … Don't worry. I'm here to help."

The sound of her high heels echoed in the parking lot as they headed to the Psychology Department. The department was small and overlooked the empty school square.

"So tell me, what brought you in this early?" she asked as she prepared two cups of coffee.

"I don't know what's going on in my life." He took a deep breath. "Weird things are happening to me all of a sudden."

"Speak," she said, then sipped her coffee. "I'm here to listen." She sat on her chair, a large brown bookshelf behind her, and smiled. "Tell me everything."

Leland knew he'd come to the right person. "A week or so ago everything started." He cleared his throat, looked straight at her eyes, then divulged, "This might sound unbelievable, but you must believe me. Voices … Many voices are whispering in my ears every day."

"Voices like what?" She leaned forward, placing her cup on the table.

"Like people. Many people talking to me at the same time. And I can't tell what they're saying."

"Well. I wonder why's this is happening to you in particular, but I can assure you it's not so weird."

A positive thought floated into Leland's head. *Great! So I'm not making things up.*

"They've been haunting me for a week now," he explained. "No matter how much I try to distract myself, I can't seem to succeed."

"I see." She pushed up her rounded eyeglasses. "Is that all?"

"No. It seems I'm the only one hearing the voices." He looked down. "Yesterday, the voices said something. For the first time, they said something I understood."

"What did they say?"

"Basement. They said basement. Our house has a basement, and it had been deserted for over ten years. But I had to go there and find out what's inside."

"And?"

"When I went there last night, at first I didn't see anything, but then." Leland paused for a moment or two. "Then … I saw Jennifer!"

Leland's skin prickled as he said it.

"What do you mean you saw Jennifer? When was that?" Dina's eyebrows met in a frown.

"Past midnight. I went there alone, and then I saw her in the basement."

"Weird," Dina said, "What did she say? I mean, Jennifer."

"Nothing. Everything went black and she disappeared."

"Have you tried contacting her?"

"I tried, but she didn't answer. And then I slept. I came here afterward."

Dina raised her eyebrows and kept silent for a few seconds. Leland's eyes were downcast. *She won't believe me.*

"Let's try to rationalize this thing," she suggested.

He didn't say anything.

"You might be facing some mental problems, maybe hallucinations, bad thoughts, or even stress, all of which might be leading you to such thoughts."

Dina dropped a bombshell, unaware. Leland raised his head. She noticed she'd irritated him, so she tried to explain more. "It's very normal, Leland. We all face problems, and sometimes these problems appear in different ways, ways that you're not used to. Maybe you need to rest, or just wait until everything gets better. You know, time heals all."

Leland wasn't quite convinced. A scream from deep within wanted to be freed. His hands were cold and his legs shivered. *I'm not crazy.*

"Or," she said loudly, dispelling Leland's unsettling thoughts. "Something strange is happening to you!"

Leland was now even more confused. Still, though, this seemed more rational than the first explanation.

"Like what?" he asked.

"From a scientific point of view, and from what I believe, I don't think something supernatural is happening to you. I don't even believe such a thing exists and have never heard of any such incident before. You need to get involved with people and think about your future." She smiled. "But … I have an old friend who dedicated most of his life to the study of supernatural events."

She took a pen and paper out of her bag and wrote a name and number. "If you're going to visit him, tell him Dina says hi."

He faked a smile, thanked her, and left the room carrying an uncomfortable feeling of insecurity. *She doesn't believe me after all. But, well, at least I told someone about it.*

Alone in the now-crowded streets, he walked, barely carrying his own body. He didn't know where to go. Leland looked up to the sky. It was blue. Pure blue. *Maybe she's right. Maybe I'm making things up ... but ... everything sounds real ... so real.* He felt his head would burst. Nothing made sense. But Leland knew what he had to do next. He grabbed his phone and dialed Jennifer's number. She answered right away.

"Hey, Jenny, thank God you picked up. We need to meet."

"Of course we do," she replied angrily.

"Behind the school in fifteen minutes?"

"Fine."

And the conversation ended, the shortest they'd ever had. Minutes later behind the school, Leland stood with his back against a graffiti-painted wall. Whether the conversation with Mrs. Dina had gone right or wrong, a heavy weight had been lifted off of his chest.

As he waited, a group of boys in his school passed by. They were talking about last night's local basketball game. He remembered he hadn't talked much about such things in a while. Not more than two weeks ago, talking about sports and upcoming video games had been interesting topics. Now, when he thought about it, they sounded ridiculous compared to the mystery occupying his mind. Leland hoped Jennifer would bring some clarifications with her. He'd be happy if she said something like, "Gotcha, you scared lil' coward."

A few minutes passed like years. Then Jennifer showed up, at last. Leland instinctively clenched his fist.

He remembered her on her knees last night, staring at him with blank eyes, and his heart skipped a beat. She stood in front of him now. Her smell was nostalgic, and it always took Leland on a trip down memory lane to when he'd first met her in primary school. The sight of her comforted him in the midst of the storm somehow. He prepared his question: *What where you doing in our basement last night?*

When the space between their heads shrank to less than a foot, Jennifer asked without greeting, "What do you think you're doing? Huh?"

"What do you mean?" The conversation was already going in the opposite direction of what he'd planned.

"Do you know how much trouble you could've caused if my dad had seen you?" she growled, frowning. Leland didn't understand any of what she was saying. *What does her father have to do with all of this?*

"Hey, wait … What are you talking about? I don't get it at all!"

"Don't play dumb, Leland." Her cheeks flushed as the blood inside her boiled. "What brought you to my house yesterday? Like, you rarely visit, and when you do, it's after midnight and without even calling."

Her speech came as a bolt of lightning. No specific answer passed his mind. Her sentence was far from what he'd expected. *I was in* my *house all night … What does this mean?*

"Hold on a second," Leland said firmly. "I'm the one who should ask you that! What were you doing in *my* basement last night?"

"I'm dead serious right now, Leland. It's not the time for some silly jokes."

"I'm not joking or anything. I saw *you* in *my* basement last night!"

"I was at *my* house all day long. If what you're saying is true, then why didn't you answer my call?"

She wasn't lying. He knew her far too well to know she was serious.

"I called you right after I saw you in the basement. You didn't answer. When you called again, I don't know what happened," Leland said, trying to find the missing piece of this maddening puzzle. "I found myself sleeping on the ground!"

"I saw your call at like twelve. I was taking a shower. I tried to call you several times but you didn't answer—and then you were there in our backyard. For God's sake, what were you thinking?"

Leland was sure he hadn't left the house. Maybe he'd been hallucinating when he heard the voices. Maybe he *hadn't* seen Jennifer. But the only thing he was sure about was that he hadn't left his house.

"I swear I didn't go to your house! I was home all day long. What was I doing in your backyard, as you claim?"

"Nothing. You were walking in circles, falling, standing up, falling again. Were you drunk or what?"

"That can't be true! I don't know what's going on Jennifer."

She turned around, discombobulated, and muttered, "We haven't seen you much lately. Whatever you were doing, it's wrong. You should stop it. It's better for everyone."

"Wait," Leland shrieked. Losing Jennifer was the last thing he wanted. "I'm not lying. I swear. I haven't done anything wrong. You know me better than anyone."

Leland paused, breathed in, out, and in, and then explained. "Lately, I've been hearing some eerie sounds. I'm the only one hearing them. You must believe me. They lead me to the basement, and that's where I saw you."

With eyes like an infant waiting for his mother's milk, he gazed at her sky-blue eyes, wide and beautiful. The tension within her eased a bit. Her warm breath stroked his cold face, and he wanted a hug more than anything.

"I believe you," she revealed. "But it doesn't make any sense. I saw you in our backyard and you saw me in your basement on the same night. And we both swore we haven't left our houses. How can this be true?"

"I wish I had an answer. I need your help, please."

She nodded and her eyes glistened. She then smiled and assured him, "You've always been there for me. And whatever this thing is, I won't leave you alone."

Leland smiled back. He knew she would never leave him, even if she weren't convinced. And he wouldn't blame her if she didn't believe him anyway. Leland took a small piece of yellow paper out of his pocket and said, "This is a name and number of a man who might help us."

"Who gave you that?"

"Mrs. Dina. I went to her this morning. I thought she could help."

"What did she say?"

"Not much. The only thing I got out of that visit was this paper. I'm not even sure if this guy can help."

Jennifer was in a quandary about what to say. She suggested, "Leland, let's wait. This thing is moving really fast, and I'm not sure I can handle it."

"Of course you can't. *We* can. We've got nothing to lose, and for a strange reason I want to know more about this. There are a lot of questions that need to be answered."

"I don't know, Leland. If this is real, I mean."

"We've been through a lot together, right?"

She nodded.

"We'll get through this—together!"

They entered the school carrying the whole world on their shoulders. They gave no courtesy smiles to anyone, as though their mouths had been sutured with metal strings. Now, Leland wasn't alone. He had gained Jennifer and it was his task to prove he hadn't been lying.

As they walked, they saw Dylan standing in the square with a book in his hand. He flipped his blonde hair, revealing his small, rounded face. He pushed up his wide-framed eyeglasses as he called, "Leland! Where have you been all that time?"

Struggling.

"I've been busy with my family," Leland replied. "What about you? What have you been doing lately?"

"Nothing much. Read like seven books in the last week. Bored." Dylan flipped his hair again. "But I'm looking forward to today's Comic-Con. It cannot be missed!"

Dylan had the best grades in the school. He told Leland that he'd received three college scholarships already. He'd won the state's contest for solving puzzles when he was a seventh-grader.

"You guys are coming to the Con, right?" Dylan asked.

"Nah." Jennifer sighed. "I'm busy."

"Same here," Leland said.

The tension within Leland and Jennifer went down a degree or two. Leland wondered if he should tell Dylan about what had happened to them. He might find it interesting instead of horrifying. *Not now. I'm not ready yet,* Leland decided.

Hours passed and the school day ended when Mr. Johnson announced, "This is the final task for you today. Don't forget about your homework. See you tomorrow."

Leland and Jennifer were ready to take a leap of faith at all costs. They needed some preparations, however. Leland texted his mother and told her he had an after-school project. Jennifer did the same. Without waiting for a reply, they called Mrs. Dina's friend. There was no answer. They went to a nearby Chinese restaurant called the Asian Noodle House. Last time they'd been there, they were with Dylan. And it was months ago.

"Kung Pao chicken as usual?" the waiter asked. It was fascinating—he still remembered their order.

"Yeah," they replied in one croaked voice.

Leland's phone rang. It was Dina's friend's number. Leland wasn't sure if this man could help him or not, but he had no other choice.

"Buckle down, Leland," Jennifer muttered.

"Hello," Leland answered.

"Hello," a gentle voice replied melodically.

"My name is Leland. I'm Mrs. Dina's student. She told me you could help."

"Help with what?"

"I can't say that on the phone."

"I'm not sure I'm the right person."

"Please, sir, you are the only one who might be able to help me."

"What do you want exactly?"

"Mrs. Dina said you're keen on studying supernatural events. I need to tell you my story, sir."

"What a stubborn kid. You're not going to waste a lot of my precious time, will you?"

"No, sir. I promise."

"Columbus Ginger Street, house number five. Come at six."

Leland thanked him, but the man didn't reply.

Jennifer tucked her blonde hair behind her ears then asked, "I've been wondering—and don't get me wrong—but maybe you were dreaming. A vivid dream or something?"

"I wasn't," Leland replied swiftly. "It was as real as I'm watching you now."

"Have you taken any medication lately? Some have horrible side effects."

"I haven't," Leland replied, putting his phone on the table. "You have to believe me."

"I do." She shrugged, "I'm just trying to find a way out."

***

Leland sat on his chair, opened a blank document on his computer, and then typed in everything that had happened from scratch. Things were getting more complicated. Now his problem wasn't with the eerie voices alone, but with what he'd seen in the basement and what Jennifer had told him. In the final paragraph, he typed: **She swore she saw me in her backyard, and I swore I saw her in my basement... and both of us hadn't left our houses for the entire day. How?**

But Leland was relieved. Whatever was going on, he wasn't facing it alone. He decided to meet Jennifer at five to go to Mrs. Dina's friend. He put his head on his desk and slept, unaware. He had to rest. He'd been wild for a pretty long time.

At first, he felt nothing. Then random pictures of sunset, dawn, rain, and various colors melting together into monochrome appeared. Then there was nothing again. Until they came haunting. The voices awakened him, whispering together in his ears, filling his head with creepy sounds and breaking his temporary peace. But something new happened. They were saying full sentences. It was very clear. All the voices chorused one thing: *The truth lies beneath the skin … The truth lies beneath the skin … The truth lies beneath the skin.*

***

It was almost six when Leland and Jennifer got out of the cab. The villas on Columbus Ginger Street were large, and most of them had big gardens. The sunset depressed Leland. It always had. It felt as if the darkness would take over the day and the world would end.

"Something new happened," he told Jennifer. "They came again. The voices. 'The truth lies beneath the skin,' they said."

"When?" she asked, putting both hands inside her pockets.

"A while ago, when I was sleeping. I swear they came."

Maybe I shouldn't have told her. But she's tough. He knew that very well. *Yet it must be hard for her to swallow all of that.*

Jennifer eyed Leland, and then she inched closer to him. He felt cold, but he didn't particularly know if it was the weather or if it was just him.

"No need to swear. I believe you. And I'll be on your side no matter what," she said. "Now let's go."

Mr. Shawnkley's house, the fifth one on the street, had four floors and large windows. The garden looked as though it had been built like a maze. Columbus Ginger Street was known to be for the wealthy.

"There." Leland pointed at a large door in the corner of the house. He knocked. Surprisingly, it opened right away. An old butler wearing a black suit stood in front of them. The breeze of air rushing from the outside pushed his hair to the back of his head. With a stoic face, he asked, "How can I help you?" His voice reminded Leland of newsmen. Firm and clear.

"We have an appointment with Mr. Shawnkley," Jennifer stated.

"Stay where you are. I'll be back," he ordered before going back inside.

The butler came back a few seconds later. He nodded as he opened the big door with one hand, allowing them to enter.

On their way to Mr. Shawnkley's room, Leland and Jennifer invested every second looking at the beauty of the architecture. Crystal chandeliers guided their way beneath perfectly sculpted roofs, on perfectly polished floors, and beside perfectly painted walls. Statues of animals, old men, and ancient Egyptian figures made everything a bit creepy. A brown door with golden borders was at the end of the corridor.

"Beside some old friends and some politicians," the butler informed, "No one has visited Mr. Shawnkley for a while."

"I barely convinced him to meet us," Leland replied. "I thought he was very busy."

"He is," the butler muttered as he opened the brown door. Leland and Jennifer entered the room. Thousands of books were on shelves that stretched along the room. Lamps designed like tree leaves protruded from the walls. On a large desk ahead of them, Mr. Shawnkley sat reading a book. Behind him were a small chimney and a porcelain horse.

"Hello," Leland said, then hesitated.

Mr. Shawnkley closed the book in his hand, took his eyeglasses off, and then scanned them from head to toe.

"So," he said. "How can I help you?" His voice was nasal.

"I've been told you study supernatural events," Leland said. "And what's happening to me might be more than supernatural. I don't think it's happened to anyone before."

Shawnkley put one hand on his chin, arched an eyebrow, then uttered, "I'm listening."

Good. He's interested. Leland told him his story from A to Z. Shawnkley nodded after every sentence, asked some questions, and hummed now and then.

"And that's everything," Leland concluded. Leland still felt cold, though there was a chimney behind Mr. Shawnkley and the room seemed warm.

"In 1844, a whole town in Asia disappeared. The event was named 'The Vanish of the Sinners.' It was a time when people believed in the existence of supernatural things. A year or two later, a group of scientists found the reason behind the disappearance. They claimed it was due to a crack in the earth. They said the earth had split and the people had been buried underneath. When they dug that area, they found the dead bodies and their theory was verified." Shawnkley explained, "In a nutshell, I'm trying to tell you that *sometimes* there's a scientific reason behind something."

"So?" Jennifer said.

"So there might be a scientific explanation for what's happening to you. And the only scientific explanation that might come across my mind is that you're facing a mental problem." Shawnkley frankly said, "But … this is not what I believe in."

Shawnkley limped as he went to one of the book-shelves and picked up a blue-covered book. Shawnkley was shorter than Leland and taller than Jennifer. He put the book on the desk and then said, "This is what *I* believe in. I've read this book five times. It contains incidents stranger than yours, way stranger."

Shawnkley handed Leland the book and then ordered, "Open page one hundred fifty-nine and read it."

Leland loudly read, "John Beskow, thirty years of age, disappeared from earth leaving no trace behind. The police stated that he had been killed and buried and that they're chasing the murderers. Beskow did not have a criminal record and he did not have debts. He was married and socially stable. His family stated he had been acting strangely in the past month, claiming to see things normal people don't."

Leland's skin prickled and his heart raced. *What's he trying to say?*

Jennifer put one finger on her lips, thinking. She commented, "So, you're saying supernatural events occur frequently but most people aren't aware of them?"

"The book in your hand was banned a year after it was released," Shawnkley explained. "People don't want to believe in these things. They often convince themselves they don't exist because they're too lazy or too afraid to chase the truth."

Shawnkley ordered the butler to serve them tea. The tea was hot and smelled like roses. Shawnkley took the book from Leland and flipped the pages. He read, "Neil Hummington attempted suicide at the age of forty-two. Reports said he was a drug addict, but his relatives and friends assured he wasn't." Shawnkley continued, "He wrote a note before he died saying, 'I'm just saving myself.' Thousands of people die every day, thousands disappear, and we don't have a clue where they are. Supernatural events are *real*."

Leland's mind played tricks with him. Dirty tricks. At first, he wanted something to assure him that he wasn't a psycho. And now that he knew about all these events and how real they were, his body boiled like an inferno. He wasn't cold anymore. Leland's shirt was glued to his back from sweat.

"With all respect," Jennifer said, "All the stories you mentioned ended with disappearances and suicide and death. If this is related to our case, then tell us what to do to avoid such outcomes."

"I'm not sure myself," Shawnkley said, then sipped his tea. "But I have a theory."

"Whatever this thing is, it's trying to tell you something," Shawnkley went on. "Don't be afraid, just listen and follow the clues. A man is his own enemy." He looked at Leland and then uttered, "You look tired and helpless. You shouldn't. Accept what's happening to you and try to find what they're trying to tell you. Don't be afraid. That's all I can say."

"Thank you, sir." Leland sighed with a surge of disappointment. *Suicide and disappearance. Is this how it's going to end?*

They left Shawnkley's room, following the butler to the exit. It was raining outside, a heavy shower. The street was empty and the sun had gone. Across the street there was a coffee shop. Leland and Jennifer bought two cups of coffee and sat on a table on the second floor, overlooking the flooded street. The smell of freshly brewed beans wafted in the air. Leland hadn't spoken a word since they'd left the mansion. He was gazing at his mug when Jennifer asked, "What's wrong?"

"I'm ... " Leland confessed, hesitantly eying her, "Afraid."

"You're not alone," she said as she changed her position and took a seat beside him. "I know it's not something easy to deal with. But we're all in this now, and we'll find what's behind this mystery together."

"Thanks, Jennifer," Leland said, pulling the mug closer to him. "I'm really glad you're in my life."

"I've been thinking. Why don't we tell Dylan about it? He's smart and we've always done things together."

"Sounds good," Leland replied as he brought the mug closer to his mouth. "Hope he can help."

***

After finishing their coffee, they took a cab and headed to Dylan's house. It was still raining heavily. Leland knew the city very well. He had lived there since he was born, but he'd never seen it this dark. The streets were empty and the shops were closed. Kids weren't playing in their backyards. Leland's eyes darted to Jennifer and saw that she was writing a text to her father telling him she'd be late.

"And we're here," the cab driver announced with an Italian accent.

Dylan's house was the smallest in the neighborhood, white with only two tiny windows. Red curtains could be seen from the outside. After knocking, Dylan's foster mother opened the door. He had been adopted when he was seven and, as far as Leland knew, they treated him like their own son. The house was tiny compared to Mr. Shawnkley's. Dylan's room was on the second floor. In the corner of his room sat a small TV. In the other corner was an old desktop computer. Posters of Japanese anime characters and some rock stars spammed the walls.

"And the Con has been canceled due to rain," Dylan said. "What brought you anyway?"

"We need your help," Leland said as he sat on Dylan's bed.

"Well … My show is about to begin now. I don't have time … Maybe tomorrow?"

"Shut up and listen," Jennifer said. "It's serious."

"Okay Jenny, *okay*." Dylan sat on the carpeted floor. "You're going to be a freakin' strict mom, I can tell that."

Leland told the whole story for the fourth time from beginning to end. This time, it didn't hurt as much as it had when he'd told it to Mrs. Dina. Dylan paid attention to Leland as if he were watching one of his favorite shows.

"Hmm … lemme think," Dylan said. "It's a tough one."

Dylan's foster mother knocked on the door. She entered and placed a tray full of pastries on his desk. "Help yourself," she said, and then left the room. Dylan took a paper and a pen and drew a man.

"The truth lies beneath the skin." Dylan hummed. "What's beneath the skin?"

"Blood?" Leland replied, lying on Dylan's bed.

"Maybe. But even if we assumed they meant blood, what would it lead us to? Nothing. We should think of something else."

Dylan drew a house then took a croissant and bit it. He gazed at the drawing, raised it up, and then added more details to it.

"What? You came up with something?" Jennifer asked.

"Not yet," Dylan replied.

Jennifer went to the window, opened it, and fresh air filled the room. The sound of rain falling on rooftops, streets, and trees was strong and clear and was, among all other things, dark.

"Well," Jennifer said, staring at the street, "If we assume the skin resembles superficial things in Leland's life, then maybe it's telling him to focus more on vital issues."

"Good try," Dylan commented, still sketching. "But I don't think this one works either."

"Okay, genius," Jennifer sighed. "Figure it out while we eat pizza."

"Pizza? What about mom's pastries?" Dylan complained, raising both hands. "That's utterly rude."

"Mine is pepperoni with extra cheese and corn on the side," Jennifer chuckled. "What do you want, Leland?"

"Make it two," Leland said. "You can still join, Dylan."

Jennifer took the pen from Dylan and then drew a pizza on the other side of the paper. "So?" she teased.

"Veggie with potato wedges," Dylan complained. "Now give me my paper back."

The shelves inside Dylan's room contained a countless number of DVDs and comic books, not to mention the virtual library on his computer. Leland wondered how Dylan had time for all of that and still got high marks.

"I think I found the answer," Dylan announced as he pushed up his eyeglasses and stared at the drawing. "No. I'm *sure* I've found the answer. And you're not going to like it."

Chapter Four

Déjà vu

"What is it?" Leland asked as he sat on the ground beside Dylan.

"Well, you said that the basement was the source of the voices. And you claim you saw Jennifer there, right?"

"I didn't claim. I'm *sure* I saw her," Leland replied.

"I need you to think outside the box," Dylan explained. "The truth lies beneath the skin. This sentence doesn't necessarily refer to real skin. Now, when you think about it, most of the events occurred in your house."

"Yeah … and?" Jennifer wondered.

"Imagine that Leland's house is the body," Dylan said, showing them the picture of the house he'd drawn. "What would be beneath this body?"

"The basement?" Jennifer answered.

"Exactly!" Dylan said. "That's it. If the house is a body, then the basement is what's beneath its skin!"

"So the voices are trying to lead me back to the basement?" Leland wondered. "But why?"

"I don't know," Dylan replied. "We should search for a sign there."

Leland didn't say anything. He remembered what he'd seen in the basement, and the hair on his neck instantly stood up. *Is it right to go there again?*

"It's Leland's choice. If he's not ready, then we're going nowhere." With her back against the wall, Jennifer crossed her arms.

"But they could have easily told me to go to the basement instead of creating this riddle," Leland said.

"You're right," Dylan said. "And that I don't have an answer for."

The day was long and tiring. Leland was too fatigued to do anything now. Jennifer was probably exhausted as well. The rain had stopped. But the streets were still empty.

"Alright, look," Leland said. "We go back home now and meet at five in the morning, in my house."

"Why five?" Dylan asked. "Sounds too early."

"I don't want my family to know about this."

***

Leland woke up when he heard an alarm ringing in his ears. He washed his face with warm water, prepared a cup of coffee, and then went downstairs. The smell of beans was fresh and tempting. Leland stopped walking, sipped, and then continued. He felt stupid for previously trying to stop himself from enjoying the greatness of this drink.

Leland grabbed his mother's car keys and went outside. Whether Dylan's theory was right or wrong, it was worth trying. He sat inside the car, waiting for Dylan and Jennifer to show up. The dawn was cold, which made Leland cherish the beverage in his hand more than ever. The glove box of the car had one CD: Linkin Park's *Hybrid Theory*. He played it, feeling the anger in the music flowing to his ears, activating his own anger, and then magically exiling it all out. Jennifer showed up, yawning on her way to the car. She opened the door and sat beside him.

"Oh my God, I'm tired," she murmured with half-opened eyes. "Why are you in the car anyways?"

"Thought I'd wait here until you guys arrived," Leland replied, lowering the volume of the music. "Where's Dylan?"

"I don't know," she said, turning the music up again. "Old school. Ha!"

A mixture of red and blue streaks of light appeared in the sky as the sun peeked out of the horizon. Leland and Jennifer got out of the car when they saw Dylan walking down the empty street toward them. The glistening rays stroked their faces as the warmth of the sun overcame the coldness of the dawn.

"All right. First of all, let's not make any noise. I don't want anyone to wake up and know you're here," Leland said.

"And let's make it fast. I haven't told my father I'm out and he'll be worried," said Jennifer.

"We need candles in case the lights went off like last time," Dylan suggested.

"You're right. Hadn't thought of that," Leland said.

The three entered the house afraid of their own shadows. They tiptoed so as not to make any noise. Jennifer held her cross-body bag as tightly as she held her breath as she muttered, "It's dark in here."

Leland brought three candles from the kitchen and a lighter, and then they marched to the basement. They walked in a small corridor. Bedrooms were on their right, the living room on their left, and the spiral stairway led to the basement at the end of the corridor. But a TV in one of the rooms was on.

"Don't worry," Leland assured. "Aunt Abbey sleeps with the TV on. Let's carry on."

"Didn't know they played *Friends* at this time," Dylan commented.

They weren't sure if they were going to find anything downstairs, but if what had happened to Leland wasn't a figment of his imagination, then the outcomes of this adventure were unpredictable. Moments of deafening silence ruled until they reached the end of the corridor.

"Be careful," Leland warned, giving Jennifer and Dylan a candle. "It's even darker down there."

He lit the candles and they went downstairs arm-in-arm, prickling with every step. Portraits hung on the walls. An irritating premonition of terror pervaded Leland's senses.

"We can still back off," Leland said. He meant what he said, and he wished they'd agree. "Maybe we should come some other time."

"We're not even sure if there's anything inside," Jennifer told him. "So let's just get in and find out if it's worth the trouble."

"You're right," Leland agreed as he opened the door of the basement. It was dark and the lights weren't working, as predicted. Leland instinctively stepped back, still staring at the darkness of the basement, anticipating someone showing up.

"I told you it was a good idea to bring candles," Dylan whispered. "Now let's search."

A thick layer of dust coated everything. They stepped forward, trying to find a clue in the mess. The problem was that they didn't particularly know what they were searching for. Leland walked slowly among the shelves that contained boxes, books, and some ripped papers. He pretended he was searching when he was only trying to hide his fear. But in fact, it was meaningless. None of his friends could see him. The radius of the candle's halo was limited. Leland could barely see his hands. He put the candle on a shelf, and then he opened a box just to find more books and ripped papers stuffed inside. He returned the box to where it was, then saw a face staring back at him.

"You freakin' scared me," Leland scolded, but in a low voice.

"I didn't find anything," Dylan said. "There's nothing but dust and papers."

"And spiders," Jennifer chimed in, standing behind Leland.

When did they all get so close to me? Leland wondered. *The results of this mission are frustrating. But at least they aren't scary.* "Okay, let's leave this place," Leland ordered.

"Wait. Where's my bag?" Jennifer asked. "I must have left it there." She pointed to a spot somewhere in the darkness. Leland and Dylan followed her.

She walked to where she'd pointed, leaned down, and then picked up her bag. When Leland saw her in that position, his heart sank into the pit of his stomach. A terrifying sense of déjà vu made him shiver. He'd seen this scene before. He'd seen Jennifer on her knees, staring at him this way. This was *exactly* what she had looked like when he'd come to the basement alone the other night. Except her eyes weren't blank now. He absentmindedly dropped his candle.

"Hey, look at this!" Jennifer cried. "How the hell didn't we see it?"

Something glittered on the ground, mostly hidden under a red carpet. A few faint rays sneaked through holes in the carpet. Dylan ran to a box he'd searched and pulled out a pair of scissors. With Jennifer's help, they tried to remove the piece of carpet covering the glittering object. Leland watched. When they removed the carpet, they saw a square, golden brick covered with indecipherable writing.

"What the hell is that?" Dylan wondered.

Leland kneeled down, touched the brick, and then everything turned to black. He couldn't see anymore—not even the candles or the glittering object.

"Jennifer! Dylan!" He shouted, but no one answered. His body fainted, and he lost his balance and fell. Leland thought he'd hit the ground, but there was no ground. Only darkness. Leland felt as if he were falling into a pit with no end, and that at any point his body would splatter against solid ground. Even though he couldn't see a thing, he closed his eyes tightly.

Thousands of people die every day. Thousands disappear, and we don't have a clue where they are. Mr. Shawnkley's sentence crossed his numb mind.

Chapter Five

Woods

Leland's eyes were closed. He felt as though a lot of time had passed, but that it had passed quickly, just like when he'd sleep for ten hours but wake up feeling like it had only been a few minutes. Long, but short.

Old memories flooded Leland's brain: he was at a park playground, his mother was wiping tears off her face after his father had died, and along with Jennifer and Dylan, they were all eating something he couldn't exactly remember on a cold, windy day. His body went numb, and he could no longer think of anything. The flash of memories ended. Leland tried to move his extremities, but it was nearly impossible.

He frowned as he tried to escape invisible, invincible chains tightly binding him. For a second or two, he choked. Sweat rolled down his face, and the salty drops ended up mostly on his lips and eventually in his taste buds.

Is this how it feels when you die?

His eyelids were heavy, as if slathered in superglue, but his ears functioned perfectly. Birds chattered and wind blew. The last thing he remembered was being in his basement with Dylan and Jennifer.

How can birds chatter and the wind blow inside a basement?

Gradually, the feelings of coldness and restriction blew over. Now he could slightly stretch his extremities and recollect his scattered thoughts.

"Can anyone hear me? Dylan … Jennifer … Are you here?" He called out despite the heaviness of his tongue and the rest of his body. No voice was meant to answer him.

Why can't I open my eyes? Where am I?

Leland slowly opened his eyes expecting to see Jennifer or Dylan, or at least himself alone in the basement. But he saw three moons and green grass and trees. Each moon was double the size of the moon he knew. One of them was a full moon, the other was a half moon, and the last was a crescent.

What's this? Am I dreaming or what?

Leland glanced at the columns of trees ahead of him. They were long and curved and nearly blocked the sky. But he couldn't see beyond the trees. *Maybe there's nothing beyond the trees but more trees.* Then, along with the sounds of birds and the wind, a wolf howled. The vividness of this place made his skin crawl.

What brought me here? How far am I from home?

He got on his feet, barely lifting his body up, and went to a tree. He touched the trunk, and it was thick and rough—and real. He walked on the grassy ground, exploring the woods. Leland glanced at the sky once more, and there were *still* three moons hanging in the starry space.

How can the sky have three moons?

"Dylan! Jennifer!" He called their names once more, his voice echoing through the wild nature. Leland hated walking among the trees without knowing where to go, but it was his best option. Maybe a road full of cars and restaurants would suddenly appear and save the day. Or maybe he'd find Jennifer and Dylan and they'd call someone for help.

Wait. My phone!

Leland took his phone out of his pocket in a hurry.

I'm a freakin' idiot. I should've used it sooner.

But there was no cellular connection, and his battery was only at one percent, even though he was sure it had been fully charged when he was in the basement.

Oh please, not now.

Leland's stomach growled. He was hungry and thirsty and lost. He walked for an hour or so when, luckily, a river appeared. It was small and lined with a few rocks. He leaned down and touched the water. Like a dog drinking from a bowl, he put his mouth on the cold, running water and drank as much as he could. He then washed his face and laid back on the grassy riverbank. River water didn't taste like bottled water. But it was fine.

What if something bad happened to Dylan and Jennifer?

He began to regret getting them involved. He presumed three possible scenarios in their case. One: Dylan and Jennifer were still in the basement, safe and sound. Two: they were in these woods and lost just like him. Three: they were somewhere totally else.

He picked up a small brick and threw it in the river. The water splashed and the moons' reflections on the river vanished.

I need to find them.

He continued walking, knowing that he was searching for a needle in a haystack. Hooting owls now rivaled the eeriness of the howling wolves. The possibility of being surprised by either caused Leland to move away from the noises.

Then, something moved behind the trees in front of him. He wasn't sure yet if it was a human or something else. The shadow stopped moving, hiding half its body behind a tree.

"Stop moving or I'll end your life," the figure behind the tree threatened.

Chapter Six

Farewell

Jennifer walked in the woods wondering where she was. Being in a dark basement was the last thing she recalled. Now she was somewhere lit by three moons. She searched for Leland and Dylan for hours but found nothing. Frustrated, she threw her dead phone at a tree.

The grass behind Jennifer crunched. She turned to find two shadows running in her direction. She ran. For whatever reason, she knew she had to run. Then she took cover behind green, dense bushes. She wasn't used to running, so her breaths quickened, and they were loud enough to be heard. She stopped breathing and hoped the darkness of the night hid her body.

Who are they? Have they been following me all the time?

Two men wearing black cloaks stood where she'd been just moments ago. They turned their heads right and left, searching. The thing she noticed now, which she hadn't when they'd charged at her, was that each of them carried a long sword with a white pommel. Jennifer exhaled, drew in air, and locked it inside once more.

Where am I?

In the blink of an eye, they disappeared. They just weren't there. Jennifer had two options: run or stay. Choosing the first, she stood on her feet and tried not to make too much noise.

Focus, Jenny. Don't do anything stupid.

But at the moment she fully stood on her feet, a rough hand grabbed her waist and began dragging her from behind.

"Let go of me!" she shrieked as she struck the figure with her elbow. He seemed to receive no damage.

I must do something or I'm going to do die!

The man wrapped a big, strong hand around her skinny waist and carried her. She kicked his knee with her heel. The man growled and his grip loosened. Jennifer bit his fingers and he let go. She then ran for her life.

She could hear him breathing behind her, his heavy legs chasing her. Jennifer's adrenaline surged and now her sympathetic system was almost fully stimulated. Her heart pounded fast and her hair stood on its ends, a fight-or-flight response. The noise behind her was getting closer until something pulled on her skirt. After stumbling over a brick, she fell to the ground. Two men towered over her. One of them sharpened his dagger with a brick, a devilish grin on his face. The other one leaned down to her.

As if I'd surrender that easy!

Jennifer punched him, then kicked him in his groin. She was about to escape when the other man grabbed her shoulder, spun her around, and then slapped her face. Jennifer's head spun. The world was now inverted. She lost her balance and fell to the ground once more. The two men carried her and bound her to a tree with a rope.

"Oh, poor Castler," the tallest said with a stern look. "What brought you out of the Castle, huh?"

Castler? What are they talking about?

"I don't know what you're talking about, but you better let me go now!" she roared, struggling to free herself. The rope pressed against her belly, nauseating her and forcing vomit out of her throat. Her helplessness made her feel pathetic and weak—and she hated being pathetic and weak.

Come on, Jenn. Come on. You can do it.

"What do you want? Money?" she asked, observing their eyes as they widened with bloodlust.

"A Castler talking about money … not a rare thing," spoke one of them, frowning with expressions full of revulsion. "Not now. When the time comes we'll get all of your silver coins and the gold caves and the rest of the stolen treasures!"

"I don't understand any of that," Jennifer panted. "Let me go!"

The rope was strong and tight. Jennifer's attempts to free herself were in vain. Staring at the well-built, tall men in front of her, Jennifer realized she had no chance to escape.

"We don't have a lot of time to waste," the short-est said. "You must die now. All Castlers must die, now or later!"

I'm not going to die here!

"Now tell us," the tallest said, "Why are you outside the Castle? You must be a spy or something. It doesn't matter. You're going to die anyway."

He sharpened his knife and his eyes shimmered with glee as he approached the powerless girl.

"I won't die here!" she yelled.

He loomed over Jennifer and showed no hesitation. Men of their kind likely killed with no remorse. Her eyes widened as the man grabbed her blonde hair and tugged, exposing her neck to the knife. She closed her eyes as the knife pressed against her skin. Right when she lost the last bit of hope to survive, the man grunted. His hands moved away. She opened her eyes and found him on the ground screaming in pain.

Dylan had come to save her. He'd broken a brick upon the man's head. The other man was far enough to let Dylan untie Jennifer, but close enough to reach them in a matter of seconds.

"Run, Jennifer, run!" Dylan ordered, freeing her.

"I won't leave you," she replied, throwing the rope away. The man in the cloak flew like a bullet train toward them.

"That's an order!" Dylan roared.

"But," Jennifer said, her voice cracking. She had never seen Dylan this angry before. *If I run away, will he survive?*

"Please, go! You're getting in my way!" Dylan shouted.

Jennifer fled. She left Dylan there alone. But she had to. If they both stayed and tried to fight, they'd both get killed. But Dylan was smart. Jennifer knew he was smart. He must have planned it ahead.

Tshjjjjt.

An atrocious sound from behind forced her to stop. She turned only her head around to witness the men in cloaks both stabbing Dylan's chest. They retracted their knives and then stabbed him again and again. Dylan spat blood.

Fear and disbelief dwelled in her chest as the world collapsed in front of her eyes. She gazed away, her head throbbing as if a hammer had been striking the back of her skull, and then she ran away. Tears leaked from her eyes and she sobbed, hoping her heart would stop squeezing and let her breathe once more.

How horrible can things get here? What have I done? I've let Dylan die!

Chapter Seven

Oremanta

Leland stepped back when the shadow threatened. But now the shadow was not behind the tree. Leland's fear seemed to encourage the shadow to step out and inch closer.

"Who are you and what do you want?" the man said, pointing a glittering object from a distance at Leland. His voice was steady, loud, and confident. Rather, it was a voice of someone who *wanted* to sound confident. Leland didn't need a clue to deduct that.

Maybe this guy is lost in these woods just like me.

"My name's Leland."

"What are you doing here?" The man lowered his dagger and moved closer to Leland. He wore dirty, ripped jeans and no shirt.

Leland shrugged. "I don't know where I am. I'm lost."

"Don't lie to me!" The man raised his dagger again.

"I'm not lying. Look at me. Do I look like I know where I am?"

The guy with the triangular, tanned face scrutinized Leland.

"No," he said, putting the dagger in the back pocket of his jeans, "You look pathetic, in fact."

"I want to get out of here. I need to find my friends."

The stranger sneered, which freaked out Leland. The pity in his eyes could only mean one thing: *I'm not going anywhere.*

"I've been lost in these woods for more than three days now," the man said. "I don't belong here. Neither do you."

"Where are we?" Leland asked, staring at the moons, and then back at the stranger again. "Is this place even real?"

"Shut up. You're too loud." The man turned around. "I have no idea where we are. But if we get caught by those cloaked men, we're dead."

Cloaked men?

"Wait," shrieked Leland, following the man. "What are you talking about?"

"Don't ask too many questions. I have no idea myself. But this place is dangerous."

Whoever this man was, he seemed like the only way for Leland to escape these woods. So he followed him, saving his few thousand questions for another time. For someone who looked to be the same age as Leland, this guy had an impressive, muscled, well-built body. But he also had a wound in his back, fresh and oozing red. Leland wondered if the cloaked men had caused the wound. The man almost disappeared behind the trees, covered by the darkness of the woods, but Leland hurried toward him, afraid he might slip his sight.

"Are you afraid?" the man teased. It was hard for Leland to see his face, but he could have sworn he was grinning.

"Yes," said Leland, sharply, "I am."

"Good," he replied, firmly this time. "You should be. This place is no game."

Leland was supposed to have gotten used to the wolves' howling by now, but still, with every howl, a shiver ascended his spine. Leland realized that the more they walked, the closer they got to the sound of an owl's hooting. He asked himself if they were intentionally going toward it or not. But the answer came faster than he thought. The man stopped and ordered Leland to do the same by moving his hand horizontally in the air. Then he took the dagger from his pocket. He stood still and raised the dagger up, pointing at something Leland couldn't see. He then swiftly threw the blade into the air. Something squeaked and then fell to the muddy ground.

"What's that?" Leland asked.

The man hurried to the thing that had fallen from above. Leland followed. The man picked up a dead owl and retained his dagger. He wiped the blood off the blade with his ripped jeans, and then he sat on a flat rock, carrying the owl from its head.

"You're lucky," the man said, extracting feathers off the owl's skin, "Having meat on your first night here."

"Just who are you?"

"My name is Jack." He peeled the skin off the owl. "I don't know how I came here. It's all too confusing for me."

"I was transferred directly from the basement of my house," Leland informed him. "This is ... surreal."

Jack, who was focusing on the owl in his hand, eyed Leland, now interested in what he'd said. But he quickly rolled his eyes back to the dead creature.

"I was in the attic of my house when everything went black," Jack revealed. "And then suddenly I found myself in this place."

Jack ripped the blood-soaked wings off and threw them at Leland. "You get the wings. I get the rest."

Leland was hungry, but the piece of meat in his hand looked far from delicious. "Aren't we cooking this?" It was more of suggestion. Leland hadn't eaten any raw meat in his previous life—not even sushi. Now, the only thing he could eat were bloody, uncooked wings.

"Eat it, boy." Jack smirked. "You're not in your fancy home anymore. This is the best thing you may find here."

Jack talked a while ago about cloaked men, but I haven't seen any of them yet. Should I trust this guy? Should I stay with him, or should I search for Dylan and Jennifer alone?

Leland wasn't a spoiled kid. He'd had to work hard to earn something. He'd had to save money to buy a phone. He'd had to help his mother raise Fred and Karla. Leland even brought the groceries to the house every Saturday. He'd worked in the summer, not necessarily because he or his family needed money, but rather because he felt responsible. He hated his father, but he couldn't deny that he'd learned so much from not having one.

"We'll get out of here," Leland said enthusiastically. "I know we will."

Jack didn't reply. He kept chewing the owl as if it were the last meal he'd ever eat. Leland gazed at the bloody wings in his hands. He had to survive, and he didn't know if he would find more food later on. There was a risk of food-borne infection from eating uncooked meat. He'd read that somewhere. But he closed his eyes and brought the wings closer to his mouth. The smell was foul. Now the meat was in his mouth. It tasted like blood and meat and fish all at once. It was sweet and bitter and disgusting. Leland threw the rest of the wings on the ground, both hands now covering his mouth. The barely chewed wad of food involuntarily came out of him.

"That's what happens the first time," Jack said, still chewing. "You'll get used to it soon."

Leland closed his eyes and took a deep breath. This night reminded him of last summer, when Jennifer, Dylan, and he had been lost on Mount Lamen. That time, they'd all been together, so it hadn't been that terrifying. It was more of an adventure.

But eating an uncooked owl isn't an adventure.

Leland spat out the remnants of the meat and wondered if Jack enjoyed his meal or just ate to survive. Leland could still taste the blood and meat. It made him feel sick.

"You're going to regret it later," Jack warned. "You'll die of hunger."

Leland pinched his hand strongly. *If I'm in a dream, won't I feel pain?* He'd seen a documentary about lucid dreams where you can control your actions and movements while dreaming. *But this can't be a dream. The air, the soil, the sounds, and even Jack are all too real.*

"I must find my friends."

"Good luck on that," Jack replied, sucking on a bone. "I hope they're not dead."

Dead? If anything bad happened to them, it's my fault. I just hope they're safe. I have to search for them and get them back home.

Leland stared at Jack. "Can I ask you a favor?"

"What?"

"Can you help me find them?"

Jack laughed, and Leland felt stupid for asking. *Why would a stranger help me find my friends? But I had to ask. I know I can't leave this guy's sight. This place is dangerous and I don't want to be alone.*

"What's so funny?" Leland asked firmly, compensating for what he thought had been a stupid question.

"Do you even trust me?"

"Yes, I trust you."

"You do?" Jack laughed more sarcastically this time. "How can you trust someone you just met?" He sharpened his dagger with a brick. "I don't want you to trust me. I might be your ally today, but tomorrow, if I had to, I'd kill you."

Somehow, Jack's words comforted Leland. *People who try to trick others often pretend they to be good, and when the right time comes, they throw their masks off. At least Jack's honest.*

"I'd do the same," Leland said.

"Good. You're starting to learn."

The little time Leland had spent in the woods had made him cherish the small things he had not so long ago: pizza, books, a cozy bed, warm baths, and safety.

Leland lay on the grass, staring at the gray-black sky. The stars were like many small pieces from a gigantic, shattered pearl stretching along the horizon. *Why do the most beautiful things appear at the most difficult times?*

Leland's chest hurt, similar to when his father had died. He felt like that every time he missed someone so much. It was the feeling of needing someone but knowing it was hard to reach him or her. Losing people hurts no matter how much you convince yourself you're good without them.

I wonder what you're doing now, Dylan and Jenny.

Leland closed his eyes and hoped he'd be back home when they reopened. He couldn't believe he could let his guard down while wild animals moaned in the darkness. The grass was itchy, but he didn't care. His consciousness slipped away faster than he thought and he slept.

Sleeping is the solution to many things, but it wasn't in this case. After an unknown period, a hand slapped Leland's face.

"Wake up and don't make a noise," Jack ordered in a hurry. He hid behind a tree and gestured for Leland to join him. Leland obeyed, but it wasn't until he stood beside Jack that he noticed the sweat all over his chest and face. He took a deep breath and looked around for a clue. The only clue he got was the sound of an approaching footstep, and that was enough to force his stomach to twist. Jack tightly squeezed the pommel of his dagger, readying himself to pounce on whoever was coming.

"Don't move," Jack told Leland in a low-pitched voice.

Leland held his breath.

A tall man, almost the tallest man Leland had ever seen, walked by them. He wore a black cloak and grabbed a long, curved sword. The cloak was ripped from the sides and the bottom edges and had too many holes. Way too many holes. The man, who was a few meters away now, shifted his eyes toward them in a stern gaze, as if he'd been searching for them for a decade. His eyes, narrow and sharp, told many things, of which the most important was that he wanted them dead.

He charged at them, pointing his sword in their direction, but Jack was ready. He dodged the man's sword, pounced on him, and almost stabbed his back. But the man struck Jack with his elbow, forcing him to fall on the ground. The unknown assailant rolled his eyes at Leland as if to say, "Stay there. I'll come for you when I'm done."

Leland had two options: run for his life or save Jack. But saving Jack was likely suicide. Out of the blue, an arrow drilled into the man's chest. He stood still, his eyes bulging while his hands tried to remove the arrow. He growled then fell dead.

"On time," a croaked voice said from behind, "Leland Hopegone was about to die."

Leland turned around and found an old man carrying a lantern. He was as tall as the man who'd attacked them. The old man had a remarkable scar on his face, stretching from his forehead and reaching down to his chin, slightly deviating to the right. His unkempt, coarse mustache perfectly matched his face. A young guy and a girl joined the old man, each carrying a lantern as well.

"You're as accurate as you were back in the days, huh?" the young guy asked the old man.

Many things confused Leland, and he didn't even have time to think of what confused him most. First, he'd randomly found this guy named Jack in the woods. Then a cloaked man had attacked them. And now another party had saved his life.

"Stay away!" Jack warned, picking up his knife and stepping back.

"Or?" The old man chuckled, playing with his mustache. He looked at the young man beside him and said, raising both eyebrows, "What a grateful kid, huh?"

"We don't have much time," said the younger man. "Let's get back before more men show up."

"Follow us," the old man instructed. "We must get back to the Castle."

"I'm going nowhere," Leland said firmly. "I must find my friends first."

He knew he *sounded* strong. But he knew even more that he wasn't really strong at that moment. His legs quivered and his heart raced, but he was lucky it was dark so they couldn't see him tremble in fear. Someone had just died right in front of everyone, and Leland seemed like the only one affected by it.

"There are no friends, dear," the old man said. "There is *a* friend. One only. Good for you she's not too far from here."

Was he referring to Jennifer? If yes, how'd he know where she was? And where was Dylan?

"Just … who are you? What do you want?" Leland asked.

"My name is Aelfgar. Aelfgar Hawx. And there are no answers here in the woods. We'll tell you everything in the Castle."

Jack's resistance had gone away at some point. He didn't want to fight Aelfgar or his companions anymore. He put his dagger into his pocket, stared at the dead man's body for the last time, then asked, "Who are the cloaked men?"

"It's a long story," the girl beside Aelfgar replied. "We must leave the woods for now. Stop asking."

Aelfgar turned around, passed the lantern to his other hand, and then ordered, "Follow me."

They all obeyed and followed the old man into the depths of the woods.

If there was one thing Leland clung to that night, it was faith. He had no idea where he was going, what that place they referred to as the "castle" was, or why men in cloaks were roaming the woods. And someone had just died right in front of him, and no one cared about it. But out of the millions of things that confused Leland, one mystery in particular kept knocking at the back of his head: *How do they know my name? How could this old man have called me Leland when I've never seen him before?*

"How far are we from Temblewood?" Leland asked.

"Temblewood?" The old man wondered, then chuckled. "What a weird name."

Am I out of Temblewood now? But even if I was, how in the world doesn't he know Temblewood? Leland knew Temblewood wasn't a very famous city, but everyone in the country definitely knew the name.

"You are—" Aelfgar said, but then swiftly placed his lantern on the ground. He pulled out his sword, producing a loud, sharp sound of steel sliding against steel. Something with large claws and red eyes ran in their direction, galloping with lust to rip their bodies into little parts.

It was a wolf—at least "wolf" was the most accurate word in Leland's mental dictionary to describe the beast about to end their lives. The wolves he'd seen before didn't have two horns sticking out of their heads, and they hadn't been as tall as him.

Aelfgar grabbed the wolf by its neck and then locked it with his elbow. With his free hand, he slit the wolf's neck then threw it away as if it was weightless. The old man returned his sword back to its sheath, carried his lantern once more as if nothing had happened, then told Leland, "You are not on Earth anymore. Welcome to Oremanta."

Not on Earth?

Chapter Eight

Sorrow

Jennifer sat on a flat rock staring at the reflection of three moons on a running river. She'd arrived at the river after running for a long enough time to ensure no one was following. She was still in a state of shock, somewhere between reality and illusion. Sometimes the mind doesn't easily accept traumatizing events. Or it just doesn't *want* to accept them.

The wind sighed heavily and the grass and leaves rustled, motivating Jennifer to turn around every time expecting Dylan to show up. But Dylan was gone and she knew that very well. *There's no way he could have survived those stabs. They were all in his chest. No. They were all in his heart.*

Until this point, she hadn't felt like crying. The most destructive feelings take time before they begin to grind one's soul. In her head, she only saw Dylan being stabbed to death, and she couldn't stop it from repeating. She shook her head, glared at the moons, and then shifted her eyes back to the running river. Tall, scary trees surrounded everything.

Tears welled up and her vision blurred. They streamed down her face, rolling on her cheeks and neck and eventually settled on her shirt. She knew this was coming. She knew she would cry. Her chest hurt and a feeling of impending doom took over everything, paralyzing the lonely girl.

Stop.

She whispered, shedding tears, and squeezing on her shirt with both hands. The pain ascended from her chest to her neck, strangulating her. She struggled to draw breath. She'd seen Dylan almost every day in the past six or seven years. *Why did he have to leave now? Why does losing people hurt? Why can't someone live without missing others?*

She'd once called him a "nerdy little coward" because he hadn't replied to a group of bullies at school. At last year's summer camp, she'd called him a chicken because he was afraid to sleep alone in a tent. But now, in one single moment, Dylan had proved he was braver than any other person she'd ever encountered. Jennifer recalled last night's conversation when he'd told her and Leland he was busy and couldn't help them. She recalled how she insisted and told him to shut up because it was serious business.

If I hadn't been so persistent, he wouldn't have died. I dragged him to this hell.

Jennifer wrapped her arms around her knees. She wondered if she would see Leland ever again, but that wasn't her top priority. *I must survive for Dylan's sake. His sacrifice must not be wasted.*

A small red flower poked out from the riverbank. Flowers had always been a part of her childhood. An old memory occupied her mind:

"It's the fifth day of the month, Dad," eight-year-old Jennifer *said excitedly.*

"I know, sweetie, but daddy is busy today."

"You can't be busy! It's Mom's day. You promised, remember?"

"I know." He kissed her forehead. "We'll go there tomorrow, okay?"

Jennifer's father took her to her mother's grave every Saturday. Her mother had died in a car accident when she was only six.

"Okay." With an unsatisfied look, she tucked her hair behind her ears and ran back to her room. Jennifer put her small face on the pillow as tears rained down from her eyes. She grabbed her teddy bear, the one she'd gotten from her mother on her fifth birthday and pressed it against her chest.

Jennifer opened her drawing book after wiping the tears away and began drawing. Of course, she drew nothing but her mom.

"Don't be afraid, Mom. Dad said you'd be okay as long as we visit you. I hope that's not a lie."

She slept on the ground with her face on one of her drawings, hugging her bear. Her internal clock woke her up when the sun rose. She hurried to her father and whispered in his ear, "It's morning, Dad. Let's go!"

"It's too early, kiddo, isn't it?"

"No, Dad! She's there all alone. Let's hurry."

He smiled. "I knew you'd say that. All right, Jenny, let's visit mom, shall we?"

"Yeah!"

The cemetery was half an hour away by car. It was a sunny Sunday and the streets were crowded.

"Dad, we forgot something."

"What is it, sweetie?"

"Flowers!"

"Oh, how did we forget those?"

"I don't know."

"But dad!"

"We'll be late if we turn back. You don't want to be late, do you?"

Once they reached the cemetery, Jennifer opened the door in a hurry and ran to her mother's grave. She brought her drawings with her and placed them over the grave then said, "Sorry we're late, Mom. We didn't bring flowers with us either. Forgive us, please. We were supposed to visit you yesterday but dad said he had a lot of work."

"Look what I found!" her dad said, placing pink flowers in her hands. "They've been in the trunk the whole time. A good surprise, isn't it?"

Jennifer placed the flowers on her mother's grave.

Then she returned to reality as a familiar voice called from behind.

"Jennifer!"

Leland! Beside him stood four figures she didn't recognize, but she didn't care about them. She hurried to Leland and placed both of her hands behind his back and hugged him. She sank her head into his chest and kept it there for a while. At last, she felt warm.

"Don't … Don't ever leave me," she sputtered, shedding tears on him. It wasn't familiar for her to cry in front of anyone, and she'd never done it before. Jennifer pressed her head tightly to his chest, and for a moment she felt she was home.

"I'm sorry, Jennifer. I really am."

His voice was calm, confident, and reassuring. But that didn't mean much. It just made everything worse. *How can I tell him about Dylan's death?*

"Who are they?" she asked.

"I don't know."

"Let's run," she whispered. Then she screamed, "Let's run!"

She slowly lifted her head up, wiped her tears away, then looked straight into his eyes, doubting her ability to talk. She looked away and hesitated before whispering again, "Dylan … is—" Jennifer choked on every word until the final one tumbled out: "Dead."

Chapter Nine

Into the Castle

Leland's blood ran cold. He looked at Jennifer with a pale face then asked, shaking her shoulders, "What do you mean?"

"He's dead. He died defending me," Jennifer replied, still looking away. "Two men wanted to kill me. He came and freed me then sacrificed himself so that I could run away."

"This can't be happening. No way," Leland yelled, walking in circles. "It's my fault ... It's mine! I'm the one to blame."

"What did they look like?" Aelfgar asked Jennifer, the wolf's blood still on his body. He wore a golden shield covered by a red cloak. His two companions wore similar shields except white cloaks engulfed their bodies. A drawing of a castle had been sculpted on the center of their shields.

"Who are you?" Jennifer shouted, still wiping her tears away.

"My name is Aelfgar Hawx. This is Warden and Utta, my companions. And we're by your side," the old man replied. "Now answer my question."

"Tall, with black cloaks."

"We must get back to the Castle. It is dangerous out here," Aelfgar said. "Let's go!"

"No," Leland said. "We're not going anywhere."

He glared at Jennifer then ordered through his tears, "Let's get Dylan and go back home."

"He's … dead," Jennifer stated, barely holding her body up. "Dylan is dead." She sounded more realistic now.

Although it was dark in the woods, Leland could see Jennifer's red eyes.

"I sense no one around," Aelfgar said. "Your friend is dead. Now let's get back to the Castle before we all die."

"Right," the girl beside Aelfgar assured. "We can't afford to stay here any longer. Hurry up."

Leland wasn't convinced. He would never leave Dylan out here in the woods, even if he were dead. That was the least he could do for his friend. But guilt quickly rose inside him, and he wasn't able to say a word or move a step.

Dylan's dead because of me. It was no one else's fault. If I hadn't told Jennifer or Dylan about what had happened to me, none of this would have happened. Dylan would still be home doing what he always did. It's all my fault.

"Let's go," Jennifer whispered to him. Her voice was fragile and weak after having seen her best friend die. And she must be afraid she'd lose her life now.

"Yeah," Leland replied softly, surrendering to the reality that if they stayed in this place any longer, he could lose Jennifer and himself. "Let's go."

"I know you have a lot of questions. We'll talk more in the Castle," Aelfgar said.

Leland didn't know what this Castle was that these strangers kept referring to. He didn't understand where they even were to begin with. In fact, his list of unanswered questions kept getting longer. He didn't know what to ask about right now, but this old man seemed to have some answers. Leland inhaled deeply, counted from one to ten in his mind, and then exhaled. His best bet was to trust these guys for now. Otherwise, he and Jennifer would be lost in the woods for days. It hurt that he'd thought of himself and Jennifer only— that he hadn't counted Dylan.

"Hold our backs," Aelfgar ordered. "Never let go. Clear?"

Aelfgar, Utta, and Warden turned their backs on Leland, Jennifer, and Jack. Leland and Jennifer held tightly onto their cloaks. Jack sighed, his eyes flaming with anger. "This is stupid," he petulantly said before holding onto Aelfgar's cloak.

Leland rapidly saw scattered images of woods, hills, valleys, and mountains. And then, in one fell swoop, they were all in front of a gigantic castle as if they'd been instantly transmitted across hundreds of miles. The walls of the castle were so high they could touch the clouds. There were hundreds, and maybe thousands, of turrets stretching along its walls. Men in white cloaks with golden shields stood near those turrets. Each had a long sword etched on his metal suit.

"Here we are," Aelfgar informed. For an instant, all the cloaked men aimed their arrows at them, but then they eased once they'd confirmed it was Aelfgar and his companions.

The Castle's brown walls held countless flaming torches. Leland's face was still pale. He eyed Jennifer, but her eyes were fixed on the high walls. She was probably thinking of Dylan, who was suddenly gone, leaving nothing but memories behind. Leland clenched his fists until his knuckles were white.

I'm sorry, Dylan.

Aelfgar went toward the Golden Gate ahead of them. It was taller and wider than any building Leland had ever seen before. Aelfgar put a hand on the gate and then pushed. It opened and dim light sneaked from the inside into the small gap.

Warden spoke, moving to the gate. "Behind this wall is our shelter. Our home. We call it the Castle, even though there is more than just a castle behind these walls. There are villages and palaces and shops. Not even a hundred warriors can open the Golden Gate. But Aelfgar is one hell of an old man."

Leland looked at Jennifer. She looked back. He went closer to her then said, staring into her blue eyes, "It's going to be fine." He wasn't sure himself. He wanted to make her feel better and stronger, but it seemed she was already on the mend.

She replied, "Yeah. We have to go with them and discover what's behind everything, but don't let your guard down. We can't fully trust anyone here."

Leland and Jennifer followed the rest toward the Golden Gate and entered the Castle. Early sunbeams marked the beginning of a new morning, and a cold breeze forced Leland to shiver. Six men stood behind the gate, three on the left and three on the right. They all bowed before Aelfgar.

"How many times have I told you not to bow?" Aelfgar sighed. "The earthlings might think I'm the ruler of the Castle." He laughed.

"Earthlings?" One guard marveled at their sight. "Good luck with that, Sir Aelfgar."

From a distance, three huge palaces with big purplish domes and four high towers appeared. Leland saw they were adorned with glistening jewels, but it was hard for him to see more details as he was too far away. Yet inside the Castle, there were cottages everywhere, and shielded men with swords astride their horses roamed the grounds.

"Let's get going," Aelfgar said. "We've got a lot of things to do, and we're out of time."

"Out of time for what?" Jennifer asked in a loud voice—the same question Leland wanted to ask. This old man, Aelfgar, and his companions, Utta and Warden, hadn't told them anything about this place except that they weren't on Earth anymore, which Leland perceived as the biggest lie he'd ever heard.

"Why can't you just wait?" Aelfgar said, chuckling and scratching the back of his head as he tried to locate the road they should take now. This gigantic place, or city, or Castle as they called it, surrounded by high walls as if it's a world within a world, didn't seem to have an end. Ahead of them was a junction where four roads met. Cottages, and what seemed like shops, lined each road.

"There," Utta said firmly as she pointed with her small hand at one of the roads. "You must have gotten old, Aelfgar."

Some people inside the Castle carried shields and swords while others were unarmed, wearing silky dresses that wrapped tightly around them. For Leland, Jennifer, and Jack—the Earthlings—all of this seemed unreal. Where are the cars and the electronics and the high buildings?

Leland gazed at the people passing by, exchanging a mutual feeling of rejection. He wore jeans and a cotton shirt, an outfit that seemed unfamiliar to whoever eyed him.

"How far are we from home?" Leland asked, avoiding eye contact.

"Galaxies away," Aelfgar replied almost instantly.

"How do you know about Earth when we didn't know this place even existed?" Jennifer asked.

"Good question, but the answer might frustrate you a little bit," Aelfgar replied. "People from Earth can reach Oremanta, but it doesn't work the other way 'round. In other words, once you're in Oremanta, you can't get back to Earth."

"Bullshit." Jack sniffed.

"We know things about Earth because of people like you, but we're not so interested in knowing more. We can't get there anyway, and we have enough problems to deal with here." Aelfgar cleared his throat. "Harvard, a friend of mine, was from Earth. He told us a lot and researched a lot. There are others who are from Earth, but it's not so common."

The glowing sphere of the sun rose above the horizon, casting bright beams over the shy dawn. The road they walked in was a hive of activity: smiths sharpened spears and polished weaponry while shopkeepers sold silky uniforms, wooden brushes, and primitive tools.

"Aelfgar!" A man shouted, grinning with excitement. "What are you doing near the walls?"

He also wore golden shields and had a noticeable dark mole on his cheek. His sword was painted black, or it was black by default. Leland thought Aelfgar was the tallest man alive, but this guy was even taller. But not everyone in the Castle was *that* tall. Warden, the man with Aelfgar, was as tall as Leland.

Aelfgar didn't reply but rather pointed with his eyes to Leland, Jennifer, and Jack, who all stood there unsure of what was going on.

"Earthlings. I see." The man with the mole sighed. "It's been a while since I've last seen some. Bad timing. They'll see nothing but blood."

"No. The timing is great. We need everything we can get right now," Aelfgar said as he looked at Leland. "Especially this one."

Me?

"We're already inside the Castle, or whatever this place is called," Jack ranted. "Now you better speak!"

"You are right. We must not waste time," Aelfgar replied. "We will split into three groups. Jack will come with me, Leland will go with Utta, and Jennifer with Warden."

"No!" Leland yelled. "Jennifer and I are staying together."

"As you like," Aelfgar said, then he ordered Utta, "Take them with you."

She nodded. Her body was small and her face was childlike. She looked as though she was fifteen, with sharp eyes and thin lips. She turned right and walked.

"Follow me, Leland, Jennifer," she ordered. Utta walked fast. Her blonde ponytail swung right and left, covering and uncovering the glistening sword fixed on her back.

"Where are we going?" Leland asked.

"Somewhere quite—my cottage. I'll tell you whatever you want there."

They walked for half an hour when Utta opened the door of her remote cottage, the only one on top of a small green hill. A rough thatched roof had bent smoothly over her home and dense, purple flowers crept toward the windows from all directions.

"Here we are," she said, entering the cottage with careful steps. Beside a window that overlooked the green hills, there was a petite, round, wooden table. Leland and Jennifer sat there as Utta went to the corner of the hut. There was a pot on a stove with something boiling inside.

"What should we do now?" Leland whispered to Jennifer. *Running away from this place is an option, but where would we go?*

"We'll have to wait and listen," Jennifer suggested, her voice strong and steady.

But Leland knew what was beyond her tune. He knew she was thinking of Dylan more than anything else right now.

"It's going to be alright," he told her. He only wished he could fake his tune as well as she did.

"If I ever become a burden, leave me and go," Jennifer acknowledged, now staring at the green hills from the dusty window. "I don't want anyone to die for me anymore."

"Shut up, Jenny," Leland replied, his voice cracking. "You're here because of me."

Utta brought them two cups of a hot drink, from which steam floated into the air.

"This is Oremanta's finest mesta," Utta said, placing the cups on the round table.

"Mesta?" Leland inquired, bringing the drink closer to his mouth.

"Taste it. It's good," Utta added. She crossed her arms, and her facial expressions tightened a bit. "Now, more importantly, let's talk about what you want to hear."

Leland sipped but Jennifer didn't. She only glared at Utta as she spoke, "You're on Planet Oremanta. In the center of Oremanta there's this Castle. Men called the Flares of Truth rule it, and whoever rules the Castle rules all of Oremanta. They're the legendary kings who controlled everything on this planet for a pretty long time," Utta explained. "People of the Castle pay the Flares of Truth much respect and appreciation, but that's not the case for everyone in this dimension."

Utta brought herself a cup of mesta and sat beside them. She cleared her throat and then went on, "People like you who came from Earth told us a lot about your home. They told us about the wars and the pollution and the racial discrimination. But we aren't so different from you. Oremanta has its own problems. Before I tell you everything about this planet, tell me what happened to you on Earth before you came here."

Leland created a blank file in his head and quickly rearranged what had happened in sequence so that he could explain it properly to Utta: the voices, the basement, him seeing Jennifer, then Jennifer seeing him, but neither of them actually being at the other person's place. And then going back to the basement with Jennifer and Dylan and seeing a glistening object beneath the carpet. Then déjà vu and landing in Oremanta.

Leland explained to the Oremantian girl what had happened to them as if he hadn't promised himself before he wouldn't tell that secret to anyone.

"I see," Utta said, placing the cup on the table as she divulged, expressionless, "That is expected. First, you must know this dimension is different than Earth. To say the least, and to keep it simple, we are in a different time and location. Things that apply on Earth might not apply here and vice versa."

"How's that related to our story?" Jennifer interrupted.

"Before I answer that, I need to confirm something," Utta replied. She brought another cup. This time it was filled with sand instead. She gave it to Leland, and instantly after he grabbed it, the sand vibrated. Leland held his tongue as she commented, "As I thought. I just wanted to make sure."

"Your soul is Oremantian," she continued. "An Oremantian soul must return to Oremanta one day. Your soul was calling you day and night to bring you here."

"What? I don't get it … I've lived my whole life on Earth," Leland gawked. Jennifer didn't say a thing, but if anything she looked as confused as Leland was.

"It doesn't matter where you lived. Your soul is Oremantian, and at some point an Oremantian soul must return to where it belongs. The voices you heard came from your soul. They led you to the closest port to Oremanta."

"What's a port?" Jennifer asked, breaking her silence.

"Earth is connected to Oremanta by ports. They cannot be activated unless someone with an Oremantian soul touches it. Not only that, but when the time comes. In other words, if Leland touched that port in the basement before his soul started to call, he wouldn't have been transported. An Oremantian soul must be mature enough to be able to transport you to Oremanta."

"Why did I come along then?" Jennifer inquired, arching an eyebrow.

"Because you were there when the port got activated. That's all."

A small chandelier hung from the ceiling, and it was almost identical to the one in Leland's house. The striking difference was that Leland's house chandelier worked by electricity and this one was probably powered by gas and fire.

"This still doesn't explain why I saw Jennifer in the basement that night, and how she saw me at the same night in her house," Leland said.

Utta stood up and put her cup near the stove. The cottage was small, but if Utta lived there alone, it fit her well. In one corner, a helical staircase led up to a half-story. From Leland's perspective, he could only see one beige sheet and a small blanket up there.

"As I told you, the time in Oremanta differs from that on Earth. We're two or three days ahead of Earth. Almost. I'm explaining this with your own counting system. If it was Sunday on Earth, then it might be Tuesday or Wednesday here."

"So, for example, if it was the second day of the month on Earth, it's the fourth in Oremanta?" Jennifer asked. She finally sipped her drink and seemed to await Utta's answer eagerly.

"Yes. Almost. Now I've told you, Leland, that your soul is Oremantian. Your soul was mature enough, and it was the time for you to come here. When you were there in the basement the first time, your soul was very close to the port that would lead you here. I assume your mind had partially connected to Oremanta. Your body was on Earth, but your mind was set two or three days ahead of its timeline because it was connected to this dimension. Because of that, you saw what would happen in your basement two days in the future. The mental connection that was established doesn't necessarily happen every time, or to everyone, I would assume. Because the second time you were in the basement, when you were with your friends, it didn't happen."

Leland needed a moment to absorb what Utta had just said, but it was weird for him to process the word 'Oremanta' in his head, to acknowledge the existence of this faraway planet as they claimed.

That's why I had déjà vu right before we were transported to Oremanta. I've already seen this moment. When I first got into the basement, I saw future *Jennifer kneeling in that spot.*

"So, when my brain became connected with Oremanta and my body was still on Earth, I witnessed what happened on Earth before it really happened. I saw Jennifer in our basement, but that was going to happen days later when we all came to the basement with Dylan?"

"Yes. Exactly."

"But then how did I see him in my backyard the same night?" Jennifer asked.

"Let's go outside," Utta said. "I like it outside."

She walked out of the cottage into the meadows and green hills. The day was brighter now and the weather was cool. Some clouds gathered in the sky, looking like a field of cotton.

Utta said, "I would assume Leland ran away when he saw what he saw in the basement because he must have been frightened. In this case, he was far away from the port, and thus his mind was no longer attached to Oremanta. He was no more mentally advanced. This attachment and detachment consumed a lot of his mental powers. He was mentally unstable. He probably rushed to your house without knowing."

"I don't recall going anywhere!" Leland said.

"Of course you don't. You were connected to a whole different dimension. How do expect yourself to remember what you were doing? You were probably in a state of delirium or confusion, something that is expected after consuming *that* much of your mental powers."

Everything made sense but didn't at the same time. It was hard for Leland to digest it all. Utta's explanation was logical, but Leland had never believed in the existence of life anywhere but on Earth. Now someone was claiming that he belonged here, in another dimension.

"I want to show you something," Utta said. "Follow me, please."

Leland and Jennifer said nothing. They just followed. She walked away from her cottage. They walked in the green fields with no cottages or people. From a distance, they could see the Castle's walls, high and mighty.

"The palaces centered in the Castle belong to the legendary leaders of Oremanta, or as we call them, the Flares of Truth. They belong to the Seven Lieutenants serving them and everyone else here. Now that you've heard what you wanted to hear, you have to listen to what *I* have to say."

Leland and Jennifer remained silent, but they exchanged looks, most of which were expressions of false assurance. They had to act that way because it was the only way they could survive in this place.

Once, back in middle school, Leland had fought with a classmate who used to pick on him every day. He'd punched that kid in the face, and that kid had punched him back on his tummy. Then the teacher, who'd promised he'd inform Leland and the other kid's parents, separated them. Leland had been hurt, not only because his tummy felt like it would burst, but also because he had no parents. He only had a mother.

He hid his pain quite well that day. His classmates considered him a winner because he hadn't wailed in pain like the other kid, although he'd wanted to cry out loud so badly. Faking things sometimes worked.

"Oremanta has a lot of natural supplies: gold, oil, pure water, and phosphate among many other things. Well, all of these supplies were harvested and distributed equally to the people of Oremanta. People worked together to survive and worshiped the leaders faithfully," Utta further explained. "But some people never get enough."

She stopped when they reached a ruined ground. There were burned cottages, wreckage, fallen trees, destroyed playgrounds, horse skeletons, and half-burned black flags.

"This is the city of Tanemba." Utta stared at the ruins and crossed her arms tightly around her chest as if she wanted to merge both sides of her rib cage. She was slightly taller than Leland's sister, Karla, who barely reached his abdomen.

"This place was once a hive of activity. Now, there is only wreckage."

"What happened?" Jennifer asked, scanning the ruins.

"Tanemba is just a simple example of what happened eight years back," Utta said, her voice weak and fragile. "Children played in the yards. They danced till the sun faded away. Shops opened every day. The people of Tanemba were the kindest. What's left now? Nothing but the souls of the good men haunting this place."

Utta walked between the ruins, and then she leaned down and picked up a small brick and gazed at it for a while, her eyes agonizing over the remainder of this place.

"There, behind that big rock, was Mr. Brown's bakery." She pointed at a big rock beside a burnt tree. "Right next to it was Mrs. Julie's candy shop and across that street Mr. Richmond, the mayor, used to scold kids who played next to his cottage. All of that's gone. Loneliness has fallen on Tanemba. This hollow feeling of being alone suddenly, I wonder if you've experienced it. One day everyone's here. The next you're alone, forever. And you know no one will be back again."

Leland knew that feeling because it attacked him every time Dylan's image popped up in his head.

Yesterday they had been eating and talking and laughing as if there were no tomorrow, and now Dylan was gone.

Utta threw away the brick she'd picked up and went on. "It's a massacre. I lost all my family and friends. I lost my whole village."

Utta's voice got progressively weaker with every sentence, so she turned around and gave them her back, a defensive mechanism against showing her weakness.

"It all began eight years ago. I was only seven. A group of people rebelled against the Flares of Truth. Those people weren't satisfied and thought they deserved much more than what they got. Day by day and night by night, that group increased. The fire of their hatred grew incredibly fast. They wanted to be the leaders of Oremanta. They created headquarters, organized themselves, and chose a leader to represent them. They worked underground and didn't expose their intentions to the public. Soon, they created bases, recruited soldiers, and developed their own army."

"And the Flares of Truth weren't aware of that?" Jennifer asked.

Utta stepped away from the ruins onto green grass again. There were no hills now, only a green land that stretched for miles. But still, from where they were, Leland could see three domed palaces centered in the Castle. *Just how big is this place?*

"At that time, it wasn't a rebellion. They worked secretly. Some news leaked about them, but no one had a clue who was leading it and where they were headquartered." Utta explained, "They planned for this rebellion day and night, and they built up quite a good arsenal in a short time. The flame of the rebellion burned taller and taller. They had only one purpose: dethrone the kings to rule Oremanta."

"What happened then?" Leland asked.

"When the rebels became fully confident in their power, they declared war. Tanemba, my city, was the first place to pay the toll. The Rebel Army's cruelty didn't exclude kids or women. Their chaos resulted in countless deaths and hundreds of refugees. Only two survived Tanemba's incident: me and Alpheus. And we don't know where he is now anyway. But Tanemba was just one example. Dozens of cities were eliminated in days."

Moments of silence followed. Leland had seen people get killed every day in the news, and he could sympathize only a little. It wasn't that he didn't care, but it hadn't directly affected *him*. But Utta's story *did* touch him. Whoever those rebels were, they did an awful thing. Killing was never, and will never be, a solution to anything.

"Who won the war?" Leland asked.

"I would be biased if I said us. Both parties have lost tremendous amounts of money, lives, and resources. However, the Rebel Army couldn't overtake Oremanta. Even though we live inside this castle, our soldiers control the main natural resources inside Oremanta. Besides that, many villages outside the Castle are under our protection. The Rebel Army lost a lot of its leaders and couldn't get what they wanted, but they aren't done yet."

Wars on Earth were never less cruel. World Wars I and II had resulted in the deaths of millions. The nuclear bombings of Hiroshima and Nagasaki had eliminated cities within seconds. Humankind had always been greedy.

"I'm telling you this because you need to know that—" Utta turned around, cleared her throat, looked straight into their eyes, and revealed, "—we're on the verge of a second war. And we need you with us. We need everyone to save Oremanta for good."

"Another war!" Jennifer marveled. She eyed Leland then Utta and said, "We've never touched a sword before. We can't help you!"

"Believe me, you can."

***

They were back again to the busy roads of the Castle before they'd even noticed. But this road was more active than the one they'd been on before. Merchants advertised their goods in a barbaric way. Beside blabbering about how good the piece of carpet, or sword, or scissors, or whatever they sold were, they would stick the item very close to the faces of people passing by, illustrating how great their items were. However, they'd take those items away once Leland, Jennifer, and Utta passed by. They'd replace their smiles with frowns, maybe because they hated Leland and Jennifer's outfits.

"Why are they staring at us like that?" Jennifer whispered to Utta.

"Because you're strangers. Castlers are afraid of strangers."

At the end of the road was a village square, where pigeons landed and took off. On a nearby stand, a man with a dark black beard wearing a white cloak preached to dozens of people.

"For the bells of war are about to ring, we Castlers must fight with all we have to defend our precious lands!" The man snarled, raising his hands up and down in the air. "Only the Flares of Truth shall rule Oremanta!"

But that hadn't captured Leland's attention as much as the large sword centered in the square had. The sword was double his height and had a golden pommel with a curved, petrified blade.

"It's called the Sword of Legends," Utta told Leland. "Only three warriors in the history of Oremanta had such a sword. We're in Eren's Square, which honors the first man who obtained it."

"Obtained?" Jennifer asked.

"To obtain this sword, one has to go for a deadly quest outside the Castle. They say whoever gets it receives an immense amount of power. Oremantians love myths, and as long as you're here you're going to hear plenty of them."

Leland knew what he wanted to tell Utta. Getting out of this place safe and sound was his top priority. Even if he felt sorry for the innocent people who got killed, the war of Oremanta was not his war, and he wouldn't be of much help anyway.

"We need your help in this," Utta requested. "We need you, Leland."

"I'm sorry," Leland replied straightaway. "This war is not ours. We'll just be in your way. I've lost a close friend of mine here. This place is dangerous. I have a family to stay with, and I have a life to get back to."

"You don't get it do you?" Utta said firmly, frowning. "There's *no way* back to Earth. When I was little, I heard stories, fairy tales, about a mythical dragon carrying people to other planets. But that's nothing but a myth, and there are hundreds of stories similar to that, none of which are true. I haven't seen or heard of any Earthling who got *back* to Earth. It *never* happened and it *never* will. You have to wake up and realize that you will stay here in Oremanta—*forever.*"

Leland didn't accept the idea of staying there forever, but he knew he shouldn't strongly oppose Utta or anyone else here. *I'm powerless, and so is Jennifer, so we shouldn't cross boundaries.*

"Even if we were to stay in Oremanta, why would we fight with you? We've never been in a battle before. This thing isn't ours," Jennifer interfered.

"The Rebel Army killed your friend out there in the woods. Don't you want your revenge?" Utta asked. "You can do more than you think. This war is yours as much as it is ours."

The square became more crowded as the preacher grew louder and angrier. He had no control over his voice now, and the more he shouted, the more the crowd interacted, cheering and approving what he said.

Utta took them somewhere more quiet to a nearby road where they sat on a concrete bench.

"The rebels are now stronger than any other time before," Utta stated. "A second war to dethrone the Flares of Truth will inevitably take place." She rose from her seat, took a look at the sky, and then sighed.

Oremanta's three moons were semi-transparent at midday, but that wasn't weird or new to Leland anymore. However, the sun was. Shiny, curved, silver haloes surrounded the sun's glowing sphere, dynamically spinning around it. *Did those just appear or have they been present all the time?*

"This war involves you more than anyone else, Leland," Utta said. "I know you don't want to participate in this. Oh god, I wished Aelfgar had told you this instead of me. What if I told you that the leader of the Rebel Army, the most fearful and cruel man in Oremanta, is Frank Hopegone?"

"My … father?"

Chapter Ten

The Decision

At first, Leland struggled to draw breath. But then he realized it was more than that: his heart hammered against his chest, his head throbbed, and he could barely stand on his feet. He was sweating profusely, and the drops rolled down his face onto his neck and the rest of his body.

Is this ... real?

Accepting this meant cruelly trashing the fact that had been implanted in his head since he was a child: that his father had died. But something crushed his insides, squeezing so hard internally he could no longer think. So he ran away, fast and random and dead inside.

"Where are you going, Leland?" Jennifer called.

But he was too distracted and confused. He didn't even think of replying.

Leland didn't know where he was going, but anywhere he could be alone would be fine. He was only aware of the tears streaming down his face and that he couldn't stop them. *I've always thought my father was dead, but now he's alive, leading a rebellion,* and *killing everyone.*

Leland walked until he found a haystack between two cottages. He sat on it, thinking of the ten years he'd spent without a father. He recalled how much it hurt whenever a friend said he went to a basketball game with his father or when there were father-son camps. He missed all of that. He missed the presence of a family leader. Leland wasn't just a seventeen-year-old spoiled kid; he was a son and a father-figure and a brother all in one. All for nothing. All because Frank was somewhere else leading a rebellion. He lay motionless on the haystack, carrying the burden of the world on his shoulders.

He couldn't recall the last time he'd cried, but it was long ago. He wiped the tears off his face and thought of nothing for a while. He'd once written a sentence in his diaries: *If my tears were made of fire, I would burn down the whole world.* He didn't quite mean it at that time, but now it made a lot of sense. His tears were hot and burning, just like his heart.

Is this what you left us for?

Leland stared at Oremanta's sky, at the three moons and the haloed sun and the now-orange sky. The men in the woods outside the Castle were Rebels. In other words, his father's men had killed Dylan. Hatred spread inside Leland like wildfire. He could no longer stay where he was. He stood up and roamed the roads of the Castle as the sun began to set.

He noticed that nothing was written in letters in Oremanta. Instead, Oremantians drew symbols. Smiths drew, or sculpted, a sword and a shield symbol.

Restaurants drew a lamb or a chicken symbol with rising steam.

Leland walked for around an hour when he saw a shop with a cup symbol on top. An old man poured a hot drink into pottery cups. A few wooden chairs were neither inside the shop nor on the street, but somewhere in between. Leland walked in. The man said nothing. He glared at Leland, then went to light the lanterns that hung from the roof.

"From Earth, ain't ya?" The old man poured a hot drink into a pottery cup and set it on Leland's table. "Do you have coins to pay with? You seem new. You haven't even changed your clothes yet."

He spoke slowly, and his voice was croaked and loud. Before he got back to the stove, he glared at Leland one more time, resentment in his eyes.

"You Earthlings brought nuffin' but pain and death to our lands. Would've been better if you'd stayed on Earth. But as they say, an Oremantian soul must get back to Oremanta."

Leland understood now why Castlers stared at him. They hated Earthlings because his father had killed their families and friends and children. Now Leland knew why there hadn't been a funeral for his father. He was gone, not dead, as his mother had said.

Does my mom know about all of this?

He sipped his drink, the so-called Mesta, and now had better knowledge of what it tasted like: milk mixed with hazelnut and chocolate, and something sour.

Leland had nothing to pay with but his silver watch. He took it off and stared at it for a moment before he offered, "Would this be okay?"

Then a silver coin landed on Leland's table and a familiar voice said, "Keep it. It might be the last thing you have from Earth. Your drink is on me." Aelfgar winked at Leland. "I don't do that very often, ya' know?"

The shopkeeper bowed when he saw Aelfgar then said softly, "I'm honored. Aelfgar Hawx visiting my humble shop? It must be a lucky day!"

"I'm just an old man," Aelfgar sighed. "Don't exaggerate." He looked at Leland and suggested, "Let's take a walk."

Leland and Aelfgar walked between the shops and the cottages with the people of the Castle who wore cloaks and mantles instead of jeans and shirts. Night had fallen on Oremanta and its lands, and the moons lit the Castle, the woods, and the dark valleys. Previously crowded roads emptied as the night took over, and hanging lanterns emitted orange circles of light. Leland and Aelfgar's shadows dragged behind them on the cobblestones. But Leland's shadow was tiny compared to Aelfgar's, and he didn't have a dark, curved mustache like the old man.

"Why did he do that?" Leland asked.

"Oh, son ... That's complicated. Men want power and wealth. Some may sacrifice everything for the sake of fortune and leadership."

Leland shivered, but he wasn't quite sure if it was due to the cold breeze of air that had just hit him or because of what he'd just heard.

"When your father talked, people listened. When he promised, he fulfilled his promises. When he ordered, people obeyed. I remember Frank very well. When he wielded a sword, he could cut down ten trees and chop off five heads all at once. But he used his powers for evil, and now we can do nothing but fight him."

For a reason he couldn't understand, Leland wanted Aelfgar to be around. Maybe it was because Aelfgar knew more about his father. *But don't be naïve, Leland. Not in this place in particular.*

"I thought he was dead my whole life. I freakin' hate him," Leland confessed. "He left us when we needed him the most."

"He didn't leave you. He had to come here the same way you came. An Oremantian soul craves its home. But what he did later was evil. Pure evil. He killed innocents and burned people alive. He wanted to rule Oremanta but he failed. Now we're on the verge of a second war with him. If he controls Oremanta, only God knows what might happen then."

The two walked until they reached Eren's Square, where Leland had been with Utta just a few hours ago. But it felt different at night. It was quiet and peaceful, and the statue of the Sword of Legends took Leland's breath away as if he were seeing it for the first time.

"Where is Frank now?" Leland asked, gazing at the sword in the middle of the square.

"No one knows. Oremanta is large and he could be anywhere outside the Castle. Anywhere."

"So you're about to have a war and you don't even know where your opponent is?"

"Yes," Aelfgar replied, then shrugged and mimicked Leland, repeating what he'd just said while tilting his head right and left. "And you don't even know where your opponent is."

Leland couldn't help but laugh. *It's weird how silly things sometimes make us laugh in the grimmest of moments.*

"Let's go to my friend, Harvard. There are important things you need to know," Aelfgar told Leland, his tune more firm and serious now. "Things mostly about *you* and your father. Things about dark times and desperate measures. Things you do not want to hear but you must."

Chapter Eleven

Genesis

Harvard's small cottage was more of a library than a home. Books were everywhere: on shelves, tea tables, and in small boxes seemingly thrown into each corner. Aelfgar had mentioned something before about Harvard, the scholar from Earth. But what could he tell Leland?

"Hawx!" a man on a rocking chair cried. "You don't come here unless you want something, bloody old scrubber!"

Harvard had a long white beard and wore a black, conical hat. A large book was nestled between his thighs. Candle sconces on each wall generated dim light in the small home.

"Well," Aelfgar muttered, moving comfortably inside the cottage and taking a seat beside Harvard. "You're right. I need something."

The veins on Harvard's hands and face engorged as he struggled to place the book on the tea table inches away from his legs.

"You bring me nothing but trouble, Hawx," Harvard said, scanning Leland head to toe. "In the name of God, what the hell is *he* doing in my home?"

"Behave yourself old man," Aelfgar chuckled. "And bring us some food. We're your guests."

Harvard stood up and put a hand on his curved back as he walked to the stove in the corner of the cottage. A large steel spoon, a fork, and a metal pot hung on the wall. Something was boiling in a pot and the smell of vegetable soup emitted from it.

"What do you want to know?" Harvard asked as he mixed the ingredients.

"You know," Aelfgar replied, as he picked the book up from the tea table. "The Keo Trait … and everything."

"The Keo Trait," Harvard hummed. "The trait of the heroic ones."

Harvard sat on his rocking chair with a bowl of soup and a glass full of a red drink. He stared at Leland as if he were reading.

Nevertheless, something's comforting in this home. Maybe it's the dim lights, or the books, or the fact that no one has a sword.

"Oh, dear," Harvard said, "And to think I'd live to see another Keo." Harvard pointed at a brown book on a dusty shelf and ordered, "Bring it here, lad."

Leland brought him the book and sat beside him.

"You must know, son," Harvard said, "Once you listen to this, there's no turning back. You have to persevere, for you have a huge weight on your shoulders."

Leland remained silent.

"All right, son, I won't talk too much. Old people are boring, I know. But you have to listen very well. Thousands of years ago, three families known as Oremanta's Blue Blood Families were powerful, skilled, and wise. A kid from the Blue Blood Families could kill three, fine adult men!"

Harvard sipped his tea then continued while looking directly at Leland. "Together, the three Blue Blood Families ruled Oremanta. They built the Castle, and they unified everyone on this planet."

Leland listened carefully, interested to hear what happened next. Even though it was too much to take in, he wanted to know more. Aelfgar went to the kitchen and brought Leland and himself a hot drink and sat to listen to the rest of the story. This time it wasn't Mesta, but only tea.

Harvard continued, "Long story short, years after the three Blue Blood Families—the Keo, the Tartan, and the Largo families—built the Castle and ruled Oremanta, the Keos decided to betray the other two families. They wanted to be the *one and only* rulers of Oremanta. Fortunately, after long battles and many deaths, the Tartans and Largos stopped The Keos. The penalty for treason is death. And so, the Keos were exterminated. But somehow, some of the Keos managed to survive and breed. And now I'm telling this story to you, a Keo!"

"I don't think I quite get it all," Leland said. "Is that why my father wants to rebel? To avenge the extermination of the Keos?"

"Maybe. Or maybe he just wanted power and authority," Aelfgar replied. "Your father is a Keo. The current leaders of Oremanta are Tartans and the Largos, which means only two Blue Blood Families are ruling Oremanta. The Keos aren't there anymore."

"Who else is a Keo?" Leland asked.

"Thus far, you and your father are the only ones we know," Aelfgar muttered. "From the time your heels touched Oremanta's soil, I knew you were a Keo. I could feel it."

"I still don't know what's so special about the Keos or the two other Blue Blood Families, whatever their names were," Leland uttered as he stood up. "It's all too much to take in. I need a place to rest."

"I warn you, son," Harvard said, "Don't tell anyone that you're a Keo. This means the death sentence for you."

"You people are mad, I swear," Leland raged. "You want my help. and you call me special, and then you order me not to tell anyone who I truly am!"

Leland turned his back on Harvard then said, "I still haven't decided to fight on your side. Don't take me for granted."

"A Keo is a Keo." Harvard sighed. "Never mind, son. Do whatever you think is right."

Leland didn't know how to process all of this, or how to deal with the anger inside. *My father must be the worst person alive in this awful place, and he's leading another war. Things are only getting worse.* Leland and Aelfgar left Harvard's place and went to Aelfgar's home. Leland's heart skipped a beat when he realized he didn't know where Jennifer was right now.

"Where's Jennifer?" he cried at Aelfgar.

"I'll bring her here to you," Aelfgar replied, opening the huge door of his cottage. "You need to rest. You're tired and exhausted, and you've seen a lot already. When you're up, you'll find Jennifer here right next to you, and we'll talk about what we're going to do next."

The old man pointed to a small ladder in the corner of the cottage. "There's a bed up there. I swore no one would sleep up there except the beautiful lady I would marry someday. Oh, I always imagined her to be blonde with slim legs and a sweet smell. He gazed at Leland, who stood without saying a word. "I don't give special offers twice by the way."

Leland went upstairs and found a bed as well as axes and daggers randomly thrown onto the floor. He laid down on the bed, closed his eyes, and wished his brain would stop buzzing.

"One more thing," Aelfgar's voice came from downstairs, "I'm not even sure the Flares of Truth or the Seven Lieutenants know you're here. They're busy preparing for the war, and they won't expect anything from you even if they knew you were here."

"Then why are you insisting on letting me fight?"

"Because *I* believe you can do something, and I don't care what everyone else thinks."

As Aelfgar left, Dylan's voice instantly played in Leland's head. Soon after, every memory they'd had together buried him alive. Gradually, and sooner than he thought, his memories were fading away, as well as

Dylan's voice. A thick cloud took over his mind and he slept.

He woke to a nightmare, one he'd dreamt a thousand times before: the rainy night his father had left for good. Thunder roared as rain flooded every roof in the small town of Temblewood. Leland asked himself why they hadn't gone to the park that day. His mother used to take him to the park for a daily walk, even on rainy days. He was seven back then, and seven-year-old kids stay in their rooms when their parents fight. He could hear them scream and shout and say words he didn't understand back then.

Leland was so afraid that he pressed his little face against the pillow and cried. And then his Aunt Abbey came in. She took Leland out of the house and told him she wanted to hang out and have fun with him. He knew she was lying. She didn't want him to hear the fight. And that was the last time he'd heard his father's voice. When Leland asked his mother about his father, she gave him lame excuses and vague answers. Sometimes she even promised he'd be back. She lied. Leland never saw his father after that. Months later, Leland's mother told him his father had passed away without even stating how he'd died.

More lies.

***

Leland woke up from his sleep when he heard Jenny's voice downstairs. He didn't know how many hours he'd slept, but the fog in his brain had dissipated. Now he *knew* what he wanted to do next—for better or for worse. He went downstairs.

Jennifer, Utta, Jack, Warden, and Aelfgar were all there.

"Leland!" Jennifer cried.

"Listen to me, everyone," Leland loudly informed, wiping the sweat off his face and rotating his stiff neck. "I want to kill Frank!"

Chapter Twelve

The Will to Fight

"What?" Jennifer roared.

"You heard me," Leland replied, stepping down the creaky wooden stairs. "And I know what I'm saying."

Jack's eyebrows met in a frown. With his back against the wall, he shouted, "Don't get carried away, punk. You were about to cry there in the woods, and now you want to kill a great leader of a huge army."

"He's not a great leader ... He's a murderer and an awful father," Leland shouted back. The heat within the cottage rose.

Jennifer stood on her feet and shrugged. "And how are you going to do it?"

That was a tough question because Leland didn't have an answer. *If I started training now, would that be enough to kill someone who's been wielding swords for years? Definitely not.*

"Before you decide on anything," Utta said, bringing her hand closer to her eyes to check her nails' alignment, "Take your time."

Leland had two choices: sit back and watch his father rip this place apart or take action to stop him. While the latter seemed nearly impossible, it was what he wanted to do. For himself. For Dylan. For his mother. And, maybe, for the people of Oremanta.

"Are you willing to leave this Castle and be out in the wild?" Aelfgar broke his silence. "Are you willing to face death and terror and cold nights?"

"Aelfgar … You can't mean—" Warden stuttered, his eyes protruding in horror. "No need to go that far! Castlers are training day and night. We've got the Seven Lieutenants and our great army. This boy won't be of much help."

"Answer me, Leland," Aelfgar said. "Would you risk your life for power?"

"I would." Leland eyed Jennifer, seeking affirmation for whatever he was signing up for. But she remained silent and expressionless.

Aelfgar's eyes shimmered with excitement. The old man was hyped for an adventure.

"You can't, Sir!" Warden loudly objected.

Warden's reaction made Leland doubt his decision. *Is there more to this than just danger?*

"How are you going to help me?" Leland asked.

"You wanted power. We'll give you power," Aelfgar answered, and then he chuckled. "Or at least we'll die trying."

"You'll die," Utta weighed in. "Have you gone mad, Aelfgar? The war is coming. You can't leave the Castle now!"

Leland eyed Jennifer again. She was still expressionless. But when her eyes caught his, her face morphed to reassurance. She gave him that, "It'll all be all right" look. His tension eased.

"I'm an old man who can't even fight. The war depends on you, the Seven Lieutenants, and our army. I can't change anything here," Aelfgar told Utta. "It is settled. We're going on a Deathly Journey to get you the Sword of Legends, kid!"

Deathly Journey? How can that sword help me kill my father?

"If we go now, can we make it before the war?" Jennifer asked.

Leland answered first. "You're not going anywhere, Jennifer. You're staying right where you are."

Chapter Thirteen

Don't You Dare Die

As Leland followed Jennifer outside, a sudden doubt crossed his mind. *Am I really willing to go that far to fight him? Why aren't I holding back at all?*

"Are you aware of what you're saying?" Jennifer roared. "You've *never* held a sword before, and now you suddenly want to get the most powerful one in this place and fight a beast who started a war by himself!"

"I know what I want, and I don't care if I die for it." *Is that true? Don't I really care about death? What am I saying?*

"Are you stupid, Leland?" Jennifer lowered her voice. "How can you even trust these people? We don't know them at all! *They* might be the bad ones!"

"They saved us in the woods. If my father wanted to help, he could have easily done it. *His* men killed Dylan, not the people of the Castle. You saw Utta's annihilated village with your own eyes!"

The dawn slowly broke over the sky as the sun's rays covered the far horizon with vivid vermillion glimmers.

"You're not making any sense." Jennifer turned away. She sat on a concrete bench and said nothing.

Leland went to her, and when he looked into her eyes, he knew what she was thinking.

"You won't lose anyone, Jennifer. Not anymore," Leland mumbled as he took a seat beside her.

"Everyone says that," she replied, turning her head away. "Tell me what would be left for me if something happened to you? You're all I've got now and you know it."

"Look at me, Jenny," Leland said. "It's my fault that you're here. If something bad happens to you, I'm the one to blame. And I won't die. I won't leave you here alone. You must know that."

"Then don't leave. Stay here with me until the war is over."

"I feel involved in this war more than anybody else. I'm going on this journey, and you're going to stay here in the Castle, safe and sound."

"I'm involved in this too. Dylan is my friend as much as he's yours. Why are you being so selfish? Do you think I'll be happy here all alone, with people I don't even know, while you're outside in the wild?"

"Please understand me, Jenny. Happiness doesn't matter now as much as *safety*. I'm doing this for myself, not for you. I can't handle losing you. I'll break down and that'll be the end. You *must* stay here. I'm Oremantian, and not only that, I'm a Keo. It's a long story that doesn't even make much sense to me, but I might be able to do something about this war."

Jennifer turned away once again. "Fine."

Fragility sifted through her voice, but she didn't cry. She stood on her feet, put both hands in her pockets, and said, "If that's what you truly want, then go for it. I won't stand in your way. But don't you dare die." She walked toward the door and then half-turned her face to him. "I swear I won't forgive you if you leave me here alone."

Leland stayed outside. He thought of every word Jennifer had said and knew she was right. But a voice within him told him to move forward. For the first time in his life, that voice was clear.

Then Aelfgar came out of the cottage. "We ought to leave soon, for the war is coming and we mustn't waste more time."

Leland eyed the big man. "What's special about the sword?"

"Everything," Aelfgar replied. "The one who gets it gains the power of a thousand men! One strike is equivalent to a thousand! The speed of the sword-wielder is incomparable. I will tell you everything on our way. We'll have plenty of time for that."

"And how do we obtain that sword?" Leland hoped he'd misheard what had to be accomplished.

"Through a Deathly Journey until we reach the legendary swordsmith. He's the one and only man who can make it. And he doesn't make it for anyone." Aelfgar sat beside Leland. "Throughout the years, many warriors have tried to obtain one, but they all ended up dead or missing. It is a very hard quest. Are you still sure you want to go for it?"

Leland nodded.

"All right, then. It is settled."

But a third voice interfered. "No, it isn't. I can't let this happen."

Chapter Fourteen

Goodbye

The sun sent its golden beams over the meadows behind Aelfgar's cottage. Leland turned around and saw Jack standing beside the door.

"I deserve that weapon more than that little boy," Jack said. "I can prove it."

"You may be stronger than him now," Aelfgar replied, "But he's more qualified, and I can't say any more about that. Utta will give you proper training if that's what you want, better than anyone else."

Aelfgar walked a few steps away from his cottage then ordered, "Follow me, Leland. We have to do a few things before we leave. Let's go."

Leland followed the old man, and then Jennifer joined the party. Jack stood in his spot, his face red as a tomato. Aelfgar took them to Harvard's cottage for the second time. The old, white-bearded man sat in his rocking chair holding a loaf of bread as if his life depended on it. He raised his head then asked, "Now what do you want, Aelfgar?"

"I need to borrow your crystal compass."

"Don't tell me … You—"

"Yes. We're going for the Sword of Legends."

"You must be crazy. The war is getting closer." Harvard played with his beard. "You're old and, unfortunately, still naïve, Aelfgar."

Aelfgar slapped Leland's back as he ordered, "Go get it, boy. It's a crystal compass upstairs." Leland obeyed.

Harvard shook as he laughed, and then said, "Oh, Aelfgar. And to think you'd go so far at this age."

"You're the only old one in this cottage. I'm still planning on marrying Helen Werkwood, if she's still alive."

"Oh." Harvard laughed. "She's dead already. But she must have had a beautiful young girl by now. You can plan on that. But the Werkwoods hate you anyway."

Leland came down the stairs with a rounded, fist-sized, effulgent crystal ball. He wondered aloud, "Why do we need this?"

"To guide us in the wild," Aelfgar replied.

Harvard picked up his loaf again then said, "You know how to use it? Once you're outside the Castle, the compass will shine green if you're on the right route and red if you're not." Harvard took a bite. "Now, do you need anything else?"

"That's all," Aelfgar replied. "Wish us luck."

"Best of it. Make it count, old scrubber!"

Leland, Jennifer, and Aelfgar left Harvard's cottage. Jennifer grabbed Leland's hand then sputtered, "I'm going with you."

Leland covered her hand with his and replied, "You're the most precious thing to me now, Jennifer. I really can't afford to lose you."

She said nothing. The three roamed the streets of Oremanta. Cottages, shops, and smiths lined the roads. A group of red-hooded men walked past. Leland was about to ask who they were when Aelfgar explained, "They are the Castle's Inner Protectors. Don't panic."

"Inner Protectors?" Jennifer wondered.

"They catch thieves and prevent the murder of innocent people and so on. You know, the people of the Castle aren't all good in the end."

A few blocks away stood a tall tower with a shielded man at its top observing the road. A nearby shop sold Oremantian clothes: silky dresses, wide pieces of fabric, and some large boots. Leland wondered how he would look in those clothes. They spent about an hour buying things they'd need for their journey. Now, the bag on Aelfgar's back was stuffed with food, water, shields, daggers, coats, and a small tent. Aelfgar had bought Leland a new sword as well.

Jennifer remained silent the whole time.

"Now," Aelfgar said, "Let's head to the Golden Gate."

"Before we leave, I want to be sure of something," Leland told Aelfgar. "I want a guarantee that Jennifer won't be harmed at all."

"You don't have to worry about me," Jennifer said.

"Look at me," Aelfgar ordered. "No harm will reach Jennifer. You have the word of Aelfgar Hawx."

Leland wasn't supposed to entrust her with them just because an old man he'd recently met said so. But Aelfgar's eyes weren't lying. *There's truth in his voice.*

They followed Aelfgar until they reached a large, empty field. Two hundred rows of warriors stood with raised heads and expanded chests. A barrel-chested man with a fully muscled body stood in front, apparently commanding the warriors. None of the men made eye contact with him.

"That's Ojoy," Aelfgar informed. "He's one of the Castle's Seven Lieutenants."

Aelfgar had told Leland that the Legendary Leaders ruled the Castle, and that below them were the Seven Lieutenants. But Leland didn't think he'd meet one that quickly. Ojoy's eyes were as sharp as a razor. He held a long whip in his hand.

"The two of you," Ojoy growled, pointing at two warriors. "Come here."

"Yes, sir!" the two warriors instantly chorused.

They hesitantly approached Ojoy, who took off his armor and ordered, "Try to kill me." Ojoy wasn't joking, and the two men seemed to know that. He was bare-handed now. He threw his whip aside, unlike the two approaching warriors, who both carried a shield and a sword.

Leland stared back and forth between Ojoy and Jennifer. She was silent, and that bothered him. He felt guilty for whatever was happening to her. *She's lost a friend, and now she's forced to stay with strangers.*

The first warrior aggressively pounced on Ojoy. The second followed right away. Ojoy dodged the first warrior's strike and then ducked and avoided the sword of the second. He then swiftly grabbed the assailant's hand and struck him with his elbow. With his left leg, he kicked the other warrior's knee and forced him to fall.

"At this rate," Ojoy's voice echoed in the field, "We're going to lose the war. I want tough men on my side."

***

Before the great Golden Gate, Jennifer, Utta, Warden, Aelfgar, and Leland stood as the wind vigorously slapped their faces.

"Take care, Leland," Jennifer said. The wind freed a few strands of hair from her red ribbon. Leland faked a smile and sealed his feelings as heavy thoughts of everything they'd been through sifted through his head.

"I will. Don't worry," Leland replied.

Tears welled in Jennifer's eyes, but she didn't cry. She clenched her fist, bit her lower lip, then muttered, "I believe in you. Don't let me down."

"I won't. I promise." Leland's skin crawled. *What if I can't keep my promise?* He gazed at Aelfgar, and then at Jennifer again and said, "Take care."

"From this moment, this girl is your responsibility," Aelfgar told Warden and Utta. "If anything bad happens to her, I won't forgive you."

Aelfgar and Leland passed through the Golden Gate as eagles and owls towered over the Castle's high walls.

"Here we go," Aelfgar said. They marched toward the dark of the woods, deeper into the dangerous side of Oremanta.

Chapter Fifteen

The Deathly Journey Begins

After several hours of walking, Leland and Aelfgar entered the woods. The trees were taller than the ones in the woods Leland had been in before. And it was much darker. With just a few steps into the gloomy woods, it became nearly impossible to march forward. Bugs and flies swarmed around them and fog blurred their vision as they walked on muddy ground. Leland could no longer see Oremanta's sun or its rings.

"It's hard to tell if it's day or night in the Woods of Gregoris," Aelfgar told Leland, killing off a dozen bugs with a swing of his formidable forearm. The flying insects were as annoying as the thoughts within Leland's head. They were also both hard to get rid of.

Am I doing the right thing? Part of him was glad that Jennifer was safe inside the Castle. The other part felt guilty for leaving her alone.

"Why are you doing this, Aelfgar?" Leland asked, observing the back of the old man as he cut their way through the woods. "Why would you leave your home and help me get the Sword of Legends?"

"Because if I didn't, no one would. And because I believe in you, little one, when none of the Castle's leaders and lieutenants do." He paused. "And because I want a hell of an adventure! It has been a while."

The crystal compass shone green. *Good. We're on the right track.*

Leland missed his warm bed, his books, and his family. He stared at his Bottega shoes, the most expensive pair of shoes he'd ever bought. Now they looked just like Aelfgar's muddy boots. Aelfgar sang the whole time, and his voice wasn't bad for a man his age.

"Oh, through the hills and the valleys we go. Under the moonlight and the sun we run!" The old man was on repeat.

Leland was dead tired by now. The soles of his feet hurt. Multiple blisters had surely formed. But at least the insects were no longer flying around them. Still, it was dark.

Aelfgar pointed at a nearby rock and said, "Enough walking for today. We'll sleep here."

They set up their small tents beside the rock. Aelfgar collected dry wood from the ground and piled them together. He shoved Leland away. With just his index finger, he set the sticks on fire.

Leland stared in awe but didn't say a word. He'd seen enough weird things that day. They settled in, the only barrier between them a small red carpet that Aelfgar had brought.

"I'll teach you how to do this later," Aelfgar said, his eyes set on the flames. "Now tell me, you still wanna get the sword?"

"Yes." Leland sounded more certain than he was.

Aelfgar darted his eyes toward him, stared at him for a couple of seconds, then said, "Then there's something you need to know. To obtain the Sword of Legends, the swordsmith Mora Geuja takes something from you in return."

"Like what?"

"I don't know. That's what I heard. It's been so many years since the last man made it through. Men are afraid to try to get it. That's why only three men have grabbed the Sword of Legends throughout Oremanta's history."

Leland switched the subject. "How do you know war is coming?"

"Because we have spies outside the Castle. We know the Rebel Army is preparing themselves very well for it. We can't afford to lose. Otherwise, the Castle will fall into their hands."

"Where's the Rebel Army anyway?"

"In a place called the Ten Domes. And before you ask *again*: we don't know where that is."

Thick gray fog swirled in the air. A wolf howled in the dark woods. And then a pack of wolves howled a unified tune. Leland shivered. He scanned the trees surrounding him, their roots deep into the ground and their trunks extending up to the sky. He wondered what was his family doing on Earth now.

How can I sleep here?

Around the heat of the glowing fire, they sat like a father and son in a camp. Aelfgar grilled two loaves of bread he'd just taken out of the satchel. They smelled good.

"When the war started between the Castlers and the Rebels, a third party formed. It wasn't only them and us."

"A third party?"

"The Pyramids of the Fallen. It's a neutral place ruled by Lord Bolt Gemini. Those who wanted to be safe and weren't willing to participate in the war lived there."

Leland wrapped his arms around his knees. He thought of Jennifer more than anything else now, and so he asked, knowing his question would get him nowhere: "Will Jennifer be safe inside the Castle?"

"As long as everyone in the Castle is safe, she will be safe. She's under Warden's protection now, and I trust that boy. But nothing is guaranteed in Oremanta."

Aelfgar's reply gave Leland some sort of comfort. Aelfgar didn't seem one-hundred percent sure, which was normal. If he were going to lie, his reply would have been more persuasive. He would have said that Jennifer would *definitely* be fine.

Aelfgar placed both of his hands behind his head and leaned against a rock. "If the Rebel Army won the war, probably none of us would be safe. Frank would exterminate the two Blue Blood Families first, the Largos and Tartans, and then he'd kill whoever disobeyed him."

"What's so special about these families?" Leland asked.

"It's hard to explain the reason for their superiority, just like it's hard to tell why someone's smart and someone else is stupid. Power is in their blood, that's for sure. To be honest, I've never met a Blue Blood aside from you and Frank, so I can't tell you much. All I know is that they ruled Oremanta for ages, and that some of them mastered deadly Moxies."

"Moxies?"

"What you saw a while ago, the fire thing, was a Moxie. And there are tons of other Moxies. Some of them barely kill a dog. Others could annihilate whole villages in a matter of seconds."

***

"I know it's hard for you to accept all of this, but you can get through it. You're smart and beautiful," Warden told Jennifer. They walked over grass until they reached Warden's cottage. No homes or shops were nearby, only hills and three large stones implanted into the grass not so far from Warden's home.

"Thank you," Jennifer replied. She would have said more if Warden had been complimenting her rather than flirting with her. She felt it and she hated it.

"These three stones were erected after the first war. They resemble courage and sacrifice and love."

Jennifer gazed at the stones, but her mind was miles away. She could not afford to care about them or anything related to this Castle. *When it's all over, will I get to see my father again? Will I get to see Leland again?*

She turned to face Warden and caught him staring at her. She didn't know how long he'd been staring, but his behavior had begun to annoy her. Falling in love with a guy in a totally different dimension was the last thing she wanted. In fact, falling in love with anyone at this time was the last thing she wanted.

"Why are we here?" Jennifer asked.

"Just thought of showing you the Three Stones—and my family. They'd love to meet you!"

"I'm sorry, Warden, but I'm dead tired and I don't feel like seeing anyone at the moment. Can we get back to the Castle's center? I need to find a place to rest."

"Of course," Warden immediately replied. "If that's what you want."

They walked back to the Castle's center. Three moons illuminated Oremanta's lands, so lamps were unnecessary, but the center was full of lamps and torches anyway. Most shops were already closed, except for Mesta shops, which seemed to Jennifer like an ancient version of bars, except that people didn't go crazy here after they drank.

"Here. This way." Warden turned right. He grabbed Jennifer's hand, pulling her to where he intended to turn.

Jennifer almost fell onto him before she balanced herself and quickly pulled her body back. She stood rooted to the spot. "Don't you ever touch me," she told him firmly. Then she walked away.

***

Somewhere in Oremanta, in a chamber devoid of light, a man in a black cloak picked up his fishtail-pommelled sword from the ground. He walked down a long hall until he stopped at a black door adorned with two humanoid skulls. The man pushed the door open and entered a larger hall full of black-cloaked men, all bowing before a king on a throne.

Silence.

"Come here, Konlaw," the king ordered.

Konlaw submissively obeyed the command and then bowed. "Yes, my lord?"

The man on the throne grinned. "Tell me. Who will rule Oremanta?"

"You, my lord. The strongest of the Keo," Konlaw said, still bowing and avoiding eye contact with his king, Frank Hopegone.

Chapter Sixteen

Foolish Humans

The morning didn't bring much change. It was still wild and dark except for some light beams that filtered through the leaves. Leland and Aelfgar packed up their tent, collected their items, and prepared to move on.

Once, Leland liked horror movies. He'd watch them alone in his room, and he loved the suspense and thrill they brought. But he always wondered how he'd feel if he were the protagonist. Now, it was as though he was living one—a scary, frightening, and dark one.

This will all be over soon.

"An important lesson that you must learn is patience," Aelfgar said as they walked through the foggy woods. "Hunting requires patience and intelligence." Aelfgar turned to face Leland and went on, "And, you will help an old man get his meal. What's better than that?"

"Hunting what?"

"A rabbit … a dear … an owl … anything edible."

When Aelfgar mentioned an owl, Leland remembered the uncooked owl he'd eaten with Jack when they had first arrived in Oremanta. It was the worst thing Leland had ever put into his mouth.

"I'm not going to hunt an owl," Leland said. "I'll go for a rabbit or deer or whatever I find. And we better eat them cooked!"

The fog gradually faded away the deeper into the woods they proceeded. A good sign of progression, Leland assumed. *Now, more importantly, how do people hunt in the woods?*

"Back in my day—" Aelfgar said, and seemed enthusiastic about what he was about to say, but then he paused and put his hand on Leland's chest, preventing him from taking a step forward.

Leland stopped.

"Can you hear it?" Aelfgar asked, gazing forward.

"Hear what?"

The old man walked a few more steps. Leland did the same. Nothing but trees and the growls of wild animals surrounded them. But then Leland heard what Aelfgar was talking about. The sound of running water infiltrated his ears.

Aelfgar stopped once again. It seemed the running water wasn't what had stolen Aelfgar's attention. He looked over his shoulder for a fraction of a second and then promptly gazed ahead again.

They marched forward for a few minutes until they reached to the source of the running water, a blood-red river. Three-foot-long blue lizards with crocodile-like heads swam in the water. Gigantic red owls perched on tree limbs. Grey frogs with strange tusks hopped around the bank.

"Forget about hunting," Aelfgar said in a low voice. "Someone's following us."

***

"I know you're pissed off, Jennifer," Utta said as they headed to her cottage, "but Warden is really a light-hearted man, and I'm sure he didn't mean to bother you."

"It's not personal," Jennifer confessed, "but I don't feel like staying with that guy."

"It is your choice. If you don't want him to train you then I'll have to find someone else to take his place." They entered Utta's home.

"Would I even make a difference?" Jennifer asked.

Before Utta replied, someone knocked. Utta opened the door, and a hand brutally pulled her outside. The small-bodied girl suddenly found herself in fighting an unknown man.

Jennifer hurried to them. "Jack! What are you doing?" she roared.

"Killing her," he replied, choking Utta with both hands.

***

"It's called the Red River," Aelfgar stated.

Fish skeletons floated on the red water's boiling surface. Bubbles popped now and then. Across the riverbank a silhouette as big as Aelfgar appeared. Now they were sandwiched. Someone, or something, had followed them from behind, and another thing had just appeared in front of them. Leland's heart raced as the monster jumped and landed on the ground not too far away from them.

Aelfgar swiftly pushed Leland behind him and pulled three daggers out of his satchel. "The Guardian of the Red River," Aelfgar said. "Don't let your guard down or we'll end up dying prematurely!"

Metal armor covered the monster's entire body, even its face. It had a tail and two red eyes, the only things that could be seen on its face. As frightened as Leland was, a small part of him was glad he was involved in something other than his thoughts. Despite his fear, this seemed like a good space to detach from the voice in the back of his head.

If I don't fight, I'm going to lose it all.

He rolled up his tattered sleeves and prepared to face the creature. Leland had a sword with him, but he'd never used one before. *There's always a first time, right? But this could be the last time too.*

The monster held a rusty silver sword in its right hand and a scarf was wrapped around its neck.

"The only way to beat this little fellow is to stab its eyes," Aelfgar said, his body in a semi-squat position, "and that's not an easy task, boy."

Aelfgar marched up to the beast as he ordered Leland, "Stay where you are. When I give you a signal, stab it in the eye. You got that?"

"All right," Leland replied. *Can I really pull this off?*

He realized this was his first engagement in a real fight to the death. If he made a mistake, they'd pay with their lives. From what he knew thus far, death in

Oremanta could happen to anyone at any time—and no one would really care.

Aelfgar ran to the giant, then midway between his starting point and the armored beast, Aelfgar disappeared.

Where the heck is he?

In the blink of an eye, Aelfgar was behind the Guardian of the Red River. He grabbed the monster by its metal-covered neck and then stabilized his head with both hands.

"Now, Leland!" Aelfgar shouted.

The monster growled and smashed the surrounding trees. Leland thought it was a final act preceding capitulation. He was mistaken. The Guardian gave Aelfgar an unforeseen punch with its elbow. Aelfgar fell on his back and roared with pain.

Leland couldn't stand there and watch. He found himself running and throwing a dagger from Aelfgar's satchel at the beast. The dagger bounced off. Leland unsheathed his sword and charged again. The Guardian raged and kicked and punched at whatever was in range. Leland proceeded forward, throwing away any of his former hesitation.

I can't even reach his eyes. What should I do?

The monster grabbed Leland by his waist and then brutally threw him against a trunk.

Leland wailed. His vision blurred and his heart pumped furiously. *Is this the end?*

Aelfgar jumped in and exchanged fast punches with the Guardian. Leland stood up, picked up his sword, and joined Aelfgar. Leland swung his sword right and left, trying to damage the Guardian, but to no avail. Then Aelfgar scrambled back and said, "Keep doing what you're doing, Leland. Buy me some time!"

Leland realized that his strikes were useless. He threw his sword away so he could move more quickly. The monster growled and attacked again. Leland barely evaded his metal fist. Leland pulled himself a few steps back and then darted his eyes toward Aelfgar. *What is he doing?*

With a straight spine, raised head, and clenched fingers, Aelfgar announced, "I didn't want to use this Moxie here. It's a waste of energy, but you leave me no choice, Guardian!"

Aelfgar spread both of his legs as wide as he could and raised his hands in parallel to the sky. He grunted like a caged beast and his body shimmered as if coated with oil. Leland felt the energy floating around Aelfgar. His eyes transformed into a blank whiteness and his forehead wrinkled. Aelfgar threw one of the knives into the sky and then punched the Guardian in its ribs, crushing the interior of its thorax.

Leland couldn't imagine that metal armor covering the Guardian's body like skin could be crushed that way. The Guardian stumbled, trying to keep his balance. Aelfgar stabbed its heart. With his other hand, he caught the knife now descending from the sky and stabbed the monster in its eyes. The Guardian roared for the last time and then fell on its back.

"That was close." Leland sighed.

Aelfgar fell on the ground, drained. He breathed in and out rapidly. Leland hadn't seen Aelfgar in that state before. Minutes later, Aelfgar muttered, still lying on the green grass, "I didn't want to use it here."

"Why didn't you use it from the start? You could've easily ended this fight."

"Because it consumes a lot of energy … and it doesn't always work," Aelfgar explained, out of breath. "And because I want you to be engaged in a real battle!"

"How do you even do all of that? I mean, that fire thing, and now this."

"By controlling the natural elements around us: wind, sand, water, and fire. By controlling those four, Moxies can be performed. Not an easy thing … and I don't think you can learn any of them in a short period." He removed a bottle from his satchel. "This should do it." He drank and then passed the bottle to Leland. "Don't drink too much."

"What's this?"

"Energy booster. We don't have a lot of it, so watch out."

Aelfgar stretched out his limbs and sighed. "Back in my day, I didn't need any of these drinks. Aging is hard."

Leland stared at the Guardian's dead body beside the riverbank. The Guardian had been their first obstacle on this journey. And it had been terrifying.

"Do you know why the river's so red?" Aelfgar asked. He shifted into a squatting position, stared at the stream of red waves, and didn't wait for Leland to answer. "It's the blood of the dead warriors trying to get the Sword of Legends." Hawx stood up then ordered, "Let's go. Our journey awaits."

***

Utta struck Jack with her elbow then sent a powerful punch to his stomach. He kneeled before her. With both elbows, she then struck his back. He fell face-first to the ground. Utta crossed her arms then firmly asked, as if Jack's assault hadn't caused her any damage, "What was *that* for?"

Pushing the ground with his knuckles, Jack stood up. His left eye was shut. He grinned, "Good. Now I know you're capable of training me."

Jennifer had come to Utta's house because of Warden's attitude. Now Jack had appeared. *Jerk.*

"You almost killed her!" Jennifer shrieked.

"Don't worry," Utta commented. "He couldn't kill me in a hundred years."

Jack frowned and said nothing.

Jennifer heard footsteps behind her. She turned to see Warden standing near the door.

"What happened here?" Warden asked.

"Nothing," Utta replied. "Why are you here?"

Warden walked a few steps in their direction, his eyes fixed on Jennifer. "We need to talk, Jennifer. I came to apologize."

When Jennifer gave it a second thought, she realized she didn't have to drag this on any longer. *He came to apologize, and that's all that matters. He became aware of the lines he shouldn't cross, and that's what's important.*

"There's nothing to apologize for," Jennifer replied. "I'm okay."

"I've been thinking about what you can do here until the war comes," Warden said. "It's hard for you to be on the front lines, so I thought of an alternative."

"What is it?"

"The Healing Squad. I can't think of any better place for you."

"What's that?"

"I'll explain everything. But first, we ought to leave for the execution. It is mandatory for everyone to witness it."

Execution?

***

Jennifer and Warden overlooked a huge training field from a high platform. Hundreds of Oremantians, warriors, old people, and children alike, awaited the execution. Lieutenant Ojoy, a man as tall as Aelfgar but obviously younger, stood before three bodies that shook like leaves. Warden hadn't told Jennifer much about Ojoy except that he'd killed about half of the Rebel Army in the first war, and that no one ever dared to look him in the eyes and talk.

With stern eyes and tight lips, Ojoy announced in a voice that reached everyone in the field, "People of Oremanta, you all came here to witness the execution of Paul, Jason, and Nento. Treachery is cured with death. Whoever breaks the rules of the Castle shall receive the same punishment. Let the traitors reside in hell!"

"What have they done?" Jennifer asked Warden.

"They are traitors. They gathered Intel for the Rebel Army. And then when they got caught, they killed Castlers as they tried to escape."

Ojoy's voice rang above the crowd. He ordered the traitors, "Kneel. This won't take too long."

The three kneeled, exposing their necks to Ojoy's sword. *What does it feel like to sit and wait for someone to take your life knowing you can't do anything about it?* Jennifer didn't turn away. With one smooth swing, three heads split from their bodies and rolled onto the ground. Blood formed a pool around them.

If I want to survive here, I need to get used to all of this. But her fists clenched, her eyes blinked, and her stomach twisted. She repressed the urge to vomit. To distract herself from what she'd just seen, Jennifer asked, "Now that we're done with this execution, what about the Healing Squad?"

Everyone chanted Ojoy's name and cheered as if nothing dire had just happened. It seemed as though Jennifer had been the only one affected by their deaths.

"Ojoy! Ojoy! Ojoy!" The crowd repeated. Some voices shouted differently: "Rot in hell!" and, "Let the ravens eat every bit of you!"

Ojoy raised one hand, ordering them to stop. They all did.

"They're dead now," he said. "No need for insults."

***

A rejuvenated Aelfgar kept his eyes on their green-shining compass. Thus far, they were headed in the right direction. It was night already, and their day had been tiring. It was the longest distance Leland had ever walked.

Aelfgar stopped, looked over his shoulders—something he'd done several times since the fight with the Guardian—and then continued walking. Whoever followed them still didn't want to show their identity.

Like moths, they were drawn into a small, moonlit spot adjacent to an old tree. Leland's muscles ached. He threw himself on the ground after they'd set up their tent and had lit torches for better vision.

"You better do something useful now and then kid," Aelfgar muttered. "Why don't you tell me a story?"

"There once was a boy named Dylan who came with his friends Jennifer and Leland to a strange planet they knew nothing about." Leland massaged his own stiff shoulders. "Dylan got killed by Leland's father, and now Leland wants to avenge his friend."

"Is that a joke? If yes, then it's not funny," Aelfgar chuckled. "On a more serious note, does Leland know he's likely to be killed doing this?"

"He does. And that's why he entrusted Jennifer's life to the hands of an old man he trusted for no reason."

Two voices behind nearby bushes stole their attention, but neither Leland or Aelfgar turned their back. They pretended as if they hadn't heard a thing. A moment of awkward silence and anticipation passed before Aelfgar ended it, keeping his voice low. "We've been followed for a pretty long distance. Whoever's following us doesn't want to hurt us. We were vulnerable during that fight with the Guardian, yet no one attacked." Aelfgar whispered, "You sleep. I'll watch."

***

"So *that's* their shallow plan. When humans become powerless, they act foolishly. Do they really think I will back off because *my son* is on the battlefield? How absurd. Why would I hold back against someone I've already left behind?"

Frank Hopegone grinned. "My heart has turned to stone. I wonder if he can handle that."

Chapter Seventeen

The Ten Domes

Somewhere in Oremanta, above a mountain where the sun never shone, sat the Ten Domes. Finding a smile in that place was like waiting for a raindrop during a drought. Bats flew everywhere, as if the domes had been built just to shelter them.

The Rebel Army lived in the Ten Domes. A high fence made of skulls protected the domes from monsters. Standing a few feet apart, guards secured every entrance. Their faces were white as ghosts, in stark contrast to their black, ripped clothes.

In the main dome, which was also the smallest of the ten, Frank Hopegone and his four assistants—Haizo, Naru, Nemat Black, and Daleo Konlaw—held the reins. Captains chosen by Frank led each of the rest of the nine domes.

Perched on a hill, the first dome overlooked the other nine. A path lined with high torches led downhill from the main dome. The shafts of the torches were made of bones. The night was cold and dark in that area of Oremanta, the only place that wasn't lit by Oremanta's three moons.

Heavy rain combined with thunder, forming an ominous melody in the darkness, grim as ever.

Konlaw stepped out of the first dome. Two men kneeled before him and chorused, "Your orders, sir?"

Konlaw thought, *Oremanta belongs to us. Evil shall bring peace. What have the supposedly good ones brought to this world?*

He ordered the men, "Tell Yoink to prepare his men. The bloody war shall start!"

***

The center of Oremanta was busy that morning, and people were noticeably anxious. A man scolded his little boy and then slapped him on his face. A woman carried her child on her back and ran into a narrow alley with a bag full of vegetables. A man walked by Jennifer and Warden and complained, "War! Again!"

"The Seven Lieutenants just declared the second war of Oremanta," Warden told Jennifer. "That's why everyone's busy buying food and clothes and weapons."

"Didn't they know about this already?" Jennifer inquired, scanning the chaos.

"They did, but the rumor about the second war has been around for so long that people ignore it. A year or two ago, we thought the Rebel Army was going to attack us again, but nothing happened. Now that the Seven Lieutenants have announced it, people are certain."

"Why are you so sure this time?"

"Because the Seven Lieutenants said so. They have their spies and intel and knowledge. They have clues."

Jennifer said nothing. A blonde woman who'd walked behind Warden had stolen her attention. Instinctively, Jennifer followed the woman.

"Where are you going?" Warden asked.

"Stay here. I'll be back."

The woman had long blonde hair, fair skin, green almond eyes, and a ravishing smile. It had been years since Jennifer had seen all of those traits in one person.

Is this a dream? she asked herself as she followed the woman.

Sleep tight, Jennifer … You have to wake up early, sweetie. The voice of Jennifer's mother reverberated in her head.

She walked fast and remembered herself doing so more than ten years ago when she had followed her mother in the supermarkets and the streets and everywhere. Warmth rose in her body as she got closer and closer to the woman. The woman dropped the bag of food she was carrying. She picked it up and Jennifer saw part of her face.

Is that … my mom? she asked herself in disbelief.

The woman walked very fast, and Jennifer absent-mindedly jogged and then ran behind her. But the street ahead was crowded. A preacher in a white cloak stood on a high stage and lectured about war and death and things that didn't matter to Jennifer at that particular moment.

She might not be dead! She probably left Earth the same way we did! But why did she have a grave on Earth? Maybe my father created that just to hide everything. Or maybe she faked her death.

Jennifer found her way out of the crowd. The woman's shadow was still within range. Jennifer ran and then tripped over a stone, but she didn't completely fall. She lifted herself up with her knuckles and followed the blonde. The distance between them narrowed.

"Hey!" Jennifer shouted. "You!"

The woman slowly turned her face around. Jennifer could swear this was her mother—her hair, her lips, her nose—were all *her*. The woman fully turned around now. Jennifer bit her lips. Tears soaked her eyes. Her heart beat so hard she felt it would come out of her chest at any moment.

It's not her.

"I'm … sorry," Jennifer apologized, then turned around and walked away. Tears streamed down her face.

The dead cannot come back. I'm just stupid to think I'd have her again. Jennifer wiped the tears from her face with her shirt. *I already settled this matter with myself a long time ago. I should stop pouring salt into my wounds.*

***

"If you're not willing to be trained by me," Utta said, her back against the door of her cottage, "then tell me right now. We'll both save time."

"The question is," Jack replied, "do you really have the ability to train me?"

Utta crossed her arms. "Actually, I'm the *only* one who can train you now. If you join the rest of the warriors, who are training daily on the field, you'll be humiliated. Don't get ahead of yourself. You're nothing. Have you ever even handled a sword in a fight before?"

Jack frowned but didn't say anything.

"The war draws near. The only way you could surpass another warrior's strength is by learning Moxies!"

Jack arched an eyebrow.

"Utilizing nature's elements to strengthen yourself, just like the one we used to transport you from the woods into the Castle."

Jack shook his head in dissatisfaction. But that was expected from someone who had just arrived from Earth, a place Utta had only heard stories about. The thing she couldn't understand was Jack's will to be stronger and to fight a war that wasn't his.

She unsheathed her sword and walked toward him. He didn't step back. Utta pointed at a large rock beside Jack then ordered, handing him her sword, "Split it."

Jack tried. The sword flew out of his hands and the rock remained whole.

"That's how weak you are. The war is no game. Someone like you would be easy prey in an epic battlefield."

Utta went inside her cottage and retrieved some rusted chainmail, a linen undershirt, and linen underpants, as well as an old pair of pointed shoes.

Silently, Jack put them on.

"I will make you stronger. But first you have to tell me, what are you after?"

Jack sneered.

***

"I think we should know who's following us," Leland muttered. The chase began to bother him, but Aelfgar insisted on waiting.

"Time always answers questions. Just trust it."

An unrealistic thought knocked at the back of Leland's head several times: Jennifer had followed them into the woods. But, knowing her, she'd rather say, "I'm coming with you, and you can't stop me," instead of sneaking behind them.

According to Aelfgar's hypothesis, which he'd told Leland earlier that morning, the mystery of who followed them could be one of two things: someone who needs their help or a trap.

"We have to reach the end of the woods before night falls. I have a plan," Aelfgar announced.

"Why don't we just fight them?" Leland suggested, still pushing for a confrontation.

"I won't do that. First of all, I don't want to waste my power. Secondly, I don't want them to run away. I want to know why they're following us in the first place."

Knowing where their foot would land was not a problem anymore, as the fog had disappeared and sunbeams found their ways through the trees.

"When the first war started, a wise man called Lord Bolt Gemini took his closest men and left the Castle. He went to an abandoned land, far away in the east, and called it the Pyramids of The Fallen. Whoever didn't want to be a part of this war went with him."

Leland thought of all the mess his father had caused. He'd started this war, and no matter what reason had driven him toward that, no matter how vulnerable his cause was, it wasn't worth it. Nothing is worth the life of others. And he'd left his family, and the one he supposedly loved, all alone in a cruel world.

Preceded by no signs of a storm, raging thunder pierced their eardrums. Heavy rain followed that was continuous and loud and scary. Leland didn't know if he should be sad that it was raining or happy that they'd found a large leaf they could hide under. Raindrops crashed around them like small balls of shattering glass.

Aelfgar took two loaves of bread out of the bag and shared them with Leland.

"They're still here," Aelfgar whispered.

Leland put both hands inside his pockets as he stared at the raindrops. He missed Jennifer now more than ever. And he missed Dylan and his family, as well as everything he had back on Earth. The sound of the rain always brought up that one fragment of memory he could never forget: the day his father left. He wished the sun would shine and the rain would stop.

Aelfgar pressed on Leland's shoulder then whispered, "Time changes things and alters one's perspective. Things that hurt you now might make you laugh in the future. Vice versa. Time is the tool of the wise ones." Aelfgar gazed into Leland's eyes then muttered, "Don't overthink, boy. It kills."

And then the rain stopped and the two started walking again. With that new start, Leland had a better glimpse of why he wanted to face his father. Avenging Dylan and his family, and saving whomever he could while here, was one thing, but the rest was for himself. He wanted to know the true reason behind Frank's motive, the mystery surrounding him, and the way he looked and talked and interacted.

"Have you ever felt … empty before?" The words escaped Leland's mouth. *I must not sound this weak.* But he did. It was as though his tongue spoke on its own, and he couldn't help it.

Aelfgar smiled, and then answered, "Of course I have. In this life, we lose people we love, and we endure a lot of hardships. What I've learned in those years is that emotions are dangerous. When you lose something you loved, it's the memories that remain, and they haunt and suffocate and bury you alive. But it doesn't really matter. What counts is what you did during that time. Were you able to carry on? Were you able to keep on living? As long as you're keeping the necessary elements in your life alive, it doesn't matter what brutal realities you go through."

Their legs moved rapidly toward an open field. Sunlight showed through the clouds at last, bringing life into everything. A great surge of energy built up inside Leland. It was the sun he'd been waiting for, the end of the gloomy wood, finally.

"Here we are. This is where the woods end!" Aelfgar announced.

A waterfall adorned with rainbows on all sides greeted them. The waterfall spouted from a gigantic rock about thirty meters tall. The pure mineral water formed a river that extended for as long as their vision could reach. Seagulls flew above the river and green tree leaves floated upon it.

However, what stole their attention wasn't the river, the rainbows, or the flying seagulls. Rather, a monster stood right in front of them holding two sharp axes in each hand, ruining the beauty of the scene.

"The Triple Skulls Monster. I've heard a lot about it," Aelfgar informed, cautiously taking a step back.

The monster drew a line on the ground.

The skull on the right roared, "You won't—"

The skull in the middle spit, "Pass."

And the left skull finished, "This line."

Aelfgar swiftly turned around then remarked, as if he had been waiting for this moment for a while, "Whoever's following us: I know what you're seeking. If you want to get out of these woods, then you ought to help us fight this monster." His voice echoed. "Unless you step out and show yourself, we won't move an inch forward."

The Triple Skulls Monster showed no reaction to Aelfgar's speech. It seemed its one and only objective was to block any movement out of the woods.

Their follower was now forced to either go back into the woods or show themselves. Or they could wait forever where they were, which could ruin Aelfgar's idea.

Ten minutes passed, but no one showed. In fact, no sounds or movements happened. There was no sign of anyone in hiding.

"Is this your plan?" Leland sighed, with a slight chuckle of teasing.

Aelfgar's face turned red. He shook his head and gazed back and forth before he spoke with an embarrassment new to Leland, "Shut up and wait. It'll work."

But Aelfgar himself couldn't wait any longer. He faced the woods and shouted, loud enough that some birds flew off of the trees, "If you do not show yourself, I will come and hunt you myself. And you don't want Aelfgar Hawx of the Golden City to come after you."

That sentence had a powerful impact. Two figures hesitantly stepped out of the woods from behind dense bushes and tall trees. The wisdom of Aelfgar had paid off at last.

Try as he might, Leland couldn't hide his shock.

Chapter Eighteen

The Song of The Wind

The boy ran as fast as his legs could endure, as if a ghost were chasing him. Once he reached the center of the Castle where the lieutenants met and resided, he leaned toward the guards protecting the gate and promptly whispered a few words. They immediately allowed him to enter. He went straight to the chamber of Agis Phoenix, the head of the Seven Lieutenants.

The scout kneeled in front of Agis and reported, "Sir, I apologize for the interruption, but I have important news."

"Speak." With crossed legs and raised eyebrows as bold as brass, the lieutenant frowned and permitted him to talk.

"Our spies detected some movement outside the Castle," he said, out of breath. "They say they've never seen such rapid movement before."

"When did that happen?"

"Just now sir," the scout informed. "We think it's the Rebel Army."

"Hmm. So they have begun. That was expected. We shall make our move as well," Agis stated, playing with his chin. "We are in a time of war." He stood up then ordered, "Go inform Ojoy. He'll know what to do on the training field. The bells will ring very soon. We have to be prepared."

"Yes, sir!"

Agis walked in circles in the empty hall, both hands behind his back, and thoroughly studied the Castle's map hung on the wall. The warriors had been training for years with Ojoy in the fields. The Healing Squad was never as ready. Movements outside the Castle were closely monitored. The walls and gates of the Castle were heavily armed and shielded. Agis wasn't worried about their preparation.

The Rebel Army knows about the Castle's powerful defenses, so how will they attack?

***

Far from the Castle's center, in a road with only a few cottages, a smith, and a market, Jennifer stood in front of Warden's home. Kids wearing silky dresses played with stones and wooden swords in an empty yard nearby. A little boy cried as he pointed his sword at his friend's neck, "I will kill you, Frank Hopegone!"

If Leland were here, Jennifer thought, *he couldn't stand the amount of hatred against his father. The pain his father had caused must have been humongous.*

"That's my little brother, Patrick." Warden pointed at the boy holding the wooden sword. Jennifer noticed Warden hadn't looked her in the eye since she'd yelled at him. She might have misjudged him. He could easily have assaulted her or kidnapped her. But he hadn't done any of that.

"I'm sorry," Jennifer told Warden. "I didn't mean to yell like that."

Jennifer forced strength into her words, even while apologizing, because she mustn't seem weak. Or at least she mustn't *sound* weak. *In a place where death is like drinking a cup of water, a lonely, fragile girl shouldn't give in to anyone.*

Warden welcomed Jennifer into the cottage. An old woman spinning a fist-sized, pink cotton ball sat on a rocking chair. A purple carpet covered the middle of the cottage and a few jars of water had been placed on top of a small wooden table in front of her.

"Welcome home, my son," the old woman muttered, her eyes on the cotton ball in her hands. "I see we have a guest today."

Warden's mother raised her head, scrutinized Jennifer, then murmured, "A beautiful guest, if I'm allowed to say."

She put the cotton ball on the table and then stood up, her hand aiding her curved spine. Her forehead wrinkled as she approached Jennifer. "My son has fallen in love, perhaps?"

"She's my apprentice. Her name is Jennifer," Warden informed.

Jennifer had agreed to come here with Warden because she didn't have anything better to do. On their way there, Warden had told her a few things about how the Healing Squad operates. But she wasn't convinced she could do anything to help in the war.

"I've packed everything. We can leave now," Warden's mother said hesitantly, her eyes awaiting her son's approval.

"We are going nowhere, mother."

"Tell him, my girl … Tell him that when the war starts, it won't recognize anyone. Children will die, girls will be raped, and wives will be widowed." Warden's mother towered over Jennifer and whispered, "Tell him, my sweet girl. I have been trying to convince him for years, yet he refuses."

"Staying behind the walls of the Castle is the safest thing for everyone," Warden exclaimed. "I've seen war, and I know its consequences."

"Your father died while he was here sitting inside the Castle. Your brothers died because of this war. Let's move to the Pyramids of the Fallen. Lord Bolt Gemini will provide us shelter and food and safety."

"We can't. It's too late. I promise you I won't die, and neither will any of my younger siblings."

Warden's mom went to the metal oven at the corner of the cottage and then brought a tray containing three pies. The smell was familiar. Jennifer didn't like pies that much, but this one looked delicious.

"I am so sorry, dear," Warden's mom told Jennifer. "We shouldn't have bothered you with our invalid arguments. Allow me to offer you an apple pie. It is the best you will ever eat."

She hadn't eaten a proper meal since coming here. Now her stomach growled. A home-cooked meal, a son arguing with his mother, and a little brother playing in the yard with his friends filled Jennifer with the warmth she had craved for her entire life: a *family*.

"Warden, Warden!" Patrick, Warden's younger brother, cried.

"What?"

"A guard wants you. He's outside!"

Warden exited at the drop of a hat, and a fully armored guard with an iron helmet recited, "Warden Yerko, this mission has been assigned to you by the name of the Seven Lieutenants. You will have the honor to inform Millory village that the war is coming, and that it isn't safe for them to stay where they are. We shall provide shelter and safety for them in the Castle."

"Yes, sir." Warden bent. The guard went away.

A rough yet fragile voice behind Jennifer cried, "Stay here, my son. I beg you! Villages outside the Castle hate us. They have a grudge against us! Don't leave!" Warden's mother begged.

"The Seven Lieutenants have put their trust in me. They don't assign anyone for such missions. I won't fail them!" Warden replied.

Warden's mother turned around. "You're just their pawn. They're using you."

Jennifer saw her tears.

***

The aura of two red-haired teenagers glistened as they left their safe spot at last. Aelfgar and Leland finally got to see the two shadows that had been following them for days. The girl's silky red hair cascaded down to her waist and tickled her eyebrows. She wore a dingy white skirt and covered the top of her body with a finely crafted shirt made of tree leaves. She tightly held a sword with both hands.

The lad's clothes were likewise comprised of fine tree leaves. A quiver of arrows was strapped to his back, and he clutched a bow. They looked terribly tired, dirty, and afraid.

Aelfgar spoke first. "You showed up, at last."

Leland wouldn't have thought that mere kids could have followed them for that long. *Why would two kids roam these gloomy woods all alone?*

"Don't you dare come one step closer!" The girl quivered, raised her sword, and pointed it at Leland and Aelfgar.

"We don't intend to harm you," Aelfgar said.

She lowered her sword for a moment but then loudly said, compensating for her moment of weakness, "What are you doing in these woods?"

"Your legs are shivering, you can barely hold a sword, and I bet you're hungry. Come here, little girl. If I wanted to hurt you, I would have done it before, wouldn't I?"

The girl gazed at her brother, then darted her eyes back to Leland and Aelfgar. "Who *are* you?"

"I'm Aelfgar Hawx, and this is Leland Hopegone," Aelfgar said. "Now, can we talk? Otherwise, I might find myself forced to do things that won't please you." Aelfgar put a hand on his pommel.

Before she could reply, the Triple Skulls Monster bounced toward them with all of its brutality. Its axes were as heavy as its body, but it carried them the way a kid would carry a lollipop. Leland thought the monster wouldn't attack them unless they tried to pass. It was aggressive and swung its ax right and left, randomly cutting off the tops of thick trees as if they were wheat straws.

"What should we do now?" Leland cried.

"Fight, of course!" Aelfgar replied.

Aelfgar scrabbled backward, so now Leland was the only one facing the monster. *Why did he do that? Why is he leaving me alone against this beast?*

"You won't learn unless you experience, young lad," Aelfgar said. "He's yours."

Leland unsheathed his sword and maintained his posture. His heart pounded rapidly and his leg quivered.

The more you feed your fear, the more you become imprisoned by it. The words of his father resonated in his head, fueling him vague wisdom and lots of anger. *Whatever it means, I mustn't give in to fear.*

Leland's sword was heavy. He pointed his blade at the monster and had enough courage to rush at it. Leland's brown hair swished back as he charged with full speed, throwing away any hesitance. That was a moment of courage for Leland, but courage alone wasn't enough to beat such a monster.

***

On the training field, Ojoy threw off his cloak and stood half naked in front of all the warriors. "I'm standing here right in front of you, unarmed. But with my hands I can rip lion's heads off their bodies and wrestle hungry beasts." He cleared his throat as he walked among the rows of warriors. "The war will soon flame up I have been told. But we are ready, aren't we?" His tone was loud and tough. "I said, aren't we?"

The warriors replied in unison, "We are!"

"Who will win this war?" Ojoy asked the closest warrior to him, pressing on his shoulder.

The warrior shouted, "We will, sir!"

"Defeat is not an option." Ojoy's veins were prominent on his forehead as he roared, "We are the rulers of Oremanta, and anyone who denies that shall receive nothing short of death!"

And then, amidst his furious speech, guards dragged two handcuffed men into the field. One of them coughed badly, and the other one had rashes all over his body. The two men, who looked weary and tired, had skipped the training session that day.

Ojoy walked circles around them. Before either could spit words of apology, he said, "Sickness is not an excuse. What is sickness compared to death? What is it compared to humiliation? Do you have wives and children?"

"Yes, sir!" the two said at once.

"Imagine your wives raped and your kids chained like slaves. Imagine everything beyond these walls burning to ashes. Tough men never rest! Weaklings do not exist in my army." Ojoy took a deep breath then ordered, "Go wear your armors and get back here. You're not going to miss the training."

***

The monster growled and spat saliva everywhere as he charged Leland. Aelfgar stood still, and the two red-haired siblings kept a safe distance as well. Leland dodged the monster, and then he turned around and stuck his sword into its back. It was like sticking a needle into a lion's haunches.

The monster didn't seem to feel the damage. Leland had only angered the beast.

Gazing at that monster flying off the handle hadn't stimulated Aelfgar to move an inch.

The monster suddenly rushed the red-haired boy and then, before he could find an escape, it grabbed the boy's skinny waist and squeezed his guts as though he were an insect.

"No, Billy!" the girl shouted. "Let him go!"

With a shrill growl it covered Billy's small, round face with stinky, green saliva. The monster then attempted to slice him in half until Leland hit him a second time.

The monster roared and then went for Leland. It was slow. Leland utilized that and dodged the attacks, then hit its back for the third time. The monster grabbed Leland by his collar and brutally threw him down. Leland felt as though a truck had crushed his bones.

Can I really face this beast alone? he asked himself as he growled, suffering pain. He looked right and left, searching for his sword, but the sword wasn't within his range. Leland glared at the Triple Skull Monster, which was gaining on him. He felt his ribs aching and his limbs throbbing. He felt helpless.

"Get up, boy!" Aelfgar ordered. "You can do it."

The old man sounds certain.

Aelfgar crossed both arms and ordered again, "You're a Keo. *Do* something."

I did something. I survived thus far fighting a deadly beast when I could barely hold a sword. Maybe that's the power of a Keo. Or maybe I'm just lucky.

Leland picked up a dagger that had fallen to the ground at the beginning of the battle and pulled himself up, barely. He knew he was fighting an uphill battle, but, subconsciously, he wanted to paddle his own canoe and win without anyone's help.

Leland went behind the monster, avoiding the monster's random hits with its sharp axes, and then he stuck the dagger into the monster's neck. Leland fell to the ground and thought the monster would do the same, but he was mistaken. The monster turned around and almost ended Leland's life when Aelfgar jumped on its back and muttered, "It's all in the heart."

With his sharp dagger, Aelfgar killed the Triple Skulls Monster.

Leland took a deep breath and wiped the sweat off his face. *That was close.*

"Why did you do that?" Leland yelled at Aelfgar.

"Do what?" Aelfgar replied as he chopped the beast to small pieces with his sword. "That's enough food for two days, I hope."

"Why did you let me fight alone?"

"Because from now till the day you die, you won't stop fighting. And for that, someone must teach you how to do it. And it happened to be poor Aelfgar Hawx."

The red-haired girl rushed to her brother and delicately leaned over his wounded body. "Are you okay, Billy?" Tears welled in her eyes.

The girl's voice was weak and afraid and charming. Aelfgar shifted his eyes to the pair, who were so similar they had to be siblings. He raised both eyebrows jealously.

"I am," the boy said. He lifted his head as he spoke.

"We need to work on our relationship," Aelfgar told Leland, guffawing with a loud wheeze. Leland shook his head and chortled before he hurried to the boy. On his knees and beside the red-haired girl, he asked, "Are you hurt?"

"I'm fine," Billy replied, standing up with difficulty. "How many times do I have to repeat myself?"

"Thank you for saving our lives." The girl blushed.

"No problem," Aelfgar replied, still chopping the monster to pieces.

"Let's go, Maya," the boy told his sister. "Our way is clear now."

But Leland didn't want them to leave, and he felt selfish for wanting them here just to fill the void within. Luckily, Aelfgar wanted them there too, but for an entirely different reason.

"You're not going anywhere," Aelfgar firmly said, his body stained with the beast's blood. "Not before you tell me why you followed us."

Billy stared at Maya, silently consulting her with his eyes. She nodded. The four sat beside a tree as the sun gradually escaped the sky. The wound on Billy's face and the bruises on Leland's body were the only remnants of battle—as well as the parts of the monster Aelfgar was grilling.

"What's your story?" Aelfgar asked as he fed dry sticks to the fire. The night was cold, but not quite dark yet.

"My name's Maya," she said. A few strands of her hair blocked her left eye as she spoke. "And this is Billy, my younger brother."

"The closest village must be miles away. I wonder how you got into the woods by yourself," Aelfgar inquired while grilling.

The smell of the monster's thighs, guts, and neck disgusted Leland. He almost threw up. But that would be embarrassing, especially when everyone else wanted to eat it badly.

"No," Billy said. "We have no village."

Aelfgar darted his eyes to the boy for a moment, but only a small fraction of his gaze reflected sympathy. Hawx quickly refocused on the flames again, flipping the meat.

Leland thought, *Maybe that's what wars bring: total destruction and loss. And maybe that's what I'm changing into: an apathetic being.*

"Why are you here?" Aelfgar asked.

"Revenge," the girl confessed with cold lips, and then asserted, "We want our revenge."

Leland couldn't believe such small, innocent lips carried so much hatred. Her eyes flamed when she talked, but her hands shook. Leland gazed at her blushing cheeks as she added, "But we don't want to be alone anymore."

"Tell me your story. We have the whole night," Aelfgar demanded, serving everyone a piece of stinky, grilled meat. The siblings tore into the meat, and Leland could tell Aelfgar was salivating.

Chewing like a starving gorilla, Billy told their story. "We lived in a village once called Rangerwest. My father was a farmer, and my mother taught little kids how to defend themselves in the woods. I was six and Maya was seven. Our house was small, but father was building a bigger, better one. We all had our dreams. I wanted to be a great warrior and Maya wanted to be a healer. All we ever wanted was to live together. We never thought we'd be separated."

Maya picked up the memory. "We heard there would be a war. The rumor spread like wildfire. My father thought we'd better leave the village, but we all refused. My mother couldn't leave the kids she was teaching. Billy and I didn't want to leave Rangerwest. We were kids. We didn't understand the meaning of war. My father himself wasn't sure if it was real or just a rumor. Anyway, we decided to stay, though some families had left their homes. My mother and father had the mindset that even if there were a war, we wouldn't be a part of it. We weren't biased to any side so no one would harm us, especially because we carry no weapons and have no intentions of killing anyone."

Billy stared at the fire and put the meat on a rock beside him. "The war eventually came, and we found ourselves among the few families that stayed in the village. We all gathered in one house, shared the same food, and had the same fate. Days passed after the war began, and we all felt comfortable because nothing bad had happened to Rangerwest thus far. Until one day, hundreds of knights invaded our peaceful village at midnight." He clenched his fist then disclosed, "Their leader had long, gray hair. His face was ugly and cruel and dirty. I'll never forget his resentful eyes. He asked 'Which side are you with?' My father and the other old men told him that Rangerwest wasn't a part of the war. The gray-haired man sneered and then ordered his men to exterminate *everyone*. Before dawn, Rangerwest was *annihilated*. Men and woman and children were killed. Houses and shops and playgrounds burned to ashes. *Nothing* remained."

"How'd you survive?" Leland asked.

"Mom and dad dug a small hole somewhere close outside the village, just to make sure there'd be a safe spot for us if anything happened. They covered it with tree leaves so that no one would notice anything. It fit our small bodies perfectly. When the knights invaded the village, mom quickly hid us there and surreptitiously went back so that they wouldn't suspect anyone had escaped outside the village. We saw nothing, but the painful screams and the smell of burning flesh were more than enough to make us tremble in fear. It was a nightmare." Billy's eyes brimmed with tears. "When the knights left, we got out and saw nothing but corpses and ashes. No one was there at all. Nothing but emptiness. We were alone, hungry, and afraid, with nowhere to run."

They all paused. In the prolonged silence, the only sounds were the fire eating wood and the owls singing in the wild.

Leland thought, *This world … is cruel. Poverty, weakness, loss, hatred … I will end all of that!*

"He's named Yoink," Aelfgar remarked. "The man with the long gray hair is Yoink, a leader in the Rebel Army."

Billy frowned but didn't mumble a word. Maya started to sing, her voice pure and clear, the brightest thing Leland had heard since arriving in Oremanta. He wished she would never stop, although he didn't understand why she had started to sing.

Quietly but clearly, she sang, "We'll hold each other's hands under three moons and burning suns. Like the wind that hears all stories, but moves on and on and on, hitting every stone, not caring where it runs."

Billy murmured, "That's the song we've slept to every night since losing our village."

"Nice voice, young girl," Aelfgar praised, then winked at Leland. "Wish this brat had one like yours."

Maya closed her eyes when she sung. The words flew from her mouth into the heart of the woods, a glimpse of innocent beauty in a place of pure hatred. She blushed when she opened her eyes.

Leland pretended he wasn't staring.

"Three days ago," Billy said, "someone stole everything we had, and that's why we followed you."

"We thought it was you," Maya told Leland. "You look kind of similar."

"Similar?" Leland queried.

"He wore blue trousers and a white shirt," Billy said. "At first, we thought it was you, and we wanted our stuff back. But then it seemed we were mistaken, yet we kept following you to get out of the woods. The boy who stole from us was blonde and way shorter and had two round glasses sticking out of his eyes." Billy chuckled. "I wonder what they were."

"A short blonde guy wearing jeans, a white shirt, and eyeglasses?" Leland asked in disbelief. "That has to be Dylan!"

Chapter Nineteen

The Messenger

"I just don't get it. I don't think I will ever!" Abbey, Leland's aunt, shouted. She'd come all the way from Todland for fun, not for this.

Ever since Leland had disappeared, Maria's mood constantly fluctuated between optimism and pessimism. But today Maria was neither.

Sitting at the small round table in the corner of her room, a cup of coffee in her hand, Maria disclosed, "You know, I've been carrying this burden for many years."

"You keep on telling mysteries, and I can't pick up all these pieces!"

"I've hidden all of that for years. I've lied to Leland. Do you know how it feels to lie?"

"We all lie sometimes, Maria."

"Then you must have understood what it feels like when all of your lies become truth."

"I … don't exactly know what you're saying."

Maria kept her eyes on the cup as a weird smile of agony slowly morphed on her face. "Imagine a cup of coffee like this cup I'm holding, and you're in the middle of a storm trying to keep this cup from falling. But everything around you tells you you're going to fail. And you don't care if you die trying. I was in a storm ten years ago and I failed. I failed again this time too."

Abbey wondered, *Is she referring to Frank?* "What are you saying?" Abbey raged. "Leland isn't dead like Frank. We'll find him and his friends!"

"Worry not," Maria said. "No one is dead. Not even Frank. But sometimes I wish they were."

***

The Seven Lieutenants of the Castle gathered in the dark brown hall of the Palace of Wrath. Guarded by dozens of well-armed men, the hall was one of two palaces in the Castle's center. The other palace, the Palace of Eternal Wisdom, had been built for the rulers of Oremanta, known as the Flares of Truth and the Legendary Leaders of the Castle and all of Oremanta. The brown hall's high roof was supported by five twisted brick pillars. Seven of the finest chairs in the Castle surrounded a deep fire pit. If one fell into the fire pit, they were unlikely to reach the bottom before their body turned to ashes. Or that's what rumors in Oremanta said. It was also said that the fire hadn't died since it was kindled.

Every lieutenant sat on his own chair except for Ojoy, who had yet to arrive. They placed their swords and their golden armor in front of them on the round table, the protocol for lieutenants' meetings.

Shadows blanketed their eyelids and gray silver bands covered their foreheads. After several moments of silence, Ojoy entered through the embellished silver door, without armor or his sword.

Lieutenant Hamlet glared at him. "You need to respect—"

Hamlet choked on his words when Ojoy looked at him through his peripheral vision, as if he'd seen a ghost. Hamlet couldn't articulate further words.

Agis Phoenix saved the situation when he announced, "With the authority given to me by the Legendary Leaders of Oremanta, I must tell you that the time has come and the bells shall ring soon. There shall be no more waiting. Let the final summit preceding war start!"

Lieutenant Hamlet didn't speak another word during the meeting.

***

Fog blurred Leland's vision. He couldn't see anything but a familiar silhouette of a man standing still not too far from him. He walked toward the shadow, unable to control his heart palpitations or the tremor in his hands. But he'd seen this figure before. He knew who that man was. And he wasn't ready to meet him yet.

"Leland," the shadow whispered. His voice echoed a few times. "Think."

Not only is the shadow familiar, but his voice is too. "Think?" Leland replied, breaking out in a cold sweat. He was sure now. *It's my father.*

"Think about *who* you are fighting for. Think about *what* you are fighting for." The whispering continued. "Don't be stupid. Don't let *them* use you." The shadow disappeared into the fog. Silence ruled.

Leland's cracked voice echoed as he stretched out his hand, calling, "Wait! Wait!" His heart pounded so hard he felt it would rupture. His eyes saw nothing but darkness, and in one fell swoop light struck him—real light.

"A nightmare?" Aelfgar queried, packing up the tent.

It seemed morning had already come, and they had to walk again. Leland's neck was stiff and his muscles were fatigued. He put the palm of his hands on his forehead. It was boiling. The dream was so vivid he could still hear his father's voice, echoing.

Think ... Think.

"What did you dream of? A lion eating up your little willy?" Aelfgar chuckled. "Get yourself together. We don't have the whole day."

"Nothing," Leland lied. "It was nothing." He hesitated to tell Aelfgar what he'd dreamed.

How would Aelfgar react if I quit the mission and not fight against my father? I'm doing this for myself, for my mother, for the innocent people who died. The Castle is not using me. No one is using me. I'm doing it because I want *to do it.*

"You look confused." Aelfgar sensed something in Leland, who was shocked by the old man's wickedly strong senses. "If you don't want to fight against your father, then don't."

Amazed, Leland abruptly looked at Aelfgar. He somehow knew what was bothering Leland. He read his mind as if he were reading a paper.

How does he know?

"Follow your heart, my son," Aelfgar said, pressing on Leland's shoulder. He smiled kindly. "If your heart tells you to fight against Frank, then follow it. If it tells you not to fight in this war, then don't. One can't do anything that's against the will of their heart," Aelfgar asserted. "If your heart doesn't synchronize perfectly with your head, you will fail."

Hundreds of crows flew and cried in the sky, not so close yet not so far from them. In Amanda's Park, the one near Leland's house on Earth, crows were always crowded on trees and fences. But the ones in Oremanta were different. They were bigger and noisier and seemed more dangerous and hungry. Aelfgar was behind him, putting some leftovers from last night's meal into his satchel.

"Where's Maya and Billy?" Leland asked, scanning the horizon.

"They went hunting for some rabbits and owls. They'll be here any moment."

"Good," Leland said as he stood up. "I gotta ask them about Dylan."

***

"I'm coming with you," Jennifer insisted. "Why are you refusing?"

Warden shook his head. "You don't get it. It's too dangerous out there. I can't risk your life!"

"I just want to see how things work." Jennifer looked away. "Who will I stay here with? It won't take us too long."

"I'll take you to the Healing Squad. That was my initial plan."

She knew staying in the safety of the Castle was the optimal decision because she knew what it was like to be in the wild. She'd seen Dylan stabbed in the heart, and it had made her shiver and tremble for days. It had made her cry and sob. But she was curious to see what laid behind the walls of the Castle other than woods. The idea of her being locked here like a prisoner bothered her.

Cold wind blew in Jennifer's face and made her crave a warm shower, a mug of hot chocolate, and a good TV show airing late at night all at once. But that would never happen now. Maybe never again.

***

The sun beamed upon Utta and Jack's faces as they stood behind her cottage. Jack was ready to take the bull by the horns. He craved power. And if this girl Utta were the only source he could gain power from, he'd stick with her.

"You're improving," Utta praised, tilting her head from side to side. "But you still haven't answered me."

"What do you want?"

"Unless they have a strong purpose here, like Leland, most of those who come from Earth prefer to stay away from fights and wars. They're always terrified and panicked, and I see nothing but fear in their eyes.

But you're different. From the get-go you wanted to be strong. What's your story?"

"Let's just start training." Jack clenched his teeth and shook his head, forcefully attempting to dissipate the one fragment of memory that engulfed his mind. *Owd…Antarctica… Why do memories hurt?*

"Make me stronger, Utta!"

"If that's your choice." Utta stepped closer to him. "I'm going to make you the strongest."

***

"Tell me, Billy, Maya," Leland asked the siblings, "what did the guy you saw look like exactly?"

They walked across green hills away from the muddy, dark woods. The sky was clear and blue and a fresh breeze of air swished Leland's brown hair around his face.

"He was blonde and short," Maya said, looking at Leland from the corner of her wide eyes. "And he wore blue trousers, just like yours."

"What else? What did he look like? Tell me more, please!"

"He looked young, very young. Oh, and I almost forgot," Maya recalled. "He had a tattoo on the back of his neck. A dragon tattoo."

That killed Leland's last hope. Dylan didn't have a tattoo. Leland knew that like he knew his own name.

Aelfgar, on the other hand, kept his eyes on the crystal compass. It glowed green, which meant they were on the right path.

Leland silently fought a wave of disappointment. It felt as though an inner war was dragging him down and burying him from within. He didn't know what was depressing him more: Jennifer being away, Dylan's death, or that he desperately wanted to kill his father.

"We have to hurry," Aelfgar ordered. "We don't have all day."

"Calm down, old man." Billy chuckled. "We do have all day."

Billy was way different than yesterday. He'd been telling jokes and smiling and teasing all day long. Leland liked that, even though he'd been the center of half of those jokes. After about an hour of fast walking on a rocky river bank, dozens of double-crested cormorant birds spread their wings. Seagulls dove in the light blue water and caught their fish. Sunbeams partially reflected on the water.

"Where are we?" Leland asked.

"The Heavenly River," Aelfgar answered. "Maybe we're closer than we think to the swordsmith."

"This place is beautiful," Maya said as she leaned down and passed her delicate fingers over the clear water. Colorful butterflies danced closer to their faces, floating right and left, up and down. The place had a refreshing smell, as if they were in a garden full of roses.

But none of that grabbed Leland's attention like Maya did.

**

"So you're asking me to accompany you outside the Castle just to protect her?" Roy smirked. "I wonder when you'll stop being afraid of everything."

"I don't know what might happen to me outside the Castle," Warden explained. "This girl has no one. And she refuses to stay here."

Roy had been Warden's close friend for years. They'd gotten to know each other shortly after the first war, and in an unfavorable place: the cemetery. They had both lost their fathers in that cursed, bloody war.

"You're taking me outside the walls just because that girl *refuses* to stay in the Castle?" Roy complained. "Have you lost your mind?"

"I haven't."

"How much will you pay?"

Warden knew it would come down to that. Roy never cared about anything but money. And if this mission could grant him a few silver coins, he wouldn't mind losing parts of his body for it.

"I never thought I'd pay you for a favor!" Warden frowned to sell the small, verbal trick so he wouldn't have to pay much.

"Favor?" Roy laughed hard then tapped his index finger on Warden's head. "We're in a time of war. Wake up. I have a mother and two little sisters, get it?"

"Three silver coins." Warden offered. "And if I don't get back, take her to the Healing Squad."

"Five." Roy's eyes glistened.

"Put on your armor. We have no time to waste."

∗∗∗

Jennifer sat on a wooden bench waiting for Warden to come out. He was inside a small shop owned by Roy, Warden's friend. Jennifer put her hands inside her pockets and wondered what it would be like to live in this place forever.

What would it be like not to see my father ever again, or walk down streets I used to walk down every day? But none of that matters now. If I cling to the past, there will be no future. All I have to do now is be as I always used to be: tough. If I show any weakness in this place, I'll be dead. I've been through a lot already, but I know myself. I can surpass anything. I might cry, I might get hurt, but no one would ever know about that. From the outside, I will show no weakness until the inside heals itself. That's how I've always done it in the past, and that's how I'm going to do it now.

It was a speech Jennifer had trained to give herself. They never had a permanent effect. She knew that failure to execute what she'd just told herself was a possibility. But even knowing that was a good thing.

Warden, at last, came out of the shop, but he wasn't alone. Roy had caramel-brown hair that reached his shoulders. A few of his teeth were black, some brown, but the majority were yellow. His nail beds were black and dirty.

Roy gazed at Jennifer from head to toes then said, "Impressive."

Now that Roy was close to her, she could smell his bad breath hitting her face. She looked him in the eye, without blinking and without fear, and said, "Want me to show you something impressive?"

Roy took a step back and raised both hands in surrender. "Easy girl." He glared at Warden and then rolled his eyes back to Jennifer and repeated, "Easy!"

She could tell that Roy, at least for now, wouldn't dare say any offensive word against her—not anymore.

"Why's he coming with us?" Jennifer asked.

"It is dangerous outside the Castle. I want to make sure that if something bad happens to me, he'll get you back here," Warden replied. "And don't worry, he's a good friend of mine. Now let's go."

The three walked until they reached the Golden Gate. Warden showed the guards the slip of paper he had, and they instantly opened its doors. The gate was so high and thick that it required five guards to open it. Jennifer remembered the day they'd first arrived in Oremanta. *Aelfgar opened it all by himself.*

"How far is the village?" Jennifer asked.

"Fortunately, it is very close to here," Warden explained. "All we have to do is deliver the message and get back to safety."

"What's the message?" Roy interrupted.

"It's a warning. The lieutenants want to warn all the villages outside the Castle that there's a war approaching."

To know she was on the right side of this war was comforting to Jennifer. Evil would never care for the lives of the innocent. But that didn't matter much. She couldn't switch sides now anyways.

"Why don't we use horses?" Jennifer suggested. "I've seen many near the gate."

"Horses make noise. We don't want that. And we're not that far from Millory."

He wasn't lying. Less than an hour later, the walls of Millory appeared before them. Two men stood in front of its high wooden gate (though not as high as the Golden Gate).

"Stay here," Warden ordered Jennifer. He swallowed and looked away. "I will go inside, deliver the message, and return to you."

Jennifer felt the fear inside Warden. *Something within him is trembling.*

"Do you need me to come with you?" she asked, and then realized her question was stupid. *What could I offer him there?*

"No," Warden firmly said. "You've come far enough already."

"I'm sorry if I hurt you before," Jennifer apologized. "Get back safe."

"If I don't come back by sunset," Warden informed Roy, "take Jennifer back to the Castle."

"Who will give me my silver coins then?" Roy asked, sharpening his dagger with a brick he'd just picked up.

"For God's sake, Roy," Warden reluctantly said, gritting his teeth. "My mother will."

***

Two well-built, well-armed guards stood before Warden near the gate of Millory. The first one leaned down, as he was a few feet taller than Warden, then asked, "What brings you to Millory?"

"I am a messenger of the Castle," Warden said.

The guard chuckled but tried hard not to show it. He whispered into the other guard's ears, and the latter chuckled as well. However, he didn't try to hide it. The first guard gazed at Warden, raised an eyebrow, and then sternly ordered, as if he hadn't chuckled at all, "Stay where you are. I can't let you in unless I ask our king."

Warden heard something off in the guard's voice. Something tricky and deceiving, but he couldn't tell what was it. He knew there was no way he'd retreat now anyway. *How shameful would that be?*

Warden's mother told him she'd prepare him a piece of warm apple pie and a cup of Mista once he got back. He told her he'd be back before the new dawn and she smiled, kissed his forehead, and told him to take care. For all of that, he mustn't fail her.

"Come in," the guard told Warden.

Warden stepped inside Millory at last. It was a small village, and he could see almost all of its cottages from where he stood. The first thing his eyes caught was a wooden statue in the middle of a round square. Behind that sat what seemed like an old throne carved from pale wood. Everything in Millory was old, cheap, and poorly polished, and quite unlike the Castle, which now seemed like a piece of heaven.

On the wooden throne sat a man with blonde hair and a notable hunchback. He glared at Warden from head to toes. As he did, a guard pushed Warden so hard that he almost fell on his face.

What the hell are they doing? Warden panicked.

"Tsh." The guard sighed in complaint. "Kneel before your king, Castler!"

Warden frowned at the guard, who was devoid of facial expressions, and then shifted his vision back to the king. With respect, Warden said, "Apologies, my lord."

"I'm Gorno Mathew, the first of his name, the king of the great village of Millory, and I ask you, Castler, what brought you to our land?" The king glared at Warden. When Gorno stood up, every guard kneeled.

It wasn't long before hundreds of people had formed a circle around the Castler too. Warden wondered where all of those faces had come from. The heat of his body rose as drops of sweat rolled down his skin.

"I came here to deliver a message from the Castle. The bells of the second war of Oremanta shall ring soon. We can offer you shelter and safety."

The king burst into annoying, condescending, wheezing laughter. The guards beside him laughed as well but then immediately stopped when the king did.

"Your unlucky day has arrived, my boy."

Warden's heartbeat quickened.

The king raised his voice so that all the people gathered in the square could hear. "The first misfortune of the war has arrived. But rest assured, what happened in the first war will not be repeated. Millory is now a solid fortress, immune to all treachery and betrayals. Millory will stand on its own, and from now on there shall be no mercy."

The people chanted and hailed. The king waved with one hand for them to stop. "The first war brought nothing but a deadly massacre to Millory. And I swear, by all that is sacred, that no one from Millory will ever be hurt again."

The king sat on his throne again. Two guards grabbed Warden and brought him closer to the king.

"I'm just a messenger!" Warden shouted.

"And what does that mean?" The king replied. "Millory was slaughtered by *refugees* in the first war. They knocked on our doors, and we gave them nothing but food and shelter. Three days later, those *refugees* slaughtered the people of Millory. A king does not repeat his mistake."

"But … wait!" Warden stuttered.

"Guards!" The king raised a hand and ordered his guards, "Treat him the way we always treat our guests."

Chapter Twenty

Solitude Breeds Hatred

"We ought to leave now," Roy told Jennifer. "He's taking too long."

Jennifer frowned and pointed her index finger to the ground. "We're staying right here. We aren't leaving before the sun sets."

"Or what?" Roy inched closer to her.

"Or," Jennifer said, staring him down, "you won't get your silver coins. If I don't get back, Warden's mother won't give you the coins."

Roy didn't reply.

Jennifer thought, *Warden really is taking too long. What if something bad has happened to him?*

"If he doesn't come by sunset," Jennifer said, "we'll have to tell the lieutenants. They need to know about this."

"*You* tell the lieutenants. *I'll* take my money."

If her mother could see her bravely dealing with what she was facing, she'd be so proud. Jennifer always wished she could have talked with her mother about her problems, or go shopping with her like girls in her school did with their mothers. It always hurt knowing she'd never see her again. When some girls in her school complained about their moms, Jennifer wanted to slap them in the face. They didn't know how lucky they were to have someone beside them all the time. This train of thought made her think of Dylan and Leland, too. Without them, she wouldn't have survived. Her eyes moistened, and she turned away, clenching her fists so tightly that her knuckles turned white.

"How long does it take to get a Sword of Legends?" Jennifer asked.

"A Sword of Legends? I've never heard of a man going after that thing and coming back alive," Roy said. "But oh, lord, if I had one, I'd sell it for a thousand golden coins!"

***

Warden was chained like a slave in a small chamber filled with spears and swords and shields and a few other weapons. If it weren't for Jennifer and Roy, who might get back to the Castle and bring reinforcements, Warden would've lost all hope of remaining alive. It had been a few hours since they'd brought him here, and no one had come to see him since.

The chamber was hot, and he was sweating as if in a sauna. He couldn't wipe the sweat off his face, which was irritating. Warden heard footsteps coming rhythmically toward his chamber. His neck was stiff and heavy, but he forced himself to lift it up. Perhaps he'd see Ojoy's face, or Aelfgar's, or even Roy's, who would definitely ask him for money after saving him. But he saw none of those.

A guard with a large mole on his cheek and thick eyebrows entered the room. He unchained Warden without mumbling a word and then supported Warden's body with his own as they left.

"Don't make any noise," the guard whispered. "I'm here to save you."

"Why do you want to save me?" Warden said, out of breath.

"I'm from the Castle," the man whispered. "I've lived in Millory for a long time, but I cannot let a Castler die this way!"

Warden felt lucky. If he could safely get outside of Millory, he swore he'd never leave the Castle again. Before they had chained him, the guards had punched and kicked Warden so hard that they left prominent, blue bruises on his skin.

"Don't tell anyone about this," the man said. "If they knew I freed you, they'd kill my children and wife before my eyes, before they'd kill me."

They walked down a poorly lit corridor similar to those in the Castle's underground prison, the Cage of the Damned. Warden had once gone there with Aelfgar to check on the prisoners of the first war. There were hundreds of them, chained, helpless, and lost. Now he was just like them.

"I won't," Warden forced a smile. "You have my word."

The end of the corridor was near. Warden saw dim light beneath the wooden door not so far away. Pain radiated throughout his body as he forced himself to walk fast. *Come on. I can do it!*

"When I reach the Castle safely," Warden said, "I'll make sure you receive what you deserve, noble man."

"That's generous of you, sir."

A few more steps and the two were in front of the door. The man opened the door with his free hand.

Fearfully, Warden thought, *Why is this door unlocked? There's a prison inside, and if the door isn't locked, chances of escape are high.*

But a moment later, Warden knew why.

The man beside him forcefully pushed him forward so that he lost his balance and fell on his knees. Hundreds of grinning faces stared at him, reluctantly, lustily, and happily all at once. And then there was Gorno Mathew, on his age-blackened wooden throne, grinning like the devil torturing a pure soul.

"You really thought you'd escape Millory?" the guard with the mole sneered. "Poor Castler."

"Silence!" Gorno Mathew ordered.

Everyone stopped talking.

The king descended from his throne and went to Warden, who was still chained. Mathew said, "We treat everyone with respect here in Millory. That's why, Castler, I will give you the right and freedom to scream when it hurts. The right to express your pain freely, my boy."

"I came here to warn you!" Warden shouted. "I came to help you! Is this how the people of Millory return the favor?"

The king chuckled, producing that annoying, wheezing sound again.

"No," the king said. "*This* is how we return the favor."

He *tsk-tsked* the guards, simultaneously raising an eyebrow and pointing with his head toward Warden.

"You know how we return the favor, right?" He turned around and walked back to his throne. "We've been betrayed once, and the king of Millory shall not repeat his mistake!" Mathew groaned on his way to the throne.

Hundreds of throats hailed at once.

My mother told me not to leave, but I'm stubborn, and now my only wish is that I'd obeyed her when I had the chance. Who will look after my family now? Who will protect them when the massacre begins? I've seen war before, and I knew very well what wars bring: death and loss, poverty and fear.

A guard kicked Warden hard on the stomach. Blood poured from his mouth and onto his neck, slowly descending to paint what was left of his armor. Warden realized his death was inevitable, and if he could salvage anything right now, it would be his family.

"Would you deliver my last will to my family?" Warden asked, one eye shut.

"Of course," the king said. He whispered into the ears of a nearby guard.

The guard went to Warden, pulled his tongue out, and then cut it off.

Blood pooled in his mouth. The pain was more than he could take. It felt as if a thousand razors had shredded his mouth. He wished he hadn't spoken.

"Now tell us your will," the king told Warden. "We are listening."

Four guards brought in a wooden platform with rollers at both ends. The man with the mole and another guard tied Warden's hands and feet at the rollers' opposite ends. Other guards stretched Warden's feet from one side of the roller while more guards stretched his hands to the opposite side.

Warden felt every joint in his body dislocating. The agonizing pain made him scream and growl. It was the worst kind of pain he'd ever felt. At any point, his legs and hands would detach from his body.

Then it happened.

Warden's wrist ruptured. Blood sprayed as his hands fell away from the rest of his body. He wished a sword would cut through his chest and kill him. The joints in his ankle tore apart, followed almost instantly by the total separation of his feet from his legs. Warden bled heavily.

The guards untied what was left of his extremities, and then one of them lifted his head up, exposing his neck. Another guard unsheathed his sword and went closer to him.

Make it end. Engulfed with regret for leaving everyone he loved behind, for not listening to his mother, and for being reckless and stubborn, Warden wanted it all to be over.

The people of Millory seemed to enjoy the show. They clapped and giggled and chanted.

"Cut his head off," the king said, "and feed it to the ravens behind the walls!"

The guard didn't hesitate.

***

Roy complained, "We must leave!"

He was right. The sun was about to set, and it was frightening to stay outside the Castle in the night. Jennifer gazed at the gate, still waiting for Warden to come out. But Warden didn't come.

Instead, a guard arrived carrying Warden's head with one hand. He threw it to the ground and closed the gate behind him. Warden's head rolled across the ground, pouring out blood.

Jennifer's face morphed from worry to horror.

Roy hoisted Jennifer onto his shoulders and ran as fast as he could back toward the Castle.

The petrified girl couldn't articulate a word.

***

Ten years ago in an abandoned dungeon beneath the Castle, fifty torch-wielding men walked behind Frank Hopegone. The dungeon had been abandoned for many long years. Just like the man they followed, the men wore ripped, black cloaks.

Oremanta didn't have many moonless nights, but on this night no moon shone. Once every few years, all three moons of Oremanta disappeared.

Hundreds of skeletons and skulls were randomly scattered throughout the dungeon. Frank Hopegone slowed down then turned around to face the men behind him.

"He who's not willing to sacrifice his life for the sake of honor, he who's not willing to step up and face the oppression, shall leave this place now." Frank's voice echoed in the dark dungeon. His voice was steady and calm, and his eyes didn't blink. "I want men on my side. I want men who do not fear death."

The cloaked men were tall and wide, and they frowned and growled like hungry beasts in reaction to Frank's words.

Frank unsheathed his sword and walked a few steps toward a man in the first row. He pointed his sword at the man's throat.

The man didn't move an inch. He stared back at Frank with eyes that didn't know fear.

Frank returned his sword back to where it belonged. "We are not afraid of death. We'd rather die than live like sheep. Wolves get to rise again and reclaim what they deserve."

Frank turned around again and repeated as he faded into the darkness of the dungeon, "Solitude breeds hatred. Hatred breeds power. Power breeds violence. And if violence is controlled by wisdom, one shall rule."

***

"With the authority given to me by Frank Hopegone, I shall tell you," Konlaw spoke to the men after Frank had left the dungeon, "from this place, on this night, our rebellion begins. We shall meet every other day, and our army must increase every night. Oppression must end, and only we can end it. Day by day, night by night, our army shall grow stronger. We shall dethrone the Legendary Leaders of the Castle and get back what's ours!"

Rebellious spirits swarmed in the dungeon.

That was the night where it had all begun.

***

A powerful sensation of *jamais vu* wrapped around Jennifer, a feeling that everything she was seeing was unfamiliar, that everything that had happened until now was just a dream, or a fragment of her imagination, that none of what she was hearing or living was real, and that when she closed her eyes and opened them, she'd be in her bed, or at school, or anywhere but in this awful place.

She closed her eyes, hoping for that to happen. Her back was against a tree trunk, alone, somewhere in the bloody Castle. Roy had left her right when they'd arrived safely behind its walls. "Now I get my coins," was all he'd said.

When she opened her eyes, she saw nothing but trees, scattered cottages, and darkness. Knowing no one was around, Jennifer cried.

Emptiness. I wonder what everyone's doing on Earth. Are they missing me and Dylan and Leland? Or have they forgotten us already?

When she felt empty and lonely in the past, she'd go out with Leland somewhere that would make them both comfortable. She wouldn't say a word, but he would understand her. They'd go to Amanda's Park at night, or to any coffee shop nearby and just sit and talk about random things until the pain ceased, or, maybe, was just temporarily forgotten.

Jennifer's amygdala was excessively stimulated, generating feelings of love, hate, nostalgia, bitterness, loneliness, and fear all mixed in a way that suffocated her and made her insides twist. She rose to her feet and walked directionless under the darkness of the night. The air around her felt like a prison, a movable cage following her wherever she went, bringing her down to her knees and bending her will every time she thought of breaking its shackles.

When someone becomes the prisoner of their own fears, nothing can break them free but their courage, Jennifer thought, clenching her hands and teeth and wondering if what she was thinking was real or just an ideal.

If they're real, why can't I apply them and break free? Because feelings are the hardest things to deal with.

She clenched her teeth and hands more strongly now.

And even though you know you don't need them, you just can't simply get rid of them. They'll be there, chasing you … haunting you … and taking the best out of you.

But then Jennifer remembered times when she'd felt bad about herself and her life. She remembered when she had thought of ending her life, times when she was alone and motherless. And, most importantly, she remembered how she had surpassed all of that and lived *without* fear. She remembered how strong she had become afterward. She remembered what she'd told herself before: *Time heals no matter how deep the wounds are. A strong person isn't the one who doesn't fear anything; it's the one who won against her fears and miseries and stood up despite all the troubles she's been through.*

Jennifer slowly opened her eyes to see only grass and cottages once again. For a moment, she wished she wouldn't wake up the next time she opened her eyes. The orange sky inked with dark blue told her it was dawn. The struggle inside her made her sick and tired.

One day I'm strong and tough and full of hope, and the other I'm down and lost and desperate. I just want this to end. I'm so sick of it.

Something moved behind her. She quickly turned around and saw a fat, white rabbit behind a tree. She stood up and walked toward it. The rabbit ran and Jennifer found herself running after it. She'd been near anorexic since the day her feet had touched Oremanta's ground, but she had to eat to survive.

The rabbit was fast, but Jennifer was *smart*. She ran parallel to it separated by columns of trees. She accelerated, bounced to the right, and kicked the rabbit so strongly that it didn't move. She looked at it, wondering what in Oremanta she was doing. Back on Earth, she would've kept such a cute creature as a pet, a friend from a different species. Now, she was about to kill it to survive.

She towered over the rabbit and grabbed its neck. Her other hand snatched the rabbit's body. She closed her eyes then broke its neck. The bones crackled and snapped, and Jennifer was sure the poor animal was no longer alive. With one hand she carried it from its tail and went back to where she'd been.

But there, on a rock, someone awaited her.

Chapter Twenty-One

Ojoy Steelhart

The Heavenly River was different than the places Leland had seen in Oremanta. The scent of flowers, the running water, the seagulls, and the fish all forced a smile upon his face.

Maya and Billy were playing near the riverbank, splashing water at each other and trying to catch some fish.

Leland looked up at the sky and stared in awe—not for the first time—at the rings surrounding Oremanta's sun. It was different than Earth's sun: he could look at it and yet not blink or turn his head away. Leland stretched his arms out, sighed, and was about to lay down on the ground when a hand firmly grabbed his face from behind, blocking his mouth. He couldn't mumble a word. A sharp knife pressed against his neck. It was so close that if he took one more breath, the knife would cut his throat open. He was paralyzed. One wrong move and he'd be as good as dead. *Who* is *this?*

"What are you going to do now, Leland Hope-gone?" a voice Leland knew very well asked.

I knew I shouldn't have trusted anyone.

***

"What do you want now?" Jennifer asked. "Haven't you got your money already?"

"I'm here to help."

"I don't need your help. Go away." Jennifer threw the dead rabbit on the ground. She looked Roy in the eyes then divulged, "And I don't have money, if that's what you're looking for." She leaned down and collected a few sticks from the ground, and then she piled them up.

A fireball slowly grew in Roy's hand. He put his flaming palm on the sticks, and they started to burn.

"Look, you're right. I love money, and I don't care about anything but money," Roy revealed. "But I don't take money I don't deserve, and I don't deserve those three silver coins now."

Jennifer placed the rabbit on the fire. Staring at its burning flesh, she asked, "What do you mean?"

"Warden wanted you in the Healing Squad. I want to get you there."

The life span of Jennifer's oversized shirt and skinny jeans were clearly coming to an end. She pulled the rabbit out of the fire with a stick.

"Staying here will do you no good," Roy insisted. "You'll find decent company there."

Roy's suggestion wasn't bad. Jennifer was sick of being alone, and she couldn't imagine living like this for days to come.

"And where's this Healing Squad?" she asked, touching the rabbit with her finger to make sure it wasn't that hot.

"Not so far from here," he answered.

Jennifer sloughed the skin and fur off the rabbit and realized she should've done that before grilling it. Too late. She ripped a leg off its body and offered it to Roy.

"All right," she said, not looking at him.

Roy took the leg without hesitation and sat beside her.

"You're pretty good for an Earthling," he said, disgustingly chewing the leg. "I mean, you're adapting really fast."

***

"We're almost there, son. We're almost there," an old man whispered to his son, carrying him on his back. The heat was unbearable. The man's face was dry and hot. It hurt every time he blinked.

"Why are we going there, father?" the son asked.

They were walking in a hot, dry, ugly, waterless desert: the Cursed Desert.

"Because," the old man muttered in staccato, "we must escape this bloody war. The Pyramids of the Fallen is our shelter now. Lord Bolt Gemini will provide us home and food. He promised."

A while later the old man noticed it from a distance. Perhaps it had been there ever since they had begun walking: the Pyramids of the Fallen. High. Mighty. Great. Powerful.

The man couldn't see details from that distance, but he could tell that the pyramids were high enough to touch the sky, wide enough they could link all parts of Oremanta, and large enough to make him believe they must have been in front of his eyes ever since they'd arrived in the Cursed Desert.

***

"What are you doing, Aelfgar?" Leland cried, the knife still pressed against his throat.

Billy and Maya didn't react at all. They just watched.

Aelfgar whispered into Leland's ears, "So what are you going to do now?"

Aelfgar's other hand, the one tightly wrapped around Leland's head, squeezed even harder, so hard that Leland felt his head would burst and everything inside his skull would splash into small pieces flying everywhere. Even though the siblings weren't showing signs of conspiracy, Leland couldn't help but think, *They had something to do with this. Otherwise, why won't they help me? Maybe they all set this up from the beginning!* Leland knew Aelfgar was strong, but he didn't know he was *that* strong. Or maybe Leland was just too weak. In any case, a knife would slit his throat if he didn't do something right now. He must react. But there was no possible way to react. Aelfgar was way too powerful for Leland.

"See?" Aelfgar said, "You're weak, Leland Hope-gone, the boy with the Keo blood."

***

The Seven Lieutenants gathered, planned, and prepared for war. Agis Phoenix, the head of the Lieutenants, declared, "We must not fail the Legendary Leaders of Oremanta, the Flares of Truth. We must not fail the people of Oremanta. This war must be won."

"Worry not," said Ojoy with a rough voice. "All of our four gates will be guarded by the finest warriors we have. From higher ground, archers will cover them. It will be impossible for the enemy to penetrate those lines."

If he had to defend all four gates of the Castle by himself and whatever laid behind its walls, Ojoy would've done it. If there was one man all Castlers trusted, it was him. In the first war, Ojoy had handled two battalions by himself before rejoining his army and slaying Bora, Frank Hopegone's former right-hand man.

Lieutenant Saneta of the Healing Squad cleared her throat and explained further, "Those units will guard our four gates. Each unit is well-balanced and has the potential to survive in the toughest of situations. The rest of the healers and defenders will line the walls, ready to aid."

Agis's gaze eased. He tapped his index finger on the round wooden table. "This leaves our main forces in the front lines, preventing the march of the enemy."

"Exactly."

Hamlet, also known as the Black Owl, chimed in. "So let's suppose our main force got destroyed outside the Castle. The enemy would have to fight the forces guarding each gate in order to get in."

"Yes," Saneta answered.

Meanwhile, the rest of the lieutenants, Charles, Jeopard, and Marquez, were mumbling and muttering in the far corner of the rounded table surrounding the fire pit, not paying much attention to what was going on.

Fast footsteps echoed in the hall. A warrior in fine armor interrupted their meeting. He bent his knees in front of Agis and requested permission to speak.

"Sir, I just received news," the warrior declared, out of breath.

"Speak up," Agis replied.

"Our messenger to Millory Village, Warden, has been killed."

Ojoy's eyes flamed. He scanned the lieutenants one by one with eyes more fearsome than the devil's. "I must leave."

***

"If you want to kill your father," Aelfgar said, still choking Leland, "you must learn how to fight. You must see death every single time you blink, and you must learn how to escape it."

Aelfgar let go of Leland.

The boy from Earth choked and coughed then fell to the ground.

Aelfgar threw a sword at him. "Never underestimate those who never underestimate anyone. Stand up and fight. Come on."

Leland picked up the sword and said nothing. He grabbed the pommel tightly with both hands and charged at Aelfgar Hawx.

The old man bent his back slightly, taking a defensive posture.

Leland's sword hit Aelfgar's, and the sound of clashing iron could be heard over miles.

"Yes, Leland, yes!" Aelfgar cried, blocking Leland's attacks. "This is how men fight."

Leland himself didn't know how he could hold a sword and fight with it this way. But a great surge of energy and rage ran in his blood, and that was enough to keep him going.

"I won't fail, old man!" Leland shouted as he pounced on Aelfgar. "With you or without you, I will make it!"

The two exchanged attacks beside the riverbank. Aelfgar then attacked Leland so powerfully that Leland's sword flew away. Aelfgar walked toward Leland, patted him on his head, and said, "*You* won't make it without *me*. But that's the spirit!"

***

The king of Millory, Gorno Mathew, sat on his throne celebrating his victory. Warden's body had been thrown in the middle of the village, headless. Like bees around a honeycomb, dozens of ravens ate his flesh.

"Yes, folks!" The king spoke to his people, who had gathered in the square to drink and celebrate. "This is what happens to anyone who tries to breach our safety."

Hundreds of throats cried, "Yeah!"

The king silenced them all with a wave of his hand. The guards surrounding the king and those near the gates raised their arrows and swords. The heads of the two guards protecting the north gate rolled down, pouring out blood.

The north gate slowly opened, and a tall man with puffed muscles stood there, alone.

"How dare you!" the king shouted. His eyes widened in fear. He shook his head. "Get him!"

"It's Ojoy!" one of the guards said, taking a few steps back.

"Get him!" the king raged. "He's only *one* man!"

Ojoy walked slowly toward the throne with the confidence of a thousand men.

Giving way, the people of Millory split into halves.

The guards rushed him.

He unsheathed his sword and looked at no one but the king.

The guards pounced on him from every direction.

Ojoy cut their heads off with his eyes still fixed on the king.

More guards came from behind.

Ojoy spun in a full circle, splitting them into halves.

"You killed … our messenger," Ojoy growled, "who came to warn you about the war."

The guards surrounding the king charged the fearless man.

Ojoy dealt with them the same way he'd dealt with their comrades. His eyes burned with anger. Blood stained his topless chest and his sword, which he pointed directly at the king. "Now, suffer the consequences."

Chapter Twenty-Two

Never Alone

Harvard placed the cup of hot Mesta on top of the table beside him. An old, leathery, dusty book was between his weary thighs. The smell of Mesta had always brought life back to the old scholar. He drank so much that it was hard to give a number for how many cups that his apprentice Ron had to wash every day.

Harvard remembered the first war, what had preceded it, and what it had resulted in as if it had happened yesterday. He'd written all of that in books only *he* could have written. That's why the Legendary Leaders of the Castle and the Seven Lieutenants paid him a monthly wage to write their history. But now, for an old man who could barely walk, he struggled to track events by himself. That's why Ron, a smart lad whom Harvard had tested many times to measure his credibility and honesty, was beside him.

Harvard opened the first page and a faint, familiar, musty smell climbed its way to his nostrils. With a blow, he wiped off a thin layer of dust across the page.

"I'm not reading this for myself," Harvard said loudly, disproportionate to the distance between him and Ron.

Ron sat on the ground inches away from Harvard with a pad and an ink pen. He'd listened to the old man read hundreds of books, and it had always fulfilled his deep desire for knowledge. But this time was different.

"Oremanta's doom began when a man rebelled against the power. But that man was a power himself," Harvard read, "for he belonged to the Keo, a Blue Blood family along with Tartan and Largo. He craved authority, but authority was meant to belong to the Tartan and Largo at the time, for the Keo were accused of treason. And that did not please him, Frank Hopegone. So he raged against the rulers."

***

"Enough for today. But from now till the war comes, we must train more often," Aelfgar informed Leland. "Go rest. We are close to the smith, and we need some power to carry on."

Leland's heart still beat fast. For a while, he thought he'd die. His neck hurt so badly he wanted a Muscadol, but there were no medications like that in Oremanta. The best thing he might find here were a few plants and warm water. He went to Billy and Maya.

Billy sank his head into the cold water and then got it out. He looked at the sun, and then at Leland, and then, abruptly, the red-haired boy fell. Billy's body shook like a fish out of water. His tongue protruded and his eyes rolled up as if his soul were slowly escaping his small body.

Maya threw herself beside him and grabbed his hand as tightly as she could. She closed her eyes and silently cried.

"What's wrong?" Leland asked.

Maya opened her eyes. They were wet and afraid— and the prettiest eyes Leland had ever seen.

"I don't know," Maya told Leland, her voice cracking. "It's happened to him once before."

Billy salivated excessively.

Unable to react, Leland sat beside Maya and grabbed Billy's other hand.

"It's going to be all right," Leland said. "Don't worry."

Leland had seen this before. *Seizures.* He didn't know how to manage it, but he could do something to alleviate it, or just comfort Maya till it stopped by itself.

"If we pour water on him, it'll go," Leland told Maya, frankly knowing this thing he'd just made up might not work.

Maya and Leland poured water onto him.

Fortunately for Leland, Billy's contractions lessened until they stopped entirely.

***

After slaughtering the guards and threatening the rest, making them hold their ground in fear of fighting the beast, Ojoy walked toward the king of Millory, Gorno Mathew.

The veins on the king's face congested, turning it red and blue. He shouted, "Come and kill him! He's only one man! Where are you, cowards?"

But no one answered. The people of Millory watched Ojoy step upon bloody corpses and walk toward their one and only king. But they didn't dare move an inch. The king grabbed a sword from one of the fallen guards and smiled a grin that reflected fear more than anything else. "You will regret this, Ojoy Steelhart!"

Ojoy said nothing until he was a few feet away from him. "It would take ten thousand men to kill Ojoy Steelhart." He pointed his sword at Gorno Mathew. "And by men, I mean true men."

Ojoy charged the king, who turned his back and ran away. Ojoy followed him, for the king was slow, Ojoy easily caught him and spun him around. Full of anger, and in a voice only the king could hear, Ojoy said, "I don't kill from the back! You lived a wasteful life. Die like a man now!"

The words encouraged Gorno. He raised his sword and charged Ojoy.

The voices in the square got louder, hailing their king.

"Now I can kill you," Ojoy told the king. "Die, lowlife."

Ojoy's sword chopped the king's head off the way sickles cut wheat: smooth and easy. He swiftly grabbed the king's head before it fell to the ground then placed it on the headless body that had just collapsed. He scanned the people standing in the square and ordered, "Bring me Warden's body."

Five men hurried to Warden's dead body and placed it on a wooden cart. They kneeled before Ojoy and said, "Apologies, my lord. Forgive us!"

Ojoy dragged the cart by its thick rope. As he walked to the gate to leave the small village, he ordered the townspeople, "Give your king a proper funeral."

***

Roy and Jennifer reached the Healing Squad Headquarter in the northwest part of the Castle, far, far away from its center. The night was cold and moonless, and Jennifer put her hands on her mouth, breathing in and out, generating whatever heat she could. She remained silent.

Roy spoke about the coins he was going to earn from Warden's mother after he delivered Jennifer to the Healing Squad.

Jennifer thought, *It's haunting how a person can be so greedy and honorable at the same time.*

He put his lantern on the ground as it was dark no more in the headquarters.

They saw three wooden huts connected by curved bridges and surrounded by a circular fence of trees. Most of its leaves were pink, though some were snow-white, and a few were orange. None were green. A hot water spring bubbled underneath the bridges. Jennifer felt its heat and wished she could take a warm bath. Hundreds of candles emitted faint light all over.

"Where's everyone?" Roy wondered.

Jennifer's blue eyes scanned the three huts. She heard noise and laughter from within.

"Inside, probably," Jennifer replied.

Roy walked onto one of the bridges and called, "Hello!"

A woman with long pink hair came out. She walked slowly, and her long, light blue dress wrapped around her like a kimono trailed along the ground. The woman reached toward Roy and Jennifer then smiled. "Welcome. Any help I could offer?"

"This is Jennifer," Roy said, "a girl from Earth."

"Earth?" The woman raised her eyebrows. "It's been a while since I met one." She inched closer to Jennifer then muttered, "Oh, poor girl. You've come in time of war and great misery."

"I am sure, my lady, that you could provide this girl home and shelter. And, maybe, train her to be one of you. A healer," Roy said.

"We would be pleased to have her here," the woman replied, "but I'm not sure she could help. Not in this war at least."

"I can help," Jennifer said.

The woman glanced at Roy and asked, "And, you are Mister …?"

"Roy. My name is Roy."

"Would you like some tea, Mr. Roy, Miss Jennifer?"

"Only a fool would say no on such a cold night."

The woman went to a concrete bench close to the spring, and then she clapped her hands twice.

Jennifer followed her instinctively.

A girl, almost the same age as Jennifer, came out of a hut with three cups of hot tea, or what seemed like tea, and gave everyone their share.

"I'm Hannah," the woman revealed, "Vice Captain of the Healing Squad."

Jennifer waited for Hannah to sip her tea, and then she sipped once Hannah did. The tea was warm and sweet and tasted like mint mixed with vanilla. Jennifer would not mind staying in this place. Thus far, it was better than Utta's cottage, the dark woods, and the rest of what she'd seen in Oremanta.

"I will leave now," Roy informed them. "I've fulfilled my mission." He turned his back and walked away. "Thank you for the tea, Lady Hannah. And if you need anything, Jennifer, ask about Roy Hollowidge in the east side of the Castle. Later."

Hannah smiled at him and nodded. She went to the hot water spring and sank her legs into it. She closed her eyes and told Jennifer, "Come here."

Rather submissively, Jennifer sat beside Hannah and also sank her legs into the spring's hot water. Warmth ascended from Jennifer's toes to her feet to her legs to her thighs, and then it covered her whole body. It was the best feeling Jennifer had ever had. She closed her eyes and lay on her back, her legs still deep in the water.

"How'd you come here?" Hannah asked.

"My friend is Oremantian. Or that's what we've been told," Jennifer replied. "I came along with him from Earth, somehow." Jennifer opened her eyes and chortled, letting go of some of what she felt. "Now that

I think of it, Earth is not so different from Oremanta. Kids starve to death every day. Men are killed with no mercy. Women are used as sex machines. Our world was rotten, but we lived on the bright side of it. Even the bright side wasn't that bright. That's all."

Hannah didn't react. She seemed in a deep state of meditation.

And so should I, Jennifer thought. She closed her eyes and thought of nothing. Or at least she tried to think of nothing. She had said too much already to Hannah.

Jennifer sighed and smiled at the starry sky. She didn't know what she had to do or what her next step was. Ironically, and temporarily, that relieved her.

"Is there a way to get back to Earth?" Jennifer asked, afraid to hear the answer. She had already heard the answer before, but she had to ask again. And she wouldn't mind asking for a thousand more times to come.

"Not in a way I know," Hannah replied.

***

The flickering green light of an approaching Aurora adorned the night sky. The green glow—glistening, re-shaping, and floating dynamically in the dark space—was hands down the most beautiful scene Leland had ever seen.

"Are you okay?" Leland asked Billy. Billy was in a postictal state of drowsiness and fatigue. Leland read somewhere that that could happen after a seizure.

"I'm fine," said Billy, turning his face away. He hadn't said much since regaining consciousness. He avoided conversations and eye contact out of shame rather than tiredness. Maybe he didn't want anyone to know his weak side, even though there was nothing to be ashamed of.

They were in The Green Hills of Vorgo, a place a half days' worth of walking from where they had been at the Heavenly River.

Aelfgar, with his back on the cold grass a few feet away from Leland, Billy, and Maya, complained, "Oh, Lord. And to think I'd be babysitting three kids at this age."

Maya delicately tucked her hair behind her ears. "You're different than what we thought you were."

"And what did you think I am?"

"I don't know. Hmm. You're just kinder than what we thought. That's all."

Aelfgar's fame reached beyond the walls of the Castle it seemed. But what had he done exactly to be that famous? Was it just for his strength? Or was there more to this man than that? Leland shifted his eyes back to the sky. He had always asked himself back on Earth if there were other planets inhabited by people and life. Now he had the answer. The universe was full of mysteries yet to be discovered. Maybe there are more than Earth and Oremanta out there in the far galaxies.

"Wanna hear a short story?" Aelfgar said, scratching his bald head. "Legends say there was a boy who smelled so bad that he couldn't sleep because of his smell. Days passed by and the boy hated himself.

People moved away from him. He didn't know why he smelled that way, and rumors started spreading that he was cursed."

"Wow, Aelfgar, what a story," Leland commented sarcastically, "And why are you suddenly telling us this?"

"Because that boy is you," Aelfgar chortled. "You smell like a rotten corpse." He threw what seemed like soap to Leland, "Clean yourself with this. Or else we won't reach the smith."

Maya, to Leland's relief, hadn't heard what Aelfgar had said. She didn't react, and she was busy cleaning the blade of her sword with the end of her clothing, standing beside Billy.

Damn it, old man. You could've delivered it more gently, Leland thought, trying hard to hide his embarrassment and refrain from laughing.

"The mountain of Olohama is so close from here. I can tell," Aelfgar said in a more serious tone. "Up at the top is where we'll find the swordsmith."

The sentence sent chills throughout Leland's body. They were one step closer to the swordsmith, which meant they were one step closer to the war, which meant they were one step closer to confronting Frank Hopegone.

Billy had fallen asleep, cuddling his silver shield.

The old man started to snore soon after.

Leland found himself alone with Maya. He looked at her, and she looked back then turned away.

"Want to take a walk?" Leland asked, hesitantly.

Maya nodded. She got up and walked beside Leland. She looked him in the eyes, slowed down, then asked curiously, "What does Earth look like?"

"It looks like, hmm … everything. Literally. There are deserts and seas and high buildings and easier ways to communicate," Leland sighed. "Gosh. I really miss it." He almost got carried away. He wanted to tell her about phones and air conditioners and refrigerators and TVs. And she wouldn't have understood any of that.

"I wish I could go there," Maya confessed. She darted her eyes down to the grass, her silky red hair covering the side of her face. "I want to leave this place."

Leland couldn't see her eyes, but he could tell she was preventing herself from crying. A cold breeze stroked their faces and then carried on, ascending and descending on the green hills.

"I don't want to lose Billy," she said, her voice even weaker now. "He's all I've got."

"You won't lose him. I'm going to get the Sword of Legends, and I'm going to save everyone," Leland uttered. "That's a promise."

"He trains every day for hours. He wants to kill Yoink, the beast who slew our village. But he stands no chance against him."

An awkward silence descended. They walked for a while, side-by-side, and then they sat on the grass. It smelled like nature: organic, raw, and odd. It was late, and they were supposed to get back now and sleep. A long tiring day awaited them. But Leland had enjoyed the night, and he didn't really care if morning fell on them.

"Now it's your turn," Leland said. "Tell me about Oremanta."

"Oremanta? I was born in an era of war and blood. If it was ever beautiful, I'm not the right person to tell you about its beauty."

"I know how you feel. It must be hard to live in this period. I've lost my friend, Dylan, and I know what it feels like to be afraid of losing someone else." *Jennifer's the last person I want to lose. What would be there for me if something happened to her?*

"You're a Keo, Leland," Maya said. "Whether you realize it or not, you can change things here. You got what it takes."

She stared at him for a moment, but it felt like ages. Her eyes reflected parts of the sky and connected times and dimensions and the beauty of all that is beautiful. On her knees, her small hands pulled the grass upward as she faced Leland, her nose almost touching his. She begged, "Save us, Leland."

***

Hannah opened the door of the hut for Jennifer. About twenty pairs of eyes stared at the newcomer. They were all girls about her same age. A pot of tea was boiling on a fireplace. Near the fireplace was a table filled with pastries and a large bottle of a dark blue drink. One girl went to the table, poured some into a pottery cup, and then she gave it to Jennifer.

"Drink," the girl said, smiling. "You must be thirsty."

Jennifer took the cup and looked at her reflection in the blue liquid. She looked worse than she'd thought. Her eyes were half-closed by default. Her skin was pale and dirty, and her hair was messier than a middle-grade student's hair after recess. Jennifer eyed Hannah, who nodded at her, assuring her that it was safe to drink.

Jennifer sipped. It tasted like grapes and strawberries. She liked it.

With her eyes, Hannah ordered two girls, and they understood what she wanted. They went through a narrow corridor to a room at its end.

"Are you from Earth?" a girl asked Jennifer.
"Yes, I am."

"But you look just like us."

"Why would I look different?"

"I don't know," the girl said, blushing. "We heard stories about the people of Earth. They said you have horns and tails and some of you could fly. But that doesn't matter. Those must be lies."

"I wish I had a tail, though," Jennifer said, and all the girls instantly laughed aloud. Jennifer felt happier in this place. Maybe because there were so many girls her age, or maybe because they seemed to accept her, or maybe because the Healing Squad Headquarter was warm and sound.

The two girls returned from the far room and waved Jennifer over. "Come with us. It's ready."

Jennifer followed the girls through a door at the end of the carpeted corridor into a bathroom with a round bathtub from which vapor reached to the ceiling. A box sat on top of a table beside the tub. One of the girls took a handful of what seemed like soap from the box and threw it into the hot water. Bubbles formed a layer on top, and a few bubbles detached and flew into the air.

"Just feel like home. Oh, and there's a clean robe in the closet beside the sink," one of them said before they left her alone and closed the door behind them.

The smell of the soap was refreshing and the bathtub was tempting. Jennifer hesitated to get into it, but then she felt silly for thinking that way. *What could be worse than what's already happened? If they wanted to kill me, they could've done it in a much easier way.*

***

"You know," Leland said as he threw himself on the grass to face the sky, "I never thought I'd live one day without the things I had on Earth. We had phones and televisions and radios and many other things. Sirens sang day and night. It was always so busy that you'd rarely think about vital things." He sighed. He knew she didn't understand what he was saying, but he said it anyways. "Everything is ready for you, and you don't know how and why and when was all of it was done. You forget your purpose in life. It's more calm here, but it's both terrifying and interesting. It's like there's nothing but you, your thoughts, and the few simple things around you."

"I didn't get half of what you said," Maya said. "What's a phone and a radio?"

"Eh." Leland sighed again and smiled. "Just a small device that connects everything to each other. Not a big deal."

"So do you like it here?" Maya inquired, lying on the cold grass beside him.

A few clouds blocked the Aurora. For a moment, Leland couldn't see anything. Then the cloud moved away, and the shining green light showed itself once more—just like every beautiful thing in this universe: not always present, but when it was, it made you think it'd been there forever.

"Not really. I *wish* I were back to all that mess again," Leland confessed, then he gazed at her in awe, as if he could find answers in the depth of her eyes. "But Oremanta has its beauty."

The sky went dark again, except this time it hadn't been caused by a cloud.

A black-cloaked man towered over Leland and Maya. He grabbed her by her head and pulled her up toward him as he pressed his dagger against her neck.

Chapter Twenty-Three

A Long Night, a New Dawn

"Good. You've learned a lot in a short time, Jack." Utta's pony-tailed blonde hair swung as she jumped off a rock in the backyard of her cottage. She carried a sword with one hand and a shield with the other. Training a stubborn boy like Jack hadn't been the easiest task assigned to her, but it hadn't been the most difficult either. *I'd rather do this than be in the Healing Squad or on the training field.*

"Make me stronger than him," Jack said. "Make me stronger than Leland."

Why does he want to be stronger than Leland? Utta asked herself. Jack had great potential. He was already wielding swords and training as if he were Oremantian-born. And he's soon to learn more. *But can I make him stronger than a Keo who might wield a Sword of Legends?*

Utta then remembered Aelfgar, outside of the Castle on a deathly journey facing beasts and cold nights and hunger. The last thing she ever wanted was to lose him. After her loss in the first war, when her city, Tanemba, had been annihilated, Aelfgar was her everything. He had taken her with him wherever he'd gone, and he'd bought her as much food and clothes and toys as she'd wanted. He'd taught her how to fight and he believed in her strength. If she could die for his sake, she'd do it. And she believed in him as much as he believed in her. That's why her worry quickly dissipated: that old man wouldn't die anytime soon.

She smiled confidently at Jack. "I will make you stronger than Leland."

***

"Let her go," Leland divulged. His tune was as firm as a judge giving an order. Without blinking, he looked at the black-cloaked man then uttered, with a fraction of a second between each word, "That is an order."

"Or what will you do, little one?" the man replied, his knife still on Maya's throat.

"I'll chop your head off and feed it to the crows." Leland tightened his fist on the pommel of his sword. He'd do it if the man didn't obey. *Maya shouldn't die. I'll do whatever it takes to save her life.*

The man brought Maya even closer to his body, grinned, and was about to slit her throat when Leland pounced forward, grabbed his face, and struck it to the ground. Leland was on top of the man, who now struck Leland's face with his elbow.

The man stood up swiftly and picked up his sword again. "You're going to regret this, brat."

Leland picked up his sword too and charged.

The man in black blocked Leland's sword, and Leland did the same to his counterattack.

He grabbed Leland's sword-wielding hand then tried to cut his head off.

Leland ducked, then punched him in his gut with his free hand.

The man bent forward so that his head was at Leland's knee.

Leland freed his hand and sent a powerful kick with his knee to the man's face.

The man retreated a few steps, bleeding.

"A Keo doesn't fear cheap men." Words flew from Leland's mouth as he walked toward the man, instinctively acknowledging the power of his blood. He pointed at the man's chest and rushed him.

The man blocked Leland once again, but Leland punched him in the face, then swiftly inserted his sword deep into the man's body. He vomited blood on Leland, and then he fell.

"That was," a far voice said, "impressive."

***

"Kill them," Frank Hopegone calmly said. "Those who disobey me shall face the ultimate punishment."

The mighty leader of the Rebel Army sat on his throne of skulls and bones as he ordered Konlaw to kill the Castle's captured spies. When Frank talked, none dared even to whisper.

The crowd of black-cloaked men knelt before him as three hostages were handcuffed and thrown in front of Frank.

Konlaw approached them, pulling his matte sword out of its scabbard.

The roof of the dome was high, and the dark walls had torches to light the place. Behind Frank's throne, flames from a fire pit extended to the ceiling.

A step away from the Castlers, Konlaw brought his blade down in a slow but fatal arc. Heads landed across the room.

Frank supported his jaw with the palm of his hand, observing the heads as they rolled on the floor, disgusted by the Castlers rather than the scene before him. Then he smiled a cold, careless smile and ordered, "Clean the ground of Castlers' filthy blood and feed their bodies to the crows."

***

"Are you okay?" Maya cried.

He couldn't have beaten that black-cloaked man with his bare strength. And the time Leland had spent with Aelfgar learning sword fighting hadn't been enough to let him win, which left one answer as to how he'd won: being a Keo. He had acknowledged it mid-fight, half-aware, proudly shouting "A Keo doesn't fear cheap men."

"I'm fine."

"Impressive, Leland!" Aelfgar praised, "I can see it growing in you, the power of Keo."

"Who was that?" Leland asked.

"A rebel," replied Aelfgar. "We must not stay here any longer. This place is dangerous. We'll start walking by sunrise."

"Thank you," Maya told Leland. "But maybe we shouldn't continue this journey with you."

"Why?"

"We're pulling you back. Can't you see?"

"Don't say that," Leland scolded. "We're in this together now."

***

Jennifer dried her wet hair with a white towel she'd found in the closet and pulled on a set of new clothes that were like Hannah's, except they were white and much smaller. When she exited the bathroom, no one was there but Hannah, sitting on a beige couch near the fireplace and reading a book.

"Everyone's sleeping," Hannah said. "I'll escort you to your room. You must be tired."

Very much so. All Jennifer needed after her shower was a cozy bed and a thick blanket. She followed Hannah, who smelled like roses and something sweet. After a few steps into another narrow corridor, she stopped.

"This is your room," Hannah murmured, pushing a door open.

"Thank you."

Hannah smiled slightly, like a mother to her child. "I know how you feel, Jennifer. It must be hard to leave everything you've ever known. But *we* are your family now. You must hate so many things here, but hatred is, sometimes, good." Hannah faced Jennifer and grabbed her hands. "You wholeheartedly love something when you, either consciously or subconsciously, have established hatred for other things. Those who do not hate will never love. Hatred makes you appreciate the things you love and cherish them. And the more you hate, the more you love. This is how it works. You can't taste love's true form unless you've tasted bitterness too."

Jennifer's eyes widened, and she didn't know what to say in reply. *Must we hate to truly love? Whether that's true or not, now isn't the right time to activate more brain cells.* Grateful for finally having good company and a decent place to stay, Jennifer smiled at Hannah and then went to bed.

***

Meanwhile, back on Earth, Abbey told Maria, "Detective Richard just called. He said they're still trying their best. But—"

"But what?"

"There aren't any clues. They've yet to find anything." Abbey put the cup of green tea she'd prepared in Maria's hand.

Maria went to the window and opened its brown curtains, viewing the empty street. She didn't say a word.

"Don't worry. We'll find them sooner or later," Abbey assured.

"They'll be gone. Just like Frank. No one stays," Maria said, pressing hard on the mug between her hands. "This is my luck in this life."

Abbey went to Maria and pressed on her shoulder. "They'll be back here, safe and sound. I promise."

Karla and Fred kicked the door open, then went to Maria and tightly grabbed her by her legs.

"He stole my doll!" Karla said to her mother. "Tell him to give it back."

Maria picked up Karla, looked at her face as if it were the last time she'd see her, and then kissed her forehead and muttered, "I'll buy you as many dolls as you want, sweetie. I'll make you happy."

Karla starred at her mother for a moment as she tucked her brown hair behind her little ears. "Where's Leland? You said he would be back soon."

Maria put her child down then looked back at the empty street. "He will, sweetie. Don't you worry. Now go to your bed. It's too late already."

***

"This is not acceptable!" Lieutenant Hamlet shouted. "We must not send more messengers anywhere."

"I agree," Chief Lieutenant Agis Phoenix calmly replied. "We cannot afford to lose anyone now. The war is near."

All the Seven Lieutenants were supposed to have gathered in the Hall by now. But Ojoy had gone on a mission outside the Castle, and Saneta was busy with the Healing Squad and final preparations for the war.

"It is not fair to judge the rest of the villages because one village broke the Vows of Men. We've sent hundreds of messengers to hundreds of villages and none have died before." Charles cleared his throat then emphasized, "As the rightful owners of the Castle, and thus the rest of Oremanta, we *must* warn the villages."

Lieutenant Charles always had a sense of justice. When the first war ended, Charles requested fair trials for every prisoner of the Rebel Army. But Ojoy had already hanged most of them and chopped off the heads of the rest.

"I get your point, Lieutenant Charles," Phoenix said. "But we have no time for that now. And we must not take any risks."

Hamlet, otherwise known as the Black Owl, walked around the fire pit with his hands behind his back. "Everyone knows the war is coming. There's no point in informing anyone. All the villages outside the Castle know about it. We shouldn't waste more men on that."

***

When the meeting ended, Lieutenant Hamlet walked outside the Hall, descended the stairs into a long corridor leading to a glass door, and then left the Palace of Wrath. A guard followed him as he did, but Hamlet dismissed him with a wave of his hand. He walked past Eren's Square and took the first narrow road on his left. The street was dirty and full of rats and leftovers, but it was empty of people, which mattered the most.

The Black Owl covered his face with a veil and walked until he reached a small cottage covered entirely by mud. He looked over his back twice before opening the black door and entering. The cottage was empty except for a round, red carpet in its middle. The Black Owl moved the carpet away, exposing a ladder that led somewhere underground. After he'd locked the cottage door, he went downstairs, though he made sure to cover the ladder with the red carpet before descending. The smell he encountered was most foul, like rotten flesh and contaminated meat and death.

"My lord." A guard kneeled before Hamlet in the underground chamber.

"How many do we have?" Hamlet asked.

"A hundred, more or less."

Hamlet stepped closer to a pile of corpses that were slowly decaying and disintegrating into threads of tissues.

"Good," he said, grinning.

***

Aelfgar placed a few daggers he'd sharpened into his big brown satchel, as well as his bedroll and a bottle of water. The satchel was half Leland's size, yet it looked like nothing more than a small bag on Aelfgar's body.

"Take this." Aelfgar threw a piece of smoked meat from last night's leftovers at Leland. "You'll need it."

Leland caught it and started to eat. He was getting used to such half-grilled, stinky food. *Maybe I'm not used to it, but I've subconsciously accepted this method of survival. I have to.*

"How did I win?" Leland asked, munching on the meat.

"You fought. And you won. That's all," Aelfgar answered.

As the green Aurora gradually died on the horizon, degrees of red and orange rays melted together in the clear Oremantian sky. It seemed that all dawns in this universe were alike. They smelt the same and felt the same: fresh, alive, and magical. Leland recalled that he'd gathered with Dylan and Jennifer for the last time on Earth at dawn, before they'd gone into the basement and had been transferred to Oremanta. The feelings he'd had then were similar to the feelings he had now—except now he was no longer with Jennifer and Dylan.

"How far are we from the smith?" Billy asked, stretching his hands and staring at the sun that showed itself at last, protected entirely and forever by three halos, silver rings spinning around a ball of heat and fire.

"The smith is on top of Olohama Mountain," Aelfgar said. He put on his cloak, picked up his satchel, and walked toward the sun as its early beams hit his face. "Let's climb Olohama and get our sword."

Leland thought Aelfgar's body could block the sun.

Chapter Twenty-Four

Rain of Olohama

The girls' noise echoed through wooden corridors, talking and giggling and shouting. The hut was a hive of activity, and Jennifer felt as if she were the only one still in bed.

What are they doing?

The sun's golden rays reflected on everything in the room, sneaking through the two small windows overlooking the hot springs. For the first time since her arrival on Oremanta, Jennifer felt relaxed while listening to the squawking birds outside. It was unlike any other sound she'd ever heard from birds before, tweeting and chattering and singing all at once.

She went to the window to satisfy her curiosity. A group of Golden Pheasant-like birds, but with longer blue beaks, were gathered around the springs. Some sat upon the pink leaves floating on the water.

Beautiful. A smile forced itself upon her lips.

The door behind her clicked open. A beautiful girl with brown skin that perfectly matched her light blue, almond-shaped eyes walked in. With enthusiasm, she said, "I'm Sara."

"Hello, Sara. I'm Jennifer."

"This is your first day here. We start our day by hunting. You skipped that, luckily."

"What do you hunt?"

"Beavers, caribou, owls, oxen. Anything edible."

Sara reminded Jennifer of a girl in her school named Jessica, the type of girl who's always happy and smiling, making everyone wonder if she'd ever cried or had gotten mad about anything.

"And what's my role here?" Jennifer inquired.

Sara scratched the back of her head and answered with a clueless smile. "The last time someone joined the Healing Squad was months ago. But I think there's a test for newcomers. No worries, though." She winked. "I'm sure it'll be easy."

"What kind of test?"

"I don't know. Really. I forgot. But I'll ask the girls. They must remember something."

Jennifer looked at Sara for a while and asked her, with a noticeable weakness in her voice she tried to hide, "Can you heal someone who's been stabbed multiple times in the heart?"

Sara paused. "The dead cannot be resurrected. I'm sorry."

***

The bone-white mountain of Olohama soared into the sky. A rug of trees filled its base, and thick layers of snow covered its peaks. Bugs and dead insects floated in the murky water of Olohama's lake, which Aelfgar and the rest were soon approaching.

Clouds blocked the sun, and the eerie howling of wild creatures made their skin prickle. Aelfgar had told them a while ago that the swordsmith lived on top of Olohama, but they couldn't imagine how someone could survive up there. Wind from all directions hit their bodies, pushing them around as though they were pieces of paper in the middle of a storm. Leland didn't understand how the climate could have changed so dramatically after only a few hours of walking.

"There!" Aelfgar pointed at a gravel road across the muddy lake. It seemed like the only route they could follow to progress forward.

"Are you sure the swordsmith is up there?" Billy asked, tightly grabbing Aelfgar's cloak.

"The compass is pointing there, and the old stories confirm it," Aelfgar replied, walking toward the gravel road.

Fortunately, there was a narrow route by the side of the lake leading to the other side. They crossed the lake, and now dense trees—as well as skulls and skeletons—lined the gravel road.

Maya gazed at the bones and the dead bodies for a moment then she clenched her fist tightly and looked away. "Who killed them?"

"Who knows?" Aelfgar wondered with a sigh, trying not to crush bones as he walked. "Beasts? Other warriors? No one knows. But we must be careful. I don't want to join their party."

They marched forward on the dreary road that was more graveyard than road. A raindrop fell on Leland's head. He gazed at the ceiling of dense tree leaves and saw millions of other drops passing through. Each drop was heavy and gray, totally contaminated with dust. He knew right away how he was going to feel about it.

He suddenly saw himself in his bed, closing his ears so as not to hear his father and mother arguing on the day that Frank had left. The sounds of falling raindrops and roaring thunder were similar to how it had been back then. Leland shook his head and focused on the road ahead. *I must be stronger than my memories.*

Aelfgar took off his cloak, and they all walked beneath it under the rain. They were so close to each other that Leland felt Billy's breathing on his neck and almost heard Maya's heartbeats.

I'm not alone in my fear.

***

Jennifer stood beside Sara at the hot springs as the rest of the girls formed a circle around Hannah and listened carefully.

Hannah had a sharp knife in her hand. She scanned the girls' faces. "To be a member of the Healing Squad, you must pass our test, Jennifer."

Jennifer was up for anything, but she didn't know why Hannah had a knife. Jennifer glanced at Sara, then at Hannah. "I'm ready."

"Good. Listen carefully, then," Hannah said, "Healing is all about your emotions and how you control them. The better you control your feelings, the better healer you are. And you don't have to be Oremantian in order to heal. You just have to be *in* Oremanta."

What do my emotions have to do with healing?

A girl with pigtails and a puffy, round face came into the circle with a creature in her hand. It was the size of an infant and cried like one. Light brown fur covered its skin, and it had a ball-like tail and two extremely wide blue eyes.

"All right," Hannah announced as she took the creature. "We shall start now."

The little thing pressed itself against Hannah's chest and stopped crying.

Jennifer and the girls silently observed Hannah as she put her knife to the creature's neck.

"Are you ready, Jennifer?" Hannah asked, as she slit the little thing's throat.

***

Raindrops kept digging into the ground, and it felt as if they were never going to stop. Leland thought he would have gotten used to it by now, but it'd been over an hour and he still couldn't stand it. The road they'd taken didn't seem to have an end either. Still underneath Aelfgar's cloak, Leland asked, "I've been wondering, Aelfgar, where's your family?" Maybe it was a way for Leland to distract himself, or he was genuinely curious to know more about Aelfgar.

"I don't have one," Aelfgar replied. "Well, technically. I lost my mother when I was a kid. She died of poisoning. I have a brother, an older brother. I've been told that, but I've never seen him. And my father is in the Castle. But he can't walk or talk anymore. He's too old now."

"I'm sorry."

"No worries, kiddo. At my age, you don't care much." Then Aelfgar's voice dropped to a whisper, but they all heard him anyway. "What I'm more concerned about now is that you haven't used the soap I've given you. We're dying here, brat."

I've already used the soap, and I did not *smell that bad to begin with.*

But Aelfgar laughed hard about it anyways.

Thunder roared like a hungry lion and mixed with the howls of wild creatures and the hoots of owls. If he hadn't been with the others, Leland would have died of fear. The mountain of Olohama was a ghost town, a place with only dead bodies and eerie sounds. The road they'd taken gradually ascended, rippling their muscles as they went upward.

"Why would someone live in this place?" Billy complained. "The swordsmith must be insane."

An hour later they came to the end of the road, a space with snowy cliffs from which behind appeared a new spiral road leading to the mountaintop. Everyone was overwhelmed with exhaustion and fatigue. They *had* to rest.

"Finally," Billy sighed.

"We'll camp there," Aelfgar notified.

"Is it safe to stay here?" Maya asked.

Aelfgar nodded. "We're tired and out of food. This is our best bet."

But resting still had to wait. Five mountain wolves appeared from the edges of the trees and from behind the snowy cliffs. The wolves had long horns, blue fur, and dark red eyes.

Something soft touched Leland's hand, melted between his fingers, and twisted around his wrist. Maya was tightly squeezing his palm, but she didn't look at him. Her eyes were fixed on the wolves. Her hand was warm and her fingers were little and delicate. She squeezed harder now, and Leland instinctively squeezed back, giving her a sign of assurance and support.

"More monsters," Aelfgar said. "Prepare yourselves."

"Let's do it," Maya added.

They had no other choice but to fight the wolves and kill them. If they couldn't find a proper thing to hunt after that, they'd eat the wolves. That was their only way to survive. Aelfgar swung his cloak back onto himself, exposing everyone's head to the rain.

The wolves' sharp claws and curved tusks were hungry for blood. They roared and groaned and prepared to attack.

The intrepid adventurers formed a circle to face the wolves and guard each other's backs.

Leland took a deep breath then lunged at one. He was no longer afraid to fight and kill. After all, he'd just fought and killed a man from his father's army.

I can do it.

The wolf evaded Leland's attack and pounced on him. Leland counterattacked with an elbow strike to the wolf's neck. It drew back a few steps, roared, and then pounced again. With his knee, Leland struck the wolf and it fell to the ground. This time, Leland didn't wait. He thrust his sword into the wolf's furry flesh and it howled for the last time.

Leland turned his face to Aelfgar and found that he'd already killed one and was locked in combat with another. Aelfgar smiled when he saw Leland. "Good job, stinky!"

Leland heard the bones of the wolf's neck detach and break.

Billy stuck two daggers into another wolf's thick mane. Its blood poured out of the holes. Leland wondered how a boy of his age could fight that way.

Maya was still struggling with her opponent. She dodged and evaded until Aelfgar kicked the wolf's underbelly with the upper part of his foot. Aelfgar split the wolf's head from its body, making it look easy.

Raindrops diluted the wolves' blood and cleansed the ground after the vicious battle. Leland hyperventilated while quickly scanning everyone. Except for some bruises, fatigue, and exhaustion, they were all fine. Leland was tired in every definition of the word. But a satisfying sensation of reward filled him. Last night he'd saved Maya's life and now he'd proven it hadn't happened by chance.

"The smith is at the end of the road," Aelfgar notified.

The narrow spiral road lacked anything more than a few natural ramparts between them and the bottom of Mount Olohama. This treacherous road was their only route to reach the peak.

"What now?" Billy inquired.

"We'll camp here," Aelfgar answered. "Tomorrow, we meet him."

***

Frank Hopegone exited the first dome, the one that overlooked the rest, and walked along the dirty road that descended to the other domes. Konlaw, Frank's most trusted right-hand man, followed him. The road was dark and unlit by Oremanta's moons. Hundreds of torches had been distributed in the Ten Domes. Black-cloaked men walking nearby kneeled when they saw Frank and Konlaw.

"Tell me, Konlaw," Frank said, "what happened to the rest of the traitors?"

"We killed most of them already," Konlaw replied, "but we kept some alive. We'll execute them tonight."

"Take me to them," Frank ordered.

Skulls and dead bodies lined the road. Crows and bats flew everywhere.

***

"Here we are," Konlaw said. "Those are the traitors, my lord."

"I see," Frank hissed. Ten men who had been chained and blindfolded had been thrown to the ground in a small tent.

"Unchain them and bring them to me."

The four wells situated behind Frank were each filled with liquid fire, a material that had been unearthed from the depths of volcanoes but intensified to be deadlier by a factor of ten. Burning stones flew off the wells and dug into the ground nearby wherever they fell.

Frank grabbed two of the traitors' heads and brought them closer to the burning wells.

"Mercy, my lord. Mercy!" one of them cried.

"Please, my lord, spare my life!" the other one begged.

Frank didn't say a word. He went closer to the well and threw them both into the raging fire.

The two men cried and growled and squealed, but shortly after there was nothing but silence and the smell of burnt flesh.

"Take care of the rest," Frank ordered Konlaw. "And let's get this done with. We have a war to win."

The leader of the Rebel Army walked away, back to his dome.

Chapter Twenty-Five

Cave of Swords

The morning was frigid, but Leland had long awaited it. Today, they'd reach the swordsmith. Leland shook his head to remove the powdered snow off his hair.

They hadn't quite prepared for such weather, but Aelfgar's cloak had kept them warm, to a certain extent. They strived to march through thick layers of snow. Snowflakes aggregated into soft balls of ice and traveled randomly with the wind across Mount Olohama. It obscured their vision and slowed them down.

"Watch your steps," Aelfgar warned. "You don't want to fall off into the bottom."

With the corner of his eyes, Leland glanced at Maya. He could tell she was concerned. She blinked often, and she couldn't take her eyes off Billy. She didn't say a word for a while.

"How long will it take him to create the sword?" Billy asked.

"I have no idea," Aelfgar answered. "Let's hope it's before the war."

***

Hundreds of families and men walked in lines in the Cursed Desert heading to the Pyramids of The Fallen. They weren't from the Castle alone but from the villages outside and the high mountains and deep valleys of Oremanta.

Lord Bolt Gemini had sent messengers all around Oremanta, promising that his land would be a shelter in the time of war. And people believed him. Or that was their only choice. If they were to stay in their homes, the chances they'd be killed were high, and they couldn't afford to lose anymore.

The heat was unbearable. A man took a flask from his satchel and poured water onto his head and then onto his little daughter's head.

As she licked the water drops that rolled down her face and onto her lips, she asked, "How long are we going to walk?"

"We're getting there, honey," he answered, eyes half-closed, as he stared at the seemingly endless desert.

***

Jennifer hadn't slept very well. She couldn't shake off what had happened yesterday. She hadn't been able to heal the creature Hannah had injured. The girls told her it was fine, and that no one ever pulled it off the first time. Sara told her that the little creature called a Merygon would turn into a monster at a year old and that anyone in the Castle who found Merygon would instantly kill it.

Jennifer walked into the hut's central room and saw Sara and Chloe, both of whom could tell Jennifer hadn't slept well.

"Don't think of anything when you try to heal," Sara instructed. "Try to focus all your energy into your hands."

"It's hard. I know," Chloe added, "but once you learn how to do it, it'll be fun."

Chloe had long black hair and brown eyes. She was skinny and tall with prominent cheekbones. She said, "Devoid yourself from all emotions. Try to think of nothing."

"How can I think of nothing?" Jennifer wondered aloud.

"That's for you to find out," Sara said.

Chloe was writing down something on paper. She then put it into an envelope and gave it to Sara. "If I were ever to die in the war, give this to my mother."

Sara took the envelope and put it under her pillow. "You will not die," Sara said.

"Shall we go now and try, Jennifer?" Chloe suggested.

Jennifer nodded. She wasn't sure she could do it again. But if there was one person in this world who could seal her feelings and control them, it was her. She followed Sara and Chloe out of the hut and into the springs. Sara informed Hannah that Jennifer was ready to try again.

"You'll make it this time," Chloe said. "I'm sure."

Hannah came to the spring with a Merygon in her hands. More girls followed Hannah, but they numbered less than yesterday.

"Are you ready, Jennifer?" Hannah asked, the knife already on Merygon's neck.

Jennifer tucked her hair behind her ears, cleared her throat, and answered, "I am."

Hannah stabbed the little creature, and it bled right away.

Jennifer placed both hands on it and closed her eyes. Merygon's body was soft and fluffy, but it was shaking and vibrating and roaring. The key to healing was to block all her thoughts, but the sound of Merygon crying was the first barrier she couldn't cross. A chain of thoughts floated in her head, and the more she tried to think of nothing, the bigger this chain grew. Her thoughts hurt.

How can I stop thinking? she asked herself.

But not long ago on Earth, she'd learned how to do it. She had learned how to ignore her thoughts and move on. It wasn't easy back then, to let go of the pain. But she'd made it, and now she had to apply that on physical ground. It was a test of her strength rather than her ability to heal.

I remember now, she recalled. *The way to ignore your thoughts and pain is to let them flow freely. Never resist. Resistance creates persistence.*

Jennifer applied the formula. She let all her thoughts swim in her head. Various pictures and sounds perpetually generated in her mind: old conversations with people she could barely remember now, dark nights when she was home alone, rainy days with Leland in a coffee shop, her mother's grave, pictures of her mother smiling. But her thoughts didn't stop there.

Jennifer remembered one particular night when she'd left home and gone to Amanda's Park, where she'd sat there alone and cried. It had been the night Jennifer became a woman. She cried because she didn't know why she was bleeding. She was frightened to death. She didn't have a mentor to tell her what or what not to do. And it hurt. A lot.

Her thoughts traveled east and west, up and down, and Jennifer didn't resist any of them. She let them form and reform and enter and exit her network of memories. At one moment, her mind shifted from a painful lane of memories to an awful avenue of imagination. She imagined Leland, blood all over his face, drawing his last breaths on top of a snowy mountain. She imagined her father, bedridden in a hospital, telling his last wishes.

But still she let her mind act the way it wanted to act. *Don't resist.* It paid off.

A moment of blankness took over everything. A peaceful state of mind descended. White clouds of nothingness inhabited her head and stayed there.

The creature stopped crying.

With her eyes still closed, Jennifer felt a strong rush of air reach her face and move her hair back. The creature was weightless now. Jennifer pressed tightly on it. She opened her eyes and everything was bright. A blue halo had formed around her hand and surrounded

Merygon. The open wound on its neck slowly closed, cell by cell and tissue by tissue.

The girls moved in slow motion. Everything moved slowly. Some girls were shouting, but she didn't know what they were saying.

Jennifer's vision got brighter and brighter until she saw nothing but white. She fell to the ground and lost her connection with everything.

***

It had taken them many hours of walking in the snow to reach the mountaintop, but the trip was worth it. Leland, Aelfgar, Billy, and Maya finally stood in front of the Cave of Swords on top of Mount Olohama. Now that they were at its peak, Olohama seemed to be the highest among the mountain ranges of Oremanta.

"We made it," Billy said, holding tightly onto Aelfgar's cloak.

The rolling waves of wind were tenacious. A fall from this height wouldn't mean death alone; it would mean your body would splash into small pieces and nothing would remain.

Two gigantic swords triple the length of Aelfgar had been erected on the right and left sides of the cave's entrance.

A wicked sensation of excitement and fear traveled down Leland's spine. He was moments away from getting the Sword of Legends.

They entered the Cave of Swords.

Chapter Twenty-Six

Mora Gueja

The compass had turned fully green, indicating that they'd reached the swordsmith. But they had no idea what awaited them inside or where the smith actually was.

"He's got to be inside, somewhere," Aelfgar muttered, leading them inside.

With stiffened muscles and weary limbs, they entered the deep, dark cave. A light shone in the distance. The cave was the warmest place they'd been in for a long time. Caves were always home to bats and wildlings, but the bats in the Cave of Swords were different. They had red wings, small horns, and apparently larger than normal skulls.

"Stay low." Aelfgar's voice echoed. "They're hungry for blood—little kids' blood."

Metal torches fixed on the cave's rugged walls appeared after a while. Leland turned around and glanced at the entrance, and he realized how far he was, not only from the entrance but from everyone he'd ever known. *Will I ever get back home?*

"When I reach your age," Billy told Aelfgar, "instead of doing this I'm going to stay in my hut with my beautiful wife and little brats running around me."

"Oh, little one," Aelfgar chuckled, "When *I* was your age, I'd seen all the wonders of Oremanta. *Twice*. When you're old, you miss all of that."

Billy glanced at Maya and said, "When the war's over, I want to take Maya to see all the wonders of Oremanta. You can join us, old man."

Aelfgar carried Billy from his waist, put him on his shoulders, and laughed. "I forgive everything, except calling me an old man."

"Let me down!" Billy begged.

"Apologize!"

Water drops fell from the ceiling. Each drop echoed and reverberated many times before its sound died.

While watching one of those drops, Leland saw him first, sitting on a high chair made of metal and iron surrounded by scorpions and snakes at the end of the cave.

"Come here," the man hissed. "Get closer."

"Where's the smith?" Aelfgar asked.

"You're standing in front of him," he answered. "I am the swordsmith, Mora Gueja, son of Beuna Gueja."

Snakes wrapped around the metal legs of his chair and climbed up to Mora's neck. Hundreds of years had been etched into every wrinkle of his half-burned face. His legs, which didn't reach the ground, swung back and forth as he asked, "Aelfgar of The Golden City, what brings you to my home?"

"I want the Sword of Legends," Leland replied.

"And you are?" Mora inquired, with hoarseness in his voice. He put his hand on a snake's head and seemed to enjoy the feeling.

"I'm Leland Hopegone—"

"—Son of Frank Hopegone" The smith took it from there. "I've heard some stories. *Interesting.*"

"How did you know?"

"Do you know why they call it the Deathly Journey, Son of *Frank*?" A wicked smile drew on his face. He jumped off his metal chair and walked toward them. "I'll tell you why."

***

All the gates of the Castle had been locked and no one was allowed to leave. Black flags had been fixed on every turret and wall surrounding the Castle. Little kids no longer played in the streets. Old men and women were confined to their homes.

Many had left the Castle and gone to the Pyramids of the Fallen, but the majority had stayed in their homes. Some people would rather die in their homeland than live somewhere else. Soldiers roamed the streets, fully armed and ready for war. A state of martial law was announced in the Castle.

***

Raindrops fell like bullets from the tar-black sky of Oremanta. Jennifer went to the small window in the room and saw sheets of rain falling on the hot springs and trees. *What's going to happen from now on?*

"You made it Jenny," Sara cried. "You healed!"

But Jennifer wasn't so happy. There was a creepy silence in Oremanta, and nature played a symphony over this deadly silence. But not everyone could hear that. Sara didn't hear that. She was acting the way she'd acted yesterday: happy and full of life. Jennifer turned around and saw Chloe on the ground, her hands around her knees and her head in between her knees. Jennifer went to her and touched her face. "What's wrong?"

"Nothing," Chloe answered, weakly.

Jennifer knew she wasn't the only one suppressed by silence. *It's the calm before the storm.*

***

"Why do you think, Leland Hopegone," Mora hissed, "I would create a sword for you?"

"Because if you don't, thousands will die," Leland answered.

"But I'll be here in the Cave of Swords, safe and sound. Do I look like I care?" he asked. "I don't give three tons of bat droppings for who lives and who dies. I've seen generations grow and die and rot only to be replaced."

"What do you want?"

"They call it a Deathly Journey, not because the road you take is too hard or because you can't reach me, but because *I kill* whomever comes to me if I'm bored. Or hungry. Or if I simply want to have fun." Mora smiled happily, seeming to recall the people he'd killed. He patted his snakes' heads as he talked, proudly enjoying their mutual affection.

Leland looked at Aelfgar, who sent him assurance through eye contact.

They'd fought monsters and had walked for miles to reach this place. If they didn't get the Sword of Legends, their effort would be in vain. Leland's palms sweat. He cleared his throat and was about to speak when the swordsmith asked, "Why do you want it?"

"To fight the Rebel Army," Leland instantly replied.

"Interesting," Mora Gueja hissed. "You want to fight your father. It's been centuries since I've seen a battle of that kind. I don't care if you deserve my sword or not. Neither do I care about this pathetic war. I don't create swords for free. That you have to know."

A snake suddenly wrapped itself around Leland's leg.

Mora glanced at the snake and then scanned Leland from head to toe.

Leland knew he was being tested. He was still sweating and his heart pounded. He took a deep breath, gritted his teeth, blinked more than he was supposed to, and then captured the snake by its head. He pressed tightly on its neck with his other hand. It was the first time Leland had ever touched a snake, but he was used to new things by now. And if he wanted the sword, he shouldn't show weakness.

The snake spat venom, hissed, and whipped Leland with its tail. Luckily, the venom projected away from Leland.

He pressed even harder on its neck now until Mora's hand reached to the snake and smoothly took it from Leland.

"Easy, kid. Easy," Mora said, his eyes on the snake. "You almost killed it."

"What is it that you want?" Aelfgar asked firmly.

"I want to live," said Mora, "and I live off powerful creatures. Now there's only *one* life I'm lusting for."

"You want me to kill someone for you?" Leland asked.

"Kind of," Mora said, sitting back in his chair. "I'll create the sword for you. And you'll go and fight with it. But I'll inject you with venom, and it will run in your body for thirty days. If you don't bring me what I want in less than that, you'll be dead, Leland Hopegone."

The sentence sent chills throughout Leland's body. He didn't say a word. Should he agree on that, his life would be at stake. But he wasn't sure he'd survive the war anyway.

"Do it," Billy said. "Do it," he repeated, pressing hard on Leland's shoulder. "We believe in you."

The decision was tough, but there was only one choice. Saying no meant letting everyone who believed in him down. He'd left Jennifer for this. He'd placed Aelfgar's life in danger for this. Maya and Billy relied on him as well. And, above all of that, Frank Hopegone, who had killed Dylan and thousands of other innocent people, would be unstoppable.

"Fine," Leland agreed. "I'll do what you want. Who is it that you want dead?"

"Come here," Mora ordered, "Only *you* must know."

Mora's breath was warm and rotten. The sword-smith thrust his lips into Leland's ears and whispered a name.

Leland stopped dead in his tracks. "Imp ... impossible."

Chapter Twenty-Seven

Farewell for Pride

"Mora Gueja, grandson of Beuna Gueja, the legendary smith who created the *first* Sword of Legends, is a fearsome man," Harvard told Ron, his apprentice, "for the Cave of Swords was a graveyard to whoever displeased him or didn't give him a good exchange for the Sword of Legends."

"A good exchange?"

"You heard it right. Mora doesn't create swords for free. That's why people die trying to get it. Or die soon *after* they get it. Because what he wants is always something beyond their capacity to give."

Harvard didn't mind the backache from constantly being in his chair as long as he was able to read books. When he was young, a long time ago, he read ten books a day. And he wasn't satisfied with it. He'd also written books about Earth because he'd once been an Earthling.

Harvard sipped his tea. "Books make you live and witness things while you're sitting on your lazy butt." Because Harvard was old, he knew passing down his knowledge was a vital step for the sake of Oremanta's history.

Three books, a pad, and an ink pen lay in front of Ron. He wrote down everything he heard, paying attention to the tiniest of details.

"I have read many books, sir," Ron told Harvard, "but I still don't know much about the Sword of Legends. How does it work? How does it make its wielder stronger?"

"That, my son, needs a whole day by itself."

***

Mora pointed at a door behind his back.

"It's only *one* Deathly Journey," Mora said to Aelfgar, Maya, and Billy. "This door will take you to the other side of the cave. It's a shortcut back to the Castle and the center of Oremanta," he instructed. "Now leave me alone with the next wielder of the Sword of Legends."

***

The other side of the cave was dark, but a dim light shone at its far end. They didn't know how long Leland would be locked in there with Mora, but they had all agreed to wait for him.

Aelfgar started a fire from a pile of wood that had been thrown into a corner of the cave. The three sat around the fireplace and grilled the remnants of the wolves they'd killed the other night.

"I wish I were the one with the smith now," Billy confessed.

"What are they doing anyway?" Maya asked.

"Who knows?" Aelfgar murmured, flipping the meat on the flames.

"Um, Aelfgar? I was wondering," Billy said, "can we train in the meantime?"

Billy had never sounded so polite before. But what he said terrified Maya and made her choke. She struggled to draw in air. Billy's thirst for revenge frightened her. She had always wanted revenge too. But now that the time had almost come, Maya feared the consequences of such an act more than anything else. Not losing her brother was more important than all the revenge she could get. But Billy was persistent.

"I want to kill Yoink," Billy said, "for what he did to our village."

Yoink. Just his name brought back awful images of the past. Maya still suffered from post-traumatic stress over what had happened to everyone she'd known. Yoink and his men had annihilated her village and burned everything to the ground. She could still hear the screams of hundreds of throats. The smell of melting flesh was still in her nostrils. She couldn't forget any of that. But she didn't want to lose more.

Maya put her head on Aelfgar's satchel and closed her eyes. In a semi-conscious state, a flashback forced itself upon her. Maya was running from a man with a knife. She pressed a loaf of bread against her chest as she ran for her life. Billy was running beside her, but he was slower. They had stolen bread from the man's shop, and now he was angry. They were hungry because they hadn't eaten anything for days. This was a few days after what had happened to their village.

The man caught Billy from behind and pulled the little kid toward him.

Maya stopped, turned around, and saw the big man scolding Billy, threatening him with the knife. She hurried to them and threw the loaf of bread into the man's eyes. Then she grabbed Billy from his hand and ran away, thinking of the precious bread she'd lost.

They didn't have a home, so they slept on pavement, haystacks, or random rooftops.

The flashback ended and Maya fell sleep. But now and then she could hear Billy and Aelfgar talking. After a length of time she didn't know, she opened her eyes and saw them training. Her vision was blurry. She closed her eyes again but slept peacefully this time.

***

Maya opened her numb eyes to the cave's ceiling. Except for the drops that regularly fell from above, she heard nothing else. She didn't know how long she'd slept, but she knew it had been far too long. She put her hand on her head. It was hot and sweaty. She scanned the area around her. The fire was out and the leftovers from yesterday's meal sat beside burned wood. Aelfgar slept on his belly not so far from her. But she didn't see Billy.

"Billy!" Maya called, walking to the dim light at the end of the cave.

"Billy?" she called again. Shy rays escaped the darkness of the dawn and sneaked into the cave's entrance, a sign of another morning. A few trees grew outside the cave, and a road descended from its entrance. And there were many villages far away from where Maya was. She was afraid to leave the cave, so she stood by the entrance and called her brother's name again. *Maybe he's hunting or peeing or just walking around. But he might be* gone *as well.* She bit her lips and cried, with lesser expectations to hear an answer, "Billy!"

Terrified by Maya's voice, birds flew off the trees. But they didn't know she was more afraid than they were. Maya went back to the cave, hoping to find Billy somehow lying there. But she only saw Aelfgar, snoring heavily.

"Aelfgar!" Maya panted, shaking the old man's body. "Wake up! Billy isn't here."

From behind the door where Leland and Mora had remained, a strong growl awakened Aelfgar. "What in the Cave of Swords was that?"

To Maya's misfortune, it was Leland's scream, not Billy's.

Chapter Twenty-Eight

The Boy and the Beast

"The Rebel Army is now attacking Velron Village, sir!" a warrior reported to Chief Lieutenant Agis Phoenix.

"How far is that?" Phoenix inquired, squeezing his chin with his index finger and thumb.

"Ten villages away, sir, outside the walls."

"We won't interfere. We offered them shelter. Lord Bolt Gemini offered them shelter. We can't act now." Agis Phoenix directed his speech to the lieutenants. "This is another warning from the Rebel Army. Prepare our men. They might reach our walls at any moment."

"Send someone to Aelfgar Hawx. He must know." With a stern gaze and a rough voice, Ojoy commented while leaving the hall, "I'll lead our forces to the Golden Gate. Get your men down there too, lieutenants. No time for chitchat."

***

Maya's blood ran cold and her limbs shook. She hurried to the end of the cave and looked in the distance, again.

Smoke and fire rose from far villages. Unable to think if that smoke had been there the first time she'd left the cave, she placed both hands on her mouth and wailed, "No! Billy!"

She had a hint as to where he was. *He must have gone to the villages hoping to find Yoink. It'll take us hours to reach the villages. And if Billy's reached there already, it'll be impossible to catch him.*

Maya fell on her knees, tears running down her face and wetting the soil beneath her.

"It's my fault," she cried.

"It's no one's fault," Aelfgar said. "We don't know where he is. He might be anywhere, and not necessarily in those villages. Calm down."

"He's not there, right? He hasn't gone to Yoink, right?" Maya asked. "He can't be there. Billy's not stupid."

"I hope not." Aelfgar put on his cloak and picked up his satchel. "We must leave Leland here. Let's hope he finds his way back."

The two left the cave and descended the single road leading to the burning villages.

***

"We'll hold each other's hands under three moons and burning suns. Like the wind that hears all stories, but moves on and on and on, hitting every stone, not caring where it runs."

The Song of the Wind replayed in Billy's head as he walked past the ruins of the burned villages. He knew where Yoink was. Men whom he'd passed had warned him not to go to Velron. Adrenaline ran through Billy's boiling blood. Every living cell inside him craved revenge. Billy's anger doubled when he stood before Velron. From outside, he heard the screams of children and the whimpering of widows.

He entered through the blood-stained gate, but no one paid him attention. The scene wasn't so different from what he'd seen years back. Smoke swam in the sky and choked the clouds. Billy could recognize Yoink among a thousand men. His long gray hair, the belt of daggers on his waist, and his dirty nails and teeth had plagued Billy's memories for years.

That monster.

Yoink stood in the middle of Velron's square, pools of blood surrounding him. "Now," Yoink growled, stepping on an old man's head, "are you ready to die?"

Ravens dug into the skulls of dead bodies. Wives begged for their husbands' freedom. Kids witnessed their fathers' deaths. Bodies had been hanged in every corner. Pain was everywhere. But it wasn't the time for Billy to agonize over all of that—it was the time to end his suffering—their suffering—for good.

"Yoink!" Billy roared.

Yoink, his army, and the villagers turned their faces to the red-haired boy standing by the gate.

"My name is Billy, and I'm here to kill you for what you did to Rangerwest."

Yoink kicked the old man's face and ordered his men to kill him.

That only added fuel to Billy's flames. And once he'd entered the village, he knew there was no turning back.

"A lion *cannot* remember every prey he's killed," Yoink groaned. "I will slit your throat. How dare you speak to me like that."

Billy heard whispers from everywhere.

"Run away, boy! Save your life!"

"Are you mad? Run!"

"Oh, lord. The young die and the old cry!"

An old woman wailed, "Someone save him!"

A man on his knees with a spear piercing his shoulder stuttered, "We'll all die in the end. They'll spare no one."

Billy stood his ground despite their words. He'd come for one single reason, and he wasn't willing to retreat.

"I will end your life here," Billy threatened, "for the sake of everyone!"

"Allow us to kill him, sir!" Yoink's subordinates requested, running at Billy.

"Stay where you are," Yoink ordered. "No one's killing him but me."

Billy's eyes glittered with vengeance. He waited no longer. With fast steps fueled by anger and pride, Billy rushed Yoink.

The latter stood still. Yoink grabbed the tip of Billy's sword with his thumb and index finger. As if he were throwing a chopstick, he sent Billy and his sword flying away.

Billy fell on his back and rolled multiple times. He felt an intensifying, dull pain on his back and shoulders. *He's strong,* Billy thought.

Everyone was staring at the fight, but everyone was silent.

I must win. Billy stood up and tightened his sweaty fist around his sword.

"Is this all?" Yoink smirked. "Prepare to die."

"I'm just starting," Billy replied, wiping dirt off his shoulders.

Yoink pounced on Billy, who swiftly dodged and scrambled behind him.

Fortunately, Yoink was slow. That was the first weak point Billy had noticed. Yoink's back was fully open now. *It's now or never.* Billy seized the chance and stabbed the beast's back.

Yoink's blood spilled on the ground, a mixture of purple and dark blue. Yoink screamed so loudly Billy thought his eardrums would tear.

"How dare you?" Yoink raged, with a devilish voice and a satanic gaze.

Billy thought his strike had been fatal, but it seemed to have done nothing but enrage the monster.

Yoink unsheathed a dagger from the belt wrapped around his waist and aimed it at Billy.

Billy blinked. When he opened his eyes, something sharp was penetrating deep into his right arm. His blood dripped onto the ground of Velron. *This is far more painful than my fall.*

Some villagers put hands on their mouths and cried. Others fell to their knees. But the majority were expressionless, masked faces that had given in to desperation. None dared to step in and help.

Billy struggled to stay balanced and struggled more to draw breath. He removed the dagger from his shoulder and threw it away. *I'll use what Aelfgar taught me, even if it means my own death.*

Billy squeezed his own neck as if choking himself to death. The veins on his face became visible and his eyes turned blank white. He felt as though his heart would break his rib cage and jump out of his chest.

"Stop!" a villager cried.

Billy recalled what Aelfgar had said: *"When you are willing to sacrifice your life for the sake of everyone, your spirit will be under your control. The Spiritual Cage is a Moxie for the selfless."*

Billy had paralyzed Yoink. Shackled by the young boy's will, the beast couldn't move any part of his body.

"What happened?" a panicked woman screamed.

"It doesn't matter," a man replied, and then threw his sword to Billy. "Finish him off, brave boy!"

Yoink's men tried to stop Billy, but the villagers of Velron had awakened. Ten men hurried to Billy and formed a circle around him.

"This boy must live," one of them said.

The fight began between the villagers and Yoink's army. Billy was still in the middle of the circle, but now more villagers had joined the party.

A villager pushed Billy from his back and into Yoink's direction.

"He's yours. Finish what you started," the villager said as he went back to the fight.

I've wanted this for too long.

Yoink was still paralyzed. Billy had never imagined he would have obtained such a Moxie. Grateful for Aelfgar's help, Billy stepped closer to Yoink. He wanted to destroy Yoink's face with a hammer, and he wanted to cut his gray hair and shove it into his mouth until he choked, and he wanted to insert a thousand needles everywhere in his body. But there was no time for all of that.

He pushed his sword into Yoink's gut.

"This is for Maya," Billy said.

He pushed it harder until the sword's tip exited through Yoink's back. Blood projected from his mouth and settled on the ground.

"And this is for everyone," Billy added.

Abruptly, a vigorous elbow strike from Yoink dispersed Billy's dream. Yoink had somehow escaped Billy's Spiritual Cage and survived his deadly stab.

The villagers stopped fighting and ran away. Some were shot in the back with arrows. Others were stabbed with swords. Few managed to escape.

How in Oremanta did he survive?

"You," Yoink growled, "will pay!"

For the first time in this fight, their swords crossed, shimmering in Velron's Square. Billy lunged, stepped back, then lunged again. *Failure now means death.* He crouched, ducked, and then charged.

Yoink perfectly blocked Billy's attacks and then swung his sword at Billy's head.

Billy ducked again. While doing so, he picked up a handful of sand and threw it at Yoink's face. *If I can't fight hard, I'll fight smart.*

Yoink staggered back, trying to locate Billy.

Billy pounced on his temporarily blind opponent and stabbed him somewhere near his previous wound.

The villagers hailed at once.

Yoink fell to his knees, severely bleeding. Strands of his long gray hair covered his weary face.

"He did it," a woman cried. "Yoink is dead!"

Yoink's men ran toward Billy and the few who remained in the square, but a voice echoed in the small village, ordering everyone, "I said ...." Yoink gasped. "Do not ... interfere!"

That's ... impossible! Will he ever die?

Yoink stood up again, eyes burning with anger. He wanted Billy's head on a platter. He rushed toward the young boy. Before he could respond, he grabbed Billy by his head and threw him as though he were weightless.

Billy landed on a statue in the square. *Am I going to die here?* Billy could no longer open his left eye. He breathed in and out, trying to fill his empty lungs. Pain radiated throughout his body, and he realized the damage that had been done was far beyond repair. *I can't surrender. I promised Maya.*

"Give me your sword," Billy ordered a villager, coughing up blood with every word. The villager threw his sword to Billy.

A mother closed her little girl's eyes and hugged her from behind. Another man looked at the sky with devastation, mumbling words Billy couldn't hear. The villagers had nothing more to offer Billy.

Don't stare at me like that. Billy clenched his fist. *I need no one's pity.*

***

"His name will be remembered for years to come. The young boy who humiliated Yoink the Beast!" From the roof of their cottage, an old man with bushy eyebrows and a dense white beard sat with his grandson, the two of them witnessing the fight.

"Close your eyes, son," the old man said. "It's over."

***

Yoink rushed Billy like a hungry lion.

Billy broke out in a cold sweat. He didn't see Yoink approaching; he saw death. He thought of his promise to Maya, that he'd protect her from everyone and that he'd kill Yoink.

I must not give up.

The two danced again in Velron Square, swinging their swords right and left, up and down. In the center of Billy's vision, he saw Yoink. In the periphery, he saw many Mayas watching him as he fought. *I won't fail her.*

Yoink threw his sword away and kicked Billy on his knee.

Billy instantly lost his balance.

Yoink punched him in the face and Billy fell. Yoink took a dagger out of his belt and roared, "Die!"

Billy blocked Yoink's dagger with his palm. The dagger stuck deep into Billy's flesh. His hand bled, and the blood fell like a waterfall.

"How long do you think you can survive?" Yoink asked, unsheathing another dagger from his belt.

"I'll fight," Billy stuttered, "until my last breath."

He blocked another strike with his left palm. Now both hands bled heavily. His left eye was still shut. Billy was on his knees with two daggers penetrating his hands. The amount of blood loss was too much. Billy's vision blurred and his head became light.

Yoink, with eyes full of revulsion, punched Billy in his chest.

The boy from Rangerwest screamed. Every inch of his small body ached. He couldn't stand the pain and the pity in the villagers' eyes and, most importantly, the endless thought of Maya being alone.

"You deserve this!" Yoink sneered, kicking him in the face.

Billy faced the ground, sniffing dust along with humiliation.

Yoink laughed and took a walk in the square, gloating and strolling in front of the villagers.

"Did you think," Yoink asked everyone, "this little kid would beat me?"

Billy's right eye swelled shut as well, and an old flashback played in his mind.

On a very cold and moonless night a week after their parents' deaths, he and Maya had sat on an abandoned rooftop in a village they didn't know the name of. Billy cuddled Maya, and they'd warmed their bodies with their own breaths. The two orphans of war had nowhere to go: no home, no family, no friends, nothing. They only had each other. And to them, that was enough.

"Don't you ever leave me," Maya had requested, her head on Billy's chest and her fingers tightly squeezing his ripped shirt.

"I won't. That's a promise," Billy replied, and then smiled from his heart. "We'll grow up together, avenge our parents, and make this world a peaceful place."

Maya laid Billy on her thighs, passed her fingers between his red hair, and sang him to sleep, the way she did every night: "We'll hold each other's hands, under three moons and the burning suns. Like the wind that hears all stories, but moves on and on and on, hitting every stone, not caring where it runs."

Yoink grabbed him by his back the way someone grabs a dead rabbit off the ground. He tightly wrapped his hand around Billy's neck and raised him high. Yoink squeezed Billy's throat and smirked. "Who won now? Tell me! Who won? Weaklings should only run and hide. I'll step on you like everyone else!"

I'm sorry, Maya. I've always been a burden.

Yoink took the last dagger from his belt and slit Billy's throat.

Chapter Twenty-Nine

War

Desperation spread in Velron like a plague. The villagers believed Yoink was an invincible tool of destruction.

Billy lay helpless with an open wound in his throat. None dared to take action.

Yoink towered over Billy and shouted, humiliating him as his soul slowly escaped his body, "And you thought *you* could kill me? I'm indestructible!"

"He fought well," a woman whispered. "But we're destined to die here."

***

A lad wearing a golden cloak entered through Velron's gate. The grip of his sword was purple. Both the blade of his sword and the shield on his chest were emblazoned with a symbol of a two-headed snake. His brown hair was spiked, and his eyes were sharp and furious.

It was Leland, the new wielder of the Sword of Legends.

Leland ran toward the crowded square, grabbing everyone's attention, and stood before Yoink.

"You want to die? Just like—" Yoink threatened, but before he could finish his sentence, Leland struck him with the pommel of his sword. Yoink instantly kneeled.

Leland leaned down to Billy, wiped the dust from his cheeks, and then mumbled, "Hold on Billy … Hold on. I'll bring help."

"Jus … just …" Billy stuttered, spitting blood, "promise me you won't leave Maya alone." Billy's hand reached to Leland's and held onto it tightly. "Tell her … I'm sorry," he said. His hands let go of Leland, and he closed his bruised eyes for good.

"I promise," Leland said, tears welling in his eyes. He glared at the contaminated sky, overwhelmed by anger and regret, and determined to end this rotten chain of hatred.

"Where's your heart?" Leland asked Yoink firmly. "How can you kill so easily? These are lives!"

Yoink was still on his knees. He pushed the ground with his knuckles, spat, and then answered, "My heart? What's a heart? Is it the thing that makes you love? That makes you weak? That makes you hold onto things you'll never get? Is it the thing that generates emotions and imprisons you within them?" he replied. "I ripped it out and left it there for dead. I'm free."

An enormous amount of energy circulated within Leland, flowing from his heart into his arteries and back to his heart again. Leland was amazed he still had stamina left in him after having run for hours to reach Velron. But that's why people wanted this sword. *Power.*

Leland showed no mercy. He pounced on Yoink, who was sluggish and slow to react. Or Leland was just too fast for him now. Yoink defended himself, barely, but he couldn't last long in this sword fight.

Leland slashed Yoink's left arm and then his right thigh. *No wonder they call it the Sword of Legends.*

Leland stepped closer to Yoink and was ready to deliver the final strike when a voice behind him called, "Wait!"

He knew the voice well: Maya. Her eyes were pepper red and her face flushed. She came from where Billy was.

"He's alive … right?" Maya asked in a fragile voice, "We can heal him, right?"

"I—" Leland stumbled over his words. "I don't know."

He lied. Billy was dead, and he knew it very well. But it's hard to tell her that, even though she probably knows Billy is gone too.

Maya took the sword from Leland's hand.

"He's mine," she said, crying.

Meanwhile, Aelfgar was engaged in a battle with Yoink's men close to Velron's gate, emitting fire, cutting heads, and saving the villagers' lives.

Yoink couldn't stand up.

Maya pushed the sword into his leg, then into his arm, and then into his chest.

"Die!" she screamed. Then she chopped his hand off his arm.

Yoink screamed in pain and bled a tank's worth of blood.

"Die!"

On his knees, wounded, humiliated, and powerless, Yoink said, "Pain ... So this is how it feels." He stuttered, breathless, staring at his own wounds. "End it."

"Never!" Maya was about to torture him more when Leland took his sword back from her.

"Enough," Leland said with sympathy to Maya's state. He plunged his sword into Yoink's heart.

"You're right," Leland said, removing the sword from Yoink's body. "Our heart is our weakness."

***

Agis Phoenix had received definitive news, so he wore his shield and picked up his sword. The Rebel Army had shown itself at last. Hundreds of rows of warriors marched toward the Golden Gate of the Castle.

"It's here," he told Hamlet, the only lieutenant with him in the hall.

"It has never been gone, Chief Lieutenant," Hamlet commented. "Once war falls, it goes on forever. The grudge never ends."

A guard walked in, bowed respectfully, and announced, "More news, sir. Seems like the Rebel Army has divided itself into three groups. They're marching from North, East, and South, sir."

"I see," Phoenix said, then glared at Hamlet. "Maybe we should divide ourselves as well. We can't let any gate fall."

"It's your choice, Chief Lieutenant," Hamlet calmly said. "But I'd suggest we stay as we are. If the main gate falls, the Castle is gone."

"What if another gate falls?"

"That would be a disaster. But if we could win the Main Gate battle, we could save the other gates as soon as the battle ends. And don't forget that every gate is already guarded, not as much as the Golden Gate, but they have protection."

"No. I can't keep the other gates with such defenses," Agis said, throwing wood into the very deep fire pit. "I'll put most of our force in the Main Gate, the Golden Gate, and divide the rest for the other gates."

"Wise decision," Hamlet praised. "No wonder you're the Chief Lieutenant."

Hamlet, the Black Owl, walked toward the door, half-turned his face, and told Agis, "I'm going to the battleground, sir. I'll inform everyone about the changes. A great fight awaits." He faced the door. Now that no one could see him, he smiled wickedly while leaving the hall, his clothes trailing behind him.

The war is just the beginning, but little do they know, the Black Owl thought.

***

Lieutenant Ojoy walked among the rows of warriors facing the Main Gate of the Castle: the Golden Gate. He scrutinized his army, randomly moving from one row to another. He stopped by a man, gazed him in the eye, and then said loudly for all his men to hear, "I smell fear." He asked the man, "Are you afraid?"

"No, sir!" the man replied even louder than Ojoy, staring at the gate in front of him without blinking.

"Good," Ojoy replied, moving to the first row. "Today, we fight for what we want! We fight for what we love! For our pride! For the Castle!" Ojoy's voice echoed throughout the field. "Die for what you want and you'll live forever!"

"Ho!" the warriors chorused in one voice.

The half-naked, barrel-chested lieutenant continued, "If any of you aren't willing to fight tooth and nail for his home, leave now." Ojoy looked at the many lines of warriors from left to right then threatened, "Because if I see any of you run away when this starts ... I swear I'll tear him apart with my own sword."

"Ho!" the warriors responded again.

***

Two men dressed in white walked side-by-side past Eren's Square in the heart of the Castle. When they reached the Palace of Eternal Wisdom, the dozens of guards protecting it cleared the way for them at once. The two men did not enter through the main gate but rather went to a high tower beside it.

One of the two took a key from his pocket and opened the door of the tower. They entered, locked the door securely behind them, and then went to the roof. From there, they could see every part of the Castle: the Palace of Eternal Wisdom, where the Legendary Leaders resided, and the Palace of Wrath, where the meetings of the Seven Lieutenants took place, and

Eren's Square, the most active spot in the Castle, and all the jeweled domes and towers and small cottages behind the Castle's walls. There was a large bell at the top of the tower. The men in white gazed at each other, nodded, and then rang it: the official announcement that the war had begun.

***

Jack gazed at his shining sword with lustful eyes. He craved the war. He wanted to test his new powers, too prideful to admit that Utta had done wonders to make him such an expert in such a short time.

When I first came here, I was strong. Now I'm one of the strongest! he thought.

"Open the gate!" Ojoy ordered.

Five guards opened the Golden Gate. Ojoy was the first to pass through. The rest of his warriors followed. Spacious fields extended for as long as his vision could reach, an empty area perfect for battle.

Six more lieutenants joined the army: Charles, Jeopard, Marquez, Saneta, Hamlet, and the Chief Lieutenant, Agis Phoenix. Except for Ojoy, who didn't wear any protection, the lieutenants wore golden armor and light gray cloaks.

There was a moment of anticipation among the army, but that didn't last for long. A thread-like line appeared from a distance. The warrior next to Jack closed his eyes and recited words Jack couldn't hear. Another warrior tightened his fingers around his spear as if holding his own life and took a step back. One warrior pressed a necklace into Jack's hand and requested, "If I die, give this to my wife. Ask for Monterraily house."

The Rebel Army's march shook the earth as they neared the Castle. Then the high-pitched, reverberating sound of a bell rang in everyone's ears.

***

The battle in Velron was over. Villagers buried the dead and began to clean their blood-filled streets. Some villagers circled Aelfgar, Leland, and Maya. A man inched closer to Leland, kneeled, and was about to kiss his hand, but Leland drew it away and got down to the man's level.

"Thank you," the man said.

Leland had no reply. He felt he didn't deserve to be thanked. He had the Sword of Legends, yet he hadn't been able to fulfill his promise and save Billy or the many other lives in Velron. The image of Billy bleeding to death was still in his head. He knew it would take too long before he could live with that. The events of today are tomorrow's memories, and memories, sometimes, are even worse than the actual events. But if Leland dwelled on that for too long, more lives would be lost. He was too ashamed to say anything to Maya, or even to look at her. He knew how she felt right now: *empty*.

"Let's head to the Castle," Aelfgar ordered.

Leland frowned as he tightly squeezed the pommel of his new sword. *I must stop the killing.*

"You must stay here, Maya," Aelfgar said. "The Castle now is too dangerous for you."

"Okay," Maya replied, not looking at anyone. Nothing mattered to her anymore, be it in Velron or the Castle or anywhere else. The damage done was far beyond repair. She went away, staring at streets she didn't know and people she'd never spoken to. But Leland followed her.

"Wait," Leland said, putting his hand gently on her shoulder. "I know how you feel. I'm sorry."

"I wish—" she replied, shedding tears she should have saved for when she was alone, "I wish I'd died with him."

Leland wrapped his hands around her as if he were crushing her bones. He was about to promise her that he would be back but thought better of it. *I can't make such a promise to someone I just failed.*

"I'll be back for you," he whispered in her ears. "I promise."

Leland didn't want to promise anything to anyone anymore, but the words had come out by themselves. Failing her twice would crush whatever remained of her soul, and that was the last thing he ever wanted to do.

"Be safe," he told her. "I have to leave now."

Leland and Aelfgar left Velron. If he lived through it all, there would be plenty of time in the future to reminisce. But now, reminiscing was only an obstacle.

The time has come, father.

***

Healers marched behind the last row of warriors. Archers lined the high walls and turrets of the Castle. The Seven Lieutenants stood in front of their men. The

Rebel Army, which had been divided into three units, united as one and approached the Castle.

Why would they divide themselves into three and then re-unite? Chief Lieutenant Agis wondered. *There has to be a trick behind that. What could it be?*

Ojoy raised his chest simultaneously with his sword. "This is our Castle, and we will fight until the bitter end!"

"Ho!" all the warriors shouted at once.

The Rebel Army was yards away now. Astonishingly, Frank Hopegone, the leader of the Rebel Army, wasn't there. Haizo, Naru, Nemat Lowblack, and Konlaw were leading the fight instead.

What does this mean? Agis asked himself again.

Konlaw, a red-bearded warrior, was the tallest and largest of them all. He had broad shoulders, a muscled, scarred body, and he didn't wear a shield, just like Ojoy. His right pupil was white, and his hair was gray and spiked. Konlaw stepped forward and announced, "It's been a while … Agis."

Agis Phoenix replied firmly, "Where is he?"

"His highness would never fight against mere men."

Phoenix turned his face to his men, "What do you call an army without a leader—"

"—The hands of the mighty leader, the new ruler of Oremanta, shouldn't touch the filthy blood of your men."

"An army without a leader is like a man without a soul!" Ojoy roared.

"Archers! Now!" Agis ordered.

At his word, a rain of arrows from both sides flooded the battlefield and blocked the sky like one large cloud.

And so, the second war of Oremanta began.

Chapter Thirty

The Heat of the Battle

Arrows pierced heads and throats and chests. Men fell to the ground one by one like dominoes. The sound of swords cutting through flesh rang in Jennifer's head. Men screamed when they killed, screamed when they were injured, and screamed even louder before they were killed. The noise in the battlefield was so terrifying Jennifer placed both hands on her ears and closed her eyes. Sara and Chloe stood beside her because she wasn't perfect in healing and still needed help. Jennifer wanted to see Leland. She had waited for him for too long. Before she opened her eyes once again, she prayed this massacre would end soon.

She opened her eyes to see a warrior's head split from his body and a hammer crush the skull of another. Swords brutally clashed together, their sounds reverberating many times before they ceased, only for more swords to clash again.

***

As the leader of his army, Phoenix had to stay alive. If the leader dies, the army loses half its strength, at least from a psychological point of view. This also meant that killing the Rebel Army's leaders would be extremely beneficial to win this battle. Agis had a huge responsibility. If the Castlers lost this war, the fate of Oremanta would change forever. The Legendary Leaders and the innocent people behind the walls would be in danger.

Where in Oremanta is Frank Hopegone? Why have they split their army and then reunited?

***

Ojoy's long, shining, silver sword turned red. He cut his way through lines of enemies, killing without mercy. *Mercy in times of war is suicide.* A shielded, black-cloaked warrior rushed him, a hammer in one hand and a sword in the other. Ojoy kicked him in his chest, forcing him to fall on his back. He then plunged his sword into his throat. Another man came at Ojoy from his back. He turned around, ducked, and then split him into halves. Ojoy marched forward through the lines until he saw an outline of a person he knew very well: Frank Hopegone.

***

Jennifer stared at the massacre with uncertain eyes. As she saw a sharp spear drill the skull of a warrior, Sara dragged a body to her. She'd never seen so many people die in such a short time. *This is awful.*

"Heal his arm. I'll heal his leg!" Sara ordered.

Jennifer tucked strands of her blonde hair behind her ears and then placed her hands on the man's arm. Once she did, the man screamed in pain. Jennifer withdrew her hands in fear. She wasn't ready, and she knew it. But she had to do it. She put her hands back on the man, closed her eyes, and tried to heal him. It was time to block her mind. She'd done it before many times, but the circumstances were different. Her current environment was deadly. The clash of swords and moaning were all she could hear. *How did the other girls do it?*

"Too slow," Sara said. "Move away. Hurry. I'll take care of him."

***

Three muscled warriors circled Ojoy. Their hands suddenly set themselves ablaze as if they'd grabbed a stick of burning wood doused in gasoline.

Fire Moxie … Impressive, not enough, though, Ojoy thought.

They rushed toward Ojoy, aiming at him with their burning hands.

Ojoy grabbed the face of one warrior, raised his whole body to the sky, and then vigorously crushed his skull into the solid ground.

Too weak.

The other two stared in disbelief. Ojoy didn't wait. He ran at them. As a defensive mechanism, they struck him with their burning hands. *Well. That was a little bit painful.* Ojoy grabbed each head with a hand and pushed them together. Blood sprayed like a fountain. Before he could take a breath, Ojoy crossed swords with another warrior and slew him with one blow.

"This is just starting!" he roared.

Someone new had joined the party. Another rebel charged at Ojoy, and Ojoy was about to deliver him to his fate when a spear plunged into the rebel's back. Ojoy got angry. He went to the warrior who'd thrown the spear and scolded, "Only cowards kill from the back. I haven't trained cowards!"

***

An arrow pierced Jack's scapula. He fell on his hands and knees as pain blazed in his shoulder. Like a toddler, Jack crawled to his fallen sword. He reached out his hands for it, but a rebel stepped on the sword and grinned at him evilly. With a hammer etched with many machetes, the rebel was about to crush Jack's head, but Jack rolled over on the ground. Fighting for his life, Jack kneed him in the place no man wants to be kicked in. Then he picked up his sword, rolled again, and bluntly inserted the sharp end into the rebel's gut.

Now on his back and facing the sky, while many bodies were falling nearby, two more men towered over Jack. Away from his sword, which was now stuck in the rebel's gut, Jack had no more options. The pain in his shoulder was unbearable. He breathed in and out heavily and had given in to defeat.

The two men's eyes glistened with satanic joy. At once, both leaned down and were about to end Jack's life when two arrows shot them in the back, with less than a fraction of a second between the two shots. They fell on Jack, dead.

"We need you! Don't die here," Utta said.

***

Because they were lined up behind the last row of warriors, the healers and archers had the best view of the battle. Clouds assembled in the bare sky, blocking sunbeams from hitting the bloodstained ground.

Jack leaned against Utta's shoulder as she made her way to Jennifer.

"What happened?" Jennifer asked, carefully laying Jack down on a wooden pad.

"Only a few scratches," Jack sarcastically said. "Can't you see my shoulder?"

If they hadn't been in the midst of war, Jennifer would've let him bleed to death. But now, every single effort mattered.

"Shut up and let me do my work," Jennifer replied. She took what remained of the spear off Jack's shoulder. He squealed. Some of the rebels had reached very close to the healers, but there was a barrier of shielded warriors who'd been tasked with protecting this last line. Jennifer closed her eyes and tried to medicate Jack.

But she failed. Again.

***

Konlaw, Nemat, and Haizo were killing machines. They'd been chosen by Frank Hopegone himself, which meant they'd been chosen for a reason. Konlaw, who was leading the Rebel Army, now raised a hand and groaned, ordering, "Destroy!"

On his word, mobile catapults launched projectiles consisting of large balls of stones. Warriors were crushed and archers on the high walls fell off the ramparts. Some of the catapults launched flaming balls of fire, squashing Castlers like ants and burning bodies alive.

**

"This is bad … This is so bad," Harvard croaked. He was so old he could barely walk by himself, yet his senses were as good as they were thirty years ago. With a spine curved like a banana, weak legs, and torn muscles, he couldn't participate in the war, even though he'd fought bravely in the first war, side by side with Aelfgar Hawx. In his old cottage south of the Castle, he walked in circles, uncertain of how to act.

"Ron!" Harvard cried. But Ron, his servant, wasn't there. He was on the battlefield. Harvard struggled to open the window and called, "Anyone here? Can you hear me?"

No one answered. But the old man had something very important to tell. Harvard hadn't sensed such a powerful aura before, and he knew very well to whom it belonged. Harvard exited his cottage and walked randomly, searching for anyone, "Hello!" he called. "Who's here?"

The streets were empty and the houses were locked. The Castle was a ghost town. *Damn it … How did this happen? How did* he *get here?*

Pain blazed in Harvard's back and his legs ached. Harvard's vision was so bad that he saw things as if they were painted over with colors. But he saw something moving by the end of the road.

"Wait!" Harvard said, walking toward the moving object. In his younger days, Harvard was a ranger. He would cross Oremanta from east to west, and he wouldn't get tired or bored. *If I'd only kept Ron here …*

The thing stopped moving and then went in Harvard's direction. The thing was a young boy carrying a jar of water. This boy, if he were lucky enough to deliver Harvard's message, would provide Oremanta a great favor.

"Ya called, old man?" the boy said rudely.

If he didn't need the boy, Harvard would have slapped him in the face. He put his hand on the boy's head, looked deeply into his eyes, and then said, "Listen carefully to what I'm about to say."

The boy nodded.

Harvard's voice dropped to a whisper. "Go to the battlefield and tell them Frank Hopegone is already inside the Castle."

Chapter Thirty-One

Deception

Aelfgar and Leland galloped toward the battlefield. The road they took, the shortcut Mora Gueja had told them about, was free of beasts and obstacles. Aelfgar stopped running and leaned against a tree.

"I'll slow you down," Aelfgar said, breathing rapidly. "Don't wait for me."

Leland knew this was better for the both of them. He could reach the Castle much faster if Aelfgar weren't with him. But Aelfgar's presence had always given him support. He needed someone like him by his side when the time would come that he'd have to kill his father.

"There's something you must know before you go," Aelfgar told him. "You're strong. But you're not strong enough to kill Frank."

Leland hadn't expected that from Aelfgar. *If that's true, then why did Aelfgar bet on his life to get the sword? And what about the myth of me being a Keo?*

"If you think you can beat your father, then you must be a fool," Aelfgar said, stressing the same point.

285

"But you could stop him. Maybe. Don't be overconfident. Frank Hopegone is different from Yoink and everything else you've ever fought before."

"Then why did I get this sword if I can't beat him?"

"Don't get me wrong," Aelfgar said, his breathing returning to normal. "You're the closest one. You're a Keo. Your instinct to live and kill and free your inner power is naturally much stronger than most other warriors in Oremanta, even if they've trained for years. It's not fair, but it's the truth. You remember what you did to the black-cloaked man in the hills that day?" Aelfgar cleared his throat and went on. "But your father is a Keo as well. You must not forget that. You have the Sword of Legends. That's a boost. But more importantly, you have the will to win. From the get-go, you wanted to do this. The pain inside you that drove you all the way through is stronger than anything else in the world. Remember why you wanted to do this in the first place."

The many days he'd spent on Oremanta had proven to Leland that his cause to fight his father had more dimensions to it than he initially supposed. In the beginning, he wanted to fight because he longed to confront the man who'd abandoned him and his family. He wanted to kill the man who'd made Leland suffer because of his own selfish agenda. He also wanted to do it for Dylan. Frank's men had killed Leland's friend. *It was because of me that Dylan died. If I hadn't gotten him into this, Dylan would be at his home playing games, watching shows, and doing what he always did.* Billy had died because of

Frank as well. Villages had been burned to ashes because of his greed. It wasn't a personal issue anymore. The fate of thousands was at stake.

"There's one more thing I want to tell you, and hold onto this as long as you're alive," Aelfgar lectured. "Not all mistakes are bad. Some have that great power to make you realize you need to change, right now."

This was not a mere sentence said by a wise man. This was a new way to perceive life. Aelfgar had forged a new concept in Leland's head. *How can someone think of his mistakes this way?*

Leland left Aelfgar behind and sprinted to the battleground. The sentence sifted through his head and repeated itself involuntarily, perpetually, for as long as he ran.

Not all mistakes are bad. Some have that great power to make you realize you need to change, right now.

***

After he'd been healed, and though still in pain but not as bad as it had been, Jack scampered back to the battle. He wiped the sweat off his face and climbed a pile of dead bodies. He viewed the mad massacre angrily, and then he raised his sword high and shouted with a voice like a thousand thunders combined, "THIS WAR … IS … OURS!"

He jumped down and cut off a man's head then picked up a spear from the ground and pierced another's chest.

***

Lieutenant Marques handled three warriors at a time. Lieutenant Jeopard had killed dozens of warriors with his fixed crossbow. Lieutenant Saneta organized the Healing Squad, and Lieutenant Charles was engaged in a deadly fight with Nemat. Only one lieutenant wasn't there fighting. The Black Owl had disappeared when the war had started.

Ojoy found Haizo, another leader of the Rebel Army, engaged in a battle. He hurried to him as if he'd found a needle in a haystack. It seemed like the kind of battle Ojoy wanted. Haizo's weapon was different than the others. Metal claws were etched on his left hand, and he carried a folding fan with sharp edges on the other. Ojoy wanted his head on a platter. Killing him meant eliminating one-quarter, if not more, of their leadership control on the battleground. Ojoy attacked.

"I'd call you the leader of the Castle," Haizo said as he scrambled back. "You're the toughest and bravest among them all."

"I don't need those words." Ojoy pounced again, giving no time for Haizo to catch a breath.

Haizo defended himself with his metal claws and steel fan. Somehow he knew where Ojoy's next strike would be, as if he could read his mind. Haizo scraped Ojoy's forearm with his claw.

Ojoy felt numbness in his shoulders that slowly spread out in his body. *Poison?* "Weakling's tricks," Ojoy divulged. "I'll tear you apart, traitor!"

Now that he was poisoned, his sword was too heavy for him, so he threw it away. In fact, Ojoy preferred sword-less ways of killing. It offered him more diverse killing methods. He lunged at Haizo, jumped, ducked, spun around slower than usual, and then he punched Haizo hard on his face, causing him to bleed from every hole. Ojoy grabbed Haizo's head as if holding a ball and broke his neck with a sharp twist.

Haizo collapsed, lifeless.

"Poison, you say?" Ojoy Steelheart spat. "Haizo is dead!"

***

Red-bearded Konlaw stood in front of Jack like a solid wall. Jack was half the size of him.

"Where to, kid?" Konlaw asked.

"Frank Hopegone! I'll end this war with my own hands!" Jack replied firmly.

"Know whom you're talking to." Konlaw chuckled and then flashed behind Jack before he could even blink. One moment he was in front of Jack; the other he was behind his back. Konlaw grabbed Jack by the back of his neck and then put his skull to the ground. "I could kill you with no effort at all." He stepped on Jack's head with his boot. "But I like to humiliate scumbags like you. You shall pick your words carefully when you talk about our mighty leader, the King of Oremanta!"

"There are no kings in Oremanta but the Flares of Truth, Legendary Leaders of the Castle!" Chief Lieutenant Phoenix shouted while pushing Konlaw away.

"We'll see about that," Konlaw said as he attacked the Chief Lieutenant.

***

In the meantime, a guard approached Saneta, the Healing Lieutenant. With a shocked, red face he whispered, "I have just received this from a little boy." The guard panted. "I must inform someone."

"Speak!"

"Harvard sent this boy, claiming—" He cleared his throat and made sure no one was eavesdropping, then he revealed, "The real Frank Hopegone isn't on the battlefield!"

"What do you mean?" Saneta frowned as she leaned closer to him. "But ... many warriors said they've spotted him on the battlefield!"

"The real one is in the Castle already! He's heading toward the Flares of Truth!" The guard dropped a bombshell. "Harvard sensed his powers, and that old man can't be mistaken! The Frank on the battlefield is probably a replica, a Moxie to deceive us!"

"This ... can't be happening."

Chapter Thirty-Two

Into the Storm

"What's wrong?" Sara asked Jennifer. "Put yourself together and do what you're supposed to do."

"I'm trying," Jennifer replied. *If it wasn't for all this killing and blood I'm seeing, I would've probably made it.* The humid air reminded her of Temblewood's summers, except her town wasn't as deadly. Jennifer heard a whisper behind her back. She didn't turn around but listened carefully, pretending to clean blood off a wooden pad.

"The real one is in the Castle already!" Now the noise of iron meeting iron was too loud. The only words she heard were, "Frank Hopegone."

Rebels sprinted in hordes toward the last few rows, which were closest to the healers and the Castle's walls. Castlers skirmished with the rebels in a bloody fight until a ball of fire rained down on both Castlers and rebels, burning thcm all to ashes. The flaming ball rolled over, grinding bodies caught along the way, and then nestled against the walls.

***

Ojoy located his next prey and galloped toward him, killing every rebel in between. Out of the blue, an arrow perforated his shoulder. He took it out, split it in two, and continued. By now, the cuts and holes on his body were countless. Haizo's poison had made Ojoy sluggish, too. But through blood, sweat, and tears, he crept closer to his target, the seemingly last obstacle in the war: Frank Hopegone.

Frank stood behind his whole army encircled by ten men. He didn't move, react, or say a word. He just grinned.

Ojoy fought all of Frank's bodyguards at once. He injured some and killed others until Lieutenant Marquez joined the party at just the right time, though Ojoy would never tell him so.

"Marquez," Ojoy gasped, "I could've finished them by myself!"

Marquez was a skilled fighter. He could handle many warriors at a time, even without a weapon, and he'd leave the fight stepping on their dead bodies.

"Careful," Ojoy teased Marquez while slaying a rebel. "It's a shame to die by traitors."

"Now!" Marquez gave Ojoy the signal. The split second when the remainders of the bodyguards surrounded Marques was all Ojoy needed to push his sword into Frank's throat.

Frank didn't even try to defend himself. He disappeared into thin air as though he hadn't even been there to begin with.

What in Oremanta is happening?

"So it's true," Lieutenant Marquez divulged, stabbing the last of the bodyguards. "The real one *is* in the Castle."

"What?" Ojoy raged. "In the Castle?"

***

Sara had just healed a half-burned warrior. She begged him, "Don't go back to the battlefield. In your current state, you won't be able to fight anymore."

The warrior nodded, stood up, picked up his sword, and then said, "Ojoy is there fighting with a poisoned body. If I were to die, I would die under his command." He returned to the battle in the canyon.

"I heard something," Jennifer told Sara. "I'm not sure, though."

"What?" Sara replied. "Quickly. No time for chitchat here."

"Leland's father—" Jennifer sputtered, "I mean, Frank Hopegone, is inside the Castle!"

"No way," Sara replied, raising both eyebrows. "Then who are we fighting now?"

***

After consecutive sword clashes—stepping forward and attacking and then stepping backward and defending—Konlaw dragged himself away from Phoenix and threatened, "This is over. Say goodbye to your Flares of Truth. It's a new era!"

With the corner of his eye, Phoenix saw Ojoy stab Frank, who disappeared like a vapor. *No way!* he marveled. *They're playing dirty!* Chief Lieutenant Agis clutched his sword at his side and then lunged at Konlaw. "All of you filthy rebels will pay!"

"You don't get it," Konlaw panted, dodging smoothly, "every moment you waste is in our favor. The throne of Oremanta is ours." Konlaw flashed behind Phoenix like a ghost.

Agis turned around, and a sword from high above was about to lay him dead in one blow, but he leaped backward at once. Konlaw's sword cut Agis's lips and nose, and he bled heavily. With a burning sensation on his cleft lips that amplified with each word, he cursed, "You bastard!"

What can we do? If Frank's inside the Castle, who will stop him? If the lieutenants leave the battlefield, we'll lose everything, Agis Phoenix thought, gritting his teeth.

"What's … this … power?" Konlaw asked as he thoroughly scanned the battlefield. A powerful, new, fresh energy had floated into the battlefield.

Why did it just suddenly appear? Who's this? Phoenix asked himself. He looked around and found an answer to his question. He smiled, and his faith was restored.

Go for it, Aelfgar's apprentice. Go for it!

***

"Can the Flares of Truth defend themselves?" Jennifer asked Sara. Among flying heads and falling corpses, one man had stolen her attention. She knew him very well, but not quite as she thought she did. There was something different about him now.

With her peripheral vision, Jennifer saw that Sara was answering her through words and gestures. And though Jennifer heard her, she didn't listen. Her vision blurred everywhere except for the warrior with the golden shield and shimmering sword. She realized how much she had missed Leland.

A half-naked man went to Leland and whispered in his ears, and then Leland ran toward the healers at the Castle's walls.

***

Leland headed to the Golden Gate of the Castle. Now he knew where his target was. Everyone fought hard to defend the Castle from the outside, but Leland had to defend it from the inside. He wasn't needed on the battlefield. He sprinted to the Golden Gate, avoiding engagement with any rebel.

But a man with a hammer blocked his way. He had a bold, round head like a cannonball. Suddenly, the cannonball fell off and flew away. Blood sprayed.

Jack cleaned his bloody sword with the headless man's clothes. "Go for him," Jack said. "You're not supposed to be here."

Leland nodded and continued to the gate. Standing with their backs against the Castle's high walls, the healers handled dozens of injured warriors. One blonde healer stared at him, and among the many healers, Leland's eyes likewise fixated on her. He smiled at Jennifer, sent her a flying two-finger wave, and then went on.

Four guards who had just received commands from Lieutenant Saneta led Leland to a hidden metal door not so far from the Golden Gate. Opening the huge entrance would certainly lead to disaster.

Leland entered the Castle, and the guards locked the small metal door behind him.

***

Leland dashed to the Palace of Eternal Wisdom at the center of the Castle. Corpses of former guards lined its roads and avenues. The Castle was bereft of life. The streets were empty, and its doors and windows were locked. A man from behind called, "Hey! You, there!"

Leland turned around and saw a guard reaching out his hand.

"Help me," he begged. The guard's face was cut from above his eye down to his chin. "Water?" he asked.

Leland looked around and found a flask of water that another guard had probably dropped. Leland gave him the flask and then went back on his way.

"Don't go! He is there," the guard warned. "You will die."

Leland said nothing and ran toward the palace, his thoughts outpacing his feet. *I am responsible now. Everyone's relying on me to end this massacre. All of Oremanta's skilled warriors are on the battlefield. Only a few remained in the Castle, but Frank's killed them all. I haven't seen my father for ten years now. How does he look now? Does he even know I'm here to kill him?*

Questions popped into his head, but, probably for the first time, he didn't want any answers. *Feeling too much right now could lead to disaster.* More than a hundred times, Leland listed every reason he had to do this. He created many barriers on his mental list, forging a high-fenced fortress against the bond he'd once had with his father.

Leland reached Eren's Square. Behind it loomed a gigantic palace with a purple, jeweled dome. A hundred ladders reached toward its entrance. He'd been here before, when he'd first arrived in Oremanta. The sky was gray, and dark clouds blocked the sun. The shadows of the pseudo-sunset dominated the empty square. Leland scanned the area, searching for a sign.

Behind Leland was a narrow avenue and ahead of him, in the heart of the square, was the statue of the Sword of Legends. Concrete cottages formed a rectangle around the open field. Eren's Square must be for the rich, because the cottages elsewhere were made of wood and not concrete.

"Are you that thirsty to kill me, son?" a familiar voice from nowhere calmly asked.

Chapter Thirty-Three

Pain

Aelfgar's legs touched the battleground. *The rebels are outnumbered—that's a good sign. But Frank isn't here. I can't even sense his powers nearby. Is he dead?*

Aelfgar formed a fireball in both hands and launched it at the rebels charging toward him. They shrieked, fell on their knees, and then collapsed, lifeless.

Chief Lieutenant Agis was engaged with Konlaw. Aelfgar joined him. He leaped on the red-bearded leader, who scrambled back and then flashed behind Aelfgar. Konlaw was too fast, but Aelfgar knew his tricks. This wasn't their first fight. Without turning around, Aelfgar kicked him in his ankle like an untamed horse. A furious round of sword-dancing started.

"Only souls filled with vengeance can change the world," Konlaw spat.

Ten years ago, when they'd first fought, Konlaw had told Aelfgar the same thing. *Maybe he's right— partially.* "You're a good man," Aelfgar panted. "Surrender and I assure you a fair trial."

Konlaw stepped backward, wiped the sweat off his face, then replied, "The world has to change. Good men want to change the world. But hurt men are the ones who actually change it."

"Enough of that," Phoenix cried, striking Konlaw and knocking his sword away. Konlaw fell on his back. Phoenix swung his weapon, but a hand had firmly grabbed his pommel.

"We don't kill from the back, Chief Lieutenant," Ojoy smirked.

"How dare you?" Agis Phoenix threatened.

Konlaw stood back on his feet, picked up his weapon, and charged at the newcomer.

Aelfgar jumped in and blocked his attack.

Barehanded, Ojoy pushed Konlaw hard on his chest, and he lost his balance. Ojoy dodged Konlaw's assault, swiftly picked up a fallen sword, and then stabbed Konlaw's chest in the blink of an eye.

"That's how we do it, Chief Lieutenant," Ojoy said.

***

It had been ten years since he'd last heard his father's voice. It resurrected a new set of abandoned memories. He recalled a childhood scene when he was sitting upon a table with his parents. Frank had cut steak into little pieces to feed them to Leland. He remembered when they were in the backyard playing soccer. Frank had taught him how to tie his shoes that day. Nostalgia inundated Leland's head.

"You've grown up … Leland." His father's voice echoed.

The square was empty. Leland was sure of that.

"Where are you? Show yourself now!" Leland demanded, searching. There was no sign of life in the square, as if he were talking to a ghost.

"Stubborn and impatient … It seems some things never change." The calm and cold voice of his father rang again. Leland's heart hammered against his chest, and his hands shivered so much he almost dropped his sword.

"Just show yourself!" Leland shouted, his voice cracking.

"And then what? You would kill your father?"

Leland bit his lips then hesitantly replied, "I'd do it … if I had to."

"Oh, son," Frank said, and Leland could swear he was grinning, "You have a grudge against me. I can tell. But why?"

"Why? That's the stupidest question I've heard. Do you have any idea how much pain you've caused?"

"Poor son … You're fragile and weak."

"I thought you were dead." Leland paused. "I wish you were *really* dead. That would have been better than this. You abandoned your family and killed hundreds just for this?"

"Just for this, you say? You mean power? Authority? Fame? Wealth?" Frank answered his own questions. "Yes. I left you for all of *this*. You make me weak and helpless. I made a beast out of myself and got rid of all the things that made me human."

"Selfish."

Fog swooped in and loomed across the square, wrapping around the cottages and statues like a vengeful phantom. Leland couldn't see anything, but the voice didn't stop.

"I think I've given you enough reasons not to hold back. There's still one more thing you need to know before you die." Frank's voice faded.

Leland sensed rather than saw the presence of someone behind him.

"Your mother. Poor Maria. She knew everything from the start. She was a good woman, I must say."

"Enough!" Leland swiftly swung his sword behind in a futile attempt to kill the shadow creeping upon him. But no one was there.

"She knew I was coming here. I wanted to raise you in Oremanta, but she didn't want to leave Earth. I didn't care much. Humans are weak and pathetic."

"You speak as if you're not human," Leland said, desperately scanning for a clue. *Where is he?*

"I'm much more than human. Once a man gets rid of his humanity, things become easier. Nothing stops you. Pain, grief, sorrow, need, solitude … They're just obstacles in the face of glory."

"I've had enough of this."

"The truth requires sacrifices. If the death of hundreds grants millions a proper life, then that's the way you should follow."

I must not hold back because of my feelings. I'm afraid of winning and I'm afraid of losing. Feelings suck. Every action and decision I take in my life are triggered by feelings. I say things I don't mean because of my feelings. I pretend to be someone else because of feelings. I just … hate to feel! I wish I had a heart that wouldn't care about anything … a heart that wouldn't feel anything. Only then could I stand up and face life without anything pulling me back. I'll try to block my feelings now. It's just better than trying to deal with them and justify why they exist.

"You're sick," Leland firmly said. "Two of my friends have died because of you. Don't you ever speak of justice!"

Leland's breath caught in his throat, and his eyes flickered as a piece of fog moved away, revealing a man wearing a black mantle. Strands of brown hair streamed down his shoulders, and the rest was pulled back into a ponytail. His wide, almond-shaped eyes hadn't changed, as if Leland had just seen him yesterday. Frank's cold smile tensed every muscle in Leland's body. The immunity he'd tried to create against this moment, in which he'd see his father for the first time in years, had vanished faster than he thought it would.

Frank's white and perfectly aligned teeth glistened as he asked, "You truly believe you can kill me with that sword?"

"I will. Not only because I have the sword, but because I have a reason." Leland's stomach twisted. His face was covered in a sheen of sweat. But he had to act. "Let's end this, now!" he roared as he ran toward his father.

Chapter Thirty-Four

Blood and Tears

Roy stole silver and gold from the fallen bodies of both allies and foes. The first thing he did after killing someone was to check if they had money or not.

Some people never change, Jennifer thought, watching him from a distance. He'd done her a favor by taking her to the Healing Squad. But he'd done it for a couple of coins too.

Four bodies fell off the ramparts and onto the ground inches away from Jennifer. She backed away. They'd been shot with arrows, and now they were dead.

Jennifer and Sara dragged their bodies to the back and piled them up against the walls. They would bury them when the war was over. Sara had told her that. Jennifer spotted a figure with a familiar outline far away and deep within the battlefield, but he wasn't engaged in any fight. The battle raged, and blood created a nontransparent membrane. Jennifer blinked, and when she opened her eyes the figure had disappeared.

She smiled.

***

Ojoy's body was numb. He could barely manage walking. The poison's effect was too much for him to handle. He could fight no more, but he didn't want to retreat or sit back, so he decided just to stand where he was. He would defend himself if someone attacked, but that was as far as he could go. If he backed off from the battleground, the spirit of his men would fall. *A leader must not fail his men.*

"Come here," Ojoy called for Jack amidst his fight. "I have something very important to tell you."

Covered in blood, Jack obeyed.

"You fought well," Ojoy said, then ordered, "Come closer."

Jack did.

Ojoy whispered some words into his ears.

Jack nodded and then went away.

***

Frank unsheathed his sword and charged at Leland. Leland growled every time their swords met, unleashing his not-quite-hidden resentment. But Frank read Leland's moves the way an old man reads his morning newspaper. Frank dodged left and right, up and down, smoothly and effortlessly. Leland felt he'd never touch him.

"You're wide open, son," Frank disclosed as he flashed behind him. "You're too young for this." Frank thrust his sword, but Leland swiftly evaded. He heard the swooshing sound of his father's sword cutting not only the air beside his ear but strands of his brown hair too. *I must beat him,* Leland encouraged himself as he advanced.

His father disappeared, and then a thick hand clutched Leland by his back and threw him into a shop's front. The glass shattered. Leland's collision with the ground wasn't as painful as the shards of glass he'd fallen upon. Leland jumped back on his feet. A few cuts on his palm and leg wouldn't be fatal. Their swords clanged in the square again.

"You're better than I thought," Frank praised.

Leland panted and gasped. "You must die," he threatened, breathing heavily.

The fog was gone, but it was still dark as more clouds assembled in the sky.

"Calm down, boy," Frank said, smiling. A navy aura surrounded Frank from head to toe, with finger-like projections on its borders, like a dark yet transparent cloud encircled him.

"Enough games, Leland. This fight must end now."

Leland squeezed the pommel of his sword as he saw his father leaping toward him. This time, Frank's face was different. His cold smile had been replaced by an angry frown. Leland felt he'd lose his balance and fall every time he blocked a strike. *What's ... this power?* Frank wasn't holding back. He wanted to kill.

"You're weak," Frank said. He flashed behind Leland, who couldn't keep up with his father's lightning speed. Then it happened. Frank's blade cut Leland's shoulder. Leland grimaced, fell on his knees, and crawled away. The pain was sharp, and it amplified as he escaped for his life on four limbs.

But Frank persisted. He plunged his sword into Leland, who rolled over and dodged the thrust. Frank plunged again. Leland rolled to the other side.

"How long do you think you can run?" Frank asked, attacking.

Leland clutched his sword to his side horizontally, blocking the strikes as he stood on his feet once more. *Defending too much will do me no good*, Leland realized. He put his strength into one strike that forced Frank to stop his consecutive assaults for a second. That was all Leland needed. He lunged and pushed his blade at Frank.

Frank evaded, but Leland delivered a powerful elbow strike to his face. Frank wiped the blood off then eyed Leland angrily as his two thick eyebrows joined. "This place is mine! A punk like you won't stop me from ruling Oremanta. I'm the strongest of the Royal Families. I'm a Keo!" Frank howled and scowled. "Allow me to show you true pain."

He kicked Leland's sword away, grabbed him by his face, and then pushed it down. Brutally, he dragged Leland's face on the cobblestones, who felt every inch of his face tearing apart.

"So … you say you tasted pain when I wasn't around, huh?" Frank sneered. "This is true pain, son."

Leland faced the ground, sniffing his own blood. Indignation possessed him. He'd gone on that deadly quest to get the Sword of Legends, but it seemed it hadn't been enough. His father was supremely overpowering. The tearing pain in his face made him sure none of his facial features remained. *But I must not surrender. Not now.* With weary limbs, Leland pulled himself up and stood on his feet, slower than a ninety-year-old man. *Why … can't I win?*

Bursting with resentment, he got his hands back on his sword. Blood dripped from his face, painting his clothes red.

"You once told me," Leland said as he charged, "the more you feed your fear, the more you become imprisoned by it."

An aura just as dark and powerful as Frank's encircled Leland. His eyes were as mad as a serial killer hunting his next victim.

"The Dark Aura appears only to a Keo bearing enough hatred and power. Leland, you surely have my blood," Frank said, fighting back. "But that's not enough. Goodbye!" Frank raged. He smoothly evaded Leland's strikes and then thrust his sharp blade into his thighs.

Leland fell on a knee, his blood pouring out.

"Now," Frank said, wearing his cold smile again, "have you tasted enough pain, my son?"

Barely breathing and with one eye closed, Leland divulged, "I can barely … call this pain." He coughed blood. "Physical pain is nothing. My body is crying, that's all. As long as the heart doesn't ache, I don't feel pain."

"Heart, feelings, emotions. You're still imprisoned by Earthling boundaries," Frank smirked. "It doesn't matter anyway. This fight is over." With steady steps, he went to Leland, aiming his sword at his heart. "You fought well, son." Heartlessly, he kicked Leland's knees. The boy collapsed to the dusty ground without resistance. "But I won't allow anything to stand against my glory. Not even my son."

It's ... hard. I can't pull it off. I can't even stand. A chain of desperate thoughts occupied his head until he saw Frank's sword arcing toward him. It was the slowest moment of his life.

"Die!" Frank uttered. The triangular, sharp end of his blade was four feet away ... now three ... two ... one. Powerless, Leland closed his eyes, certain of his death. The sound of penetrated flesh rang in his ears, but it wasn't his own.

Chapter Thirty-Five

Anything but the Rain

Frank ripped a long, sharp arrow out of his shoulder. Racked with pain and unable to move, Frank half-turned his face to the back and saw Aelfgar Hawx.

"It doesn't matter if you hit me from behind. It doesn't matter if you're two or three or even a whole army," Frank ranted. "In the end, I will be the new ruler of Oremanta!"

Aelfgar and Frank exchanged strikes. Leland watched the fight, disbelieving his eyes. *If Aelfgar hadn't helped me, I'd be dead by now. My father didn't even hesitate.* Leland's heart raced, and he felt he'd lose consciousness at any point. *I ... almost died.* Leland couldn't escape the thought.

His father and mentor fought to the death. Frank evaded Aelfgar's sword, ducked, and then delivered an uppercut to the old man. Leland was sure Aelfgar's jaw had been broken by the blow. Aelfgar scrambled back, breathed in and out, and then charged again.

"Mere warriors like you could never kill me," Frank howled, striking Aelfgar again.

Aelfgar couldn't do anything but defend himself. He had no chance of delivering a direct hit to Frank. He kept dodging, evading, and stepping back. But at one point, Frank's hits weakened and the pace of his strikes lessened.

"It's poisoned," Aelfgar said. "The arrow is poisoned, Frank. Surrender and you live. Fight and you die."

By that time, Leland had managed to pull himself up. He joined Aelfgar. Frank still dodged multiple strikes, now from Aelfgar and Leland. Whenever his sword hit Leland's, Leland almost dropped his.

"Know who you're talking to," Frank told Aelfgar with a condescending gaze. Choosing to disregard his poisoned state, he pounced on Aelfgar and slashed his chest. Blood sprayed. Aelfgar cried in pain. Yet the cut was only superficial.

"Surrender," Leland suggested, jumping in and giving Aelfgar a chance to take his breath. Leland wished Frank would surrender. Not because he didn't want to kill him, but because he believed he couldn't. Frank was overpowering both Leland and Aelfgar. They'd barely caused him any damage.

"Surrender?" Frank looked at Leland out of the corner of his eyes, forcing him to feel as if he were nothing.

Fear shivered down Leland's spine, almost causing him to beg for mercy. *But a word like "mercy" isn't in Frank's dictionary*, Leland believed.

It seemed Aelfgar had psychologically recovered from his injury. His sword clanged with Frank's once more.

Frank unsheathed a dagger from a hidden belt under his mantle and, as he fought Aelfgar, defended himself against Leland. Leland swiftly went behind Frank, who was now sandwiched. Confused and unable to defend his back, Frank felt Aelfgar's blade sink into his flesh. His blood fell all over the cobblestone ground. He frowned and shrieked in pain. He jerked Aelfgar's sword out of his flesh and stumbled backward.

"The fight is over," Leland said, in an attempt to persuade him to surrender. "Don't resist."

"I'm the one who decides when it's over," Frank replied, giving Leland a more condescending look than the one he'd given Aelfgar. Frank reeled on his way to Leland. The poison was taking over. Frank fell on a knee, but swiftly pushed himself up and attacked once more.

"I would give *anything* for glory," Frank stuttered, striking like a maniac. He smashed Aelfgar's face with his elbow as he simultaneously defended himself against Leland. Aelfgar was fully open now, but Frank pounced on Leland instead and vigorously pummeled him. Leland was sure another blow would be fatal.

Frank kicked Leland on his chest, and he fell on his back. Drawing in air became hard. Leland felt he was a hundred feet underwater. With one eye shut, Leland witnessed his father angrily approaching. He had no more tricks up his sleeve.

Then a spear pierced Frank's back. Leland saw Utta raise her hands in triumph behind his father.

"You are," Frank said coldly as he spun around in circles, "cowards!"

He tightened his fist around the spear behind his back and took it out. Then he began another round with Aelfgar, fighting with that spear. Frank injured Aelfgar's shoulder and thigh.

Aelfgar pulled himself to the back, barking.

Leland wanted to end this now. It was hard for him to see his father that way, no matter the depth of the grudge he had against him.

Utta shot an arrow at Frank's chest and another at his abdomen.

Frank spat blood, but he didn't fall.

Aelfgar raised a hand, ordering Utta not to shoot anymore. She stopped.

Frank dropped his spear.

Leland clutched his sword and then went, hesitantly, toward his father. Then he did it. Leland thrust his sword deep into his father's chest.

Frank, with Leland's sword shredding his insides, leaned over his son. He smiled—not the cold, evil smile—but a father's smile. It reminded Leland of the beautiful days when they'd all been together. He had missed this face, a lot.

With bloody hands, Frank brought Leland's ears closer to his mouth, then he whispered, and that was the last thing Leland heard from his father before he collapsed onto the ground, dead.

Leland's head was light. He could no longer see what lay around him. He fell, not on the ground, but on Jennifer. She'd come when he'd needed her the most. Leland gazed at her blue eyes and saw the home he'd craved for so long.

She pressed his head against her thighs as he lay on the cobblestone. "Time to rest, hero," she whispered, playing with his hair.

Rain fell from heights unknown and washed away all the blood and the pain and the grudge. Nostalgia inundated Leland along with a contradicting mixture of satisfaction, regret, joy, and misery that dwelled in his chest like a whirlwind. Leland's blurry vision saw, in slow motion, spherical raindrops collide with the ground then spray out into small pieces and disappear into thin air. His eyes shut down involuntarily, and everything turned black. But he could still hear the rain falling on the cottages and the palaces and the dead bodies and his school and Amanda's Park and the empty streets of Temblewood City. A thumping sound got louder and louder in his ears. And then he heard nothing.

Chapter Thirty-Six

The End of a Great Battle and the Mighty Plan

Outnumbered, outmatched, and leaderless, the Rebel Army had no hope of victory. Rebels fought for the sake of survival now, not glory.

Chief Lieutenant Agis Phoenix raised a hand and announced, "This is over. Drop your weapons and we shall take you as prisoners."

"Prisoners? Never!" a rebel cried, fighting till an arrow pierced his throat.

Most of the rebels didn't surrender, but a few dropped their weapons and raised their hands. The ones who didn't were shot with arrows and spears. The war was over.

Led by Castlers through the Golden Gate that had just been opened, the prisoners walked in line, manacled. The Castle had lost much during the war. Lieutenants Marquez and Charles had been killed, and Lieutenant Hamlet, the Black Owl, was missing in action. Besides that, more than half the army had been slaughtered. Canons and fireballs had heavily damaged the walls. The Golden Gate would have to be reconstructed. Most of the barracks and towers had been destroyed as well. Many who survived had suffered an injury, be it a chopped limb, a cut on the chest, or wounds elsewhere on their bodies.

Castlers didn't celebrate the victory. No warrior had left the battlefield without losing someone. In fact, the psychological injuries and post-traumatic effect of this war would last for years. But they'd won, and now they had the honor of proudly getting back home to their families.

The prisoners walked inside, but a wave of anxious woman, children, and some old men walked along the opposite side. They hurried to the bloodstained field, searching for their husbands and sons and fathers—or whatever remained of them. Misty rain fell on Oremanta, cleansing nature from the damage done by humans' greed.

Ravens landed on corpses, eager for flesh. Besides thrusting their beaks into open wounds, they dug into skulls and pulled out eyes. But they were cowards and flew off when wailing families approached. They'd go to another corpse that hadn't been found yet, or, luckily for the ravens, had no one to search for them. They did what their instincts told them to do.

One warrior towered over a dead body and then said in a fragile voice, "Rest in peace." He closed his dead brother's eyes.

"They haven't died for nothing," another warrior told him, squeezing his shoulder. They stared at all the dead bodies and rivers of blood. Along with the other warriors, they began to bury the corpses.

***

That night, Jennifer wrapped her hands around her knees and gazed at the gleaming moons' reflection on the springs below the empty Healing Squad Headquarter. Lieutenants Saneta and Hannah had taken all the girls somewhere to celebrate the great work they'd accomplished on the battlefield. Jennifer hadn't healed anyone, so she didn't want to be with them celebrating a false victory. Also, Leland had been severely injured, and she didn't want to leave him anymore. Oremanta's three moons gathered in the night sky, beautifully hung like three silver chandeliers.

"If I stay one more day with you," a voice behind her said, "I'll be just like you—silent and boring."

Sara giggled.

"You didn't go?" Jennifer asked.

"No," Sara replied, sitting beside Jennifer and sinking her legs into the hot water. "They said all lieutenants would be there. I hate official gatherings. They're boring."

Candles lined the round borders of the springs. Jennifer liked how the flames swung whenever air came, and no matter how strong the breeze was the flames would go back to where they'd been or fade out trying.

Internal strength is rare, and rare things are often beautiful. For the one with great strength can overcome one's own fears and obstacles; hence, foreign hordes of subtle negativities, often

disguised as mountains of evil enemies, are nothing but a tasteless
meal that needs more salt and a bit of pepper.

Jennifer smiled to herself and went to check on
Leland.

***

Leland was alone in the moonlit room. Many empty
beds lay beside him. He gazed at the starry night sky
through a small window. The thumping was still in his
ears. Leland repressed his urge to throw up. Whatever
had happened in the war was something he'd never
acknowledge. He'd done it for a purpose, and now that
it was over, everything related to it must be forgotten.
Leland swore to himself he wouldn't talk about that
tragedy to anyone.

"Hello," Jennifer said, entering the room with a
candle in her hand. Aelfgar followed her. Bandages
covered Leland from head to toe.

"How you doin', little one?" Aelfgar asked, taking a
seat beside him.

Leland darted his eyes toward the window, and a
fresh breeze hit his face.

"Look," Aelfgar said, "I know it's hard, but you
have to move on."

Leland eyed him, nodded, then turned his face
away again. Aelfgar had many bandages all over him
too.

"I'll take you to a place I really like," Aelfgar said.
"Can you walk?"

"I don't know."

"He can't," Jennifer chimed in. "He needs time."

"All right then," Aelfgar said, standing up. "Tell me if you feel pain." Aelfgar quickly picked up Leland and carefully placed him on his own back.

Leland wondered how Aelfgar could do that despite his wounds and cuts. Leland's body ached, but he didn't tell Aelfgar.

"Are you all right?" Jennifer asked Leland, who held Aelfgar's back like a frog.

"I am." Leland faked a smile as Aelfgar led them outside.

Thousands of stars shimmered across the sky. On a green hill away from the Castle's center, away from the people, away from everything, Aelfgar carefully put Leland's body on the grass. The sky appeared so close that Leland felt he could touch the stars.

Aelfgar towered over Leland and said, "You saved thousands. Be proud of yourself." He gave them his back and walked away. "Wait here. I'll be back in a moment."

Leland's heart sank like an anchor every time he remembered a scene from the fight. It would have been much better if Frank hadn't smiled before he died. A strange cocktail of emotions flowed within Leland's chest.

"I wonder if we'll ever get back home," Jennifer said. "Just ... how far are we from Earth?"

Leland paused then gave his best answer. "Who knows? Maybe we're really galaxies away."

"I've really missed you," Jennifer confessed, turning her face to his side.

"I missed you too. What have you been doing all this time?"

"Roaming around," she said. "And then I got to the Healing Squad. But I failed there too."

"You didn't fail. I'm sure."

Jennifer lay on her back and spread her hands and legs. "We made a big mistake on Earth. We shouldn't have pursued this."

"It was my fault. I belong here. An Oremantian soul must get back to Oremanta one day they say. But you're not supposed to be here."

"I belong where you belong."

"I don't know if this will help, but an old man once told me not all mistakes are bad. Some have that great power to make you realize you need to change, right now."

A streak of gray light crossed the sky, leaving a long, glowing trail that slowly faded into the nothingness of space. Leland loved shooting stars. He'd seen only a few back on Earth. He imagined this one crossing galaxies and settling permanently on Earth's sky as a souvenir from the universe.

"Maybe we shouldn't think too much of Earth," Leland said. "There are more things here to be solved."

"What do you mean?"

Aelfgar returned with three cups in his hands. The drinks were hot, and the wavy vapor smelled good.

"Where'd you get this from?" Jennifer asked, sipping.

"A farmer friend. I bet he didn't even know there was a war. All he does is farm, eat, sleep, and repeat," Aelfgar complained. "And he earns more than I do!"

"Oh, I need to tell you something," Jennifer said suddenly. She put her cup on the grass and tucked her hair behind her ears. "I'm not sure about this. I probably shouldn't even tell you now. You're not ready, and I don't want to disappoint you in case it isn't true."

"Speak, Jennifer. What's wrong?" Leland said.

"I saw a figure in the battlefield very similar to—" Jennifer paused for a while. "I don't want to raise our hopes up, but …"

"Yeah," Leland replied, looking away. "Dylan is alive."

"What's wrong?" Jennifer said, "Why aren't you happy?"

"Of course I'm happy," Leland stuttered. "I guess I have to tell you this. There's no way around it."

Aelfgar and Jennifer didn't comment.

"For me to obtain the Sword of Legends, Mora Gueja the swordsmith injected venom into my blood." Leland paused, bit his lips, then went on. "And for me to get the antidote, I have to bring him what he wants. If I don't, I'll be dead in a month."

"We won the war, Leland," Aelfgar said calmly. "Do you think it's hard for us to give him what he wants? A month is a pretty long time. Don't worry. We'll do whatever it takes."

"What he wants is something I can't afford," Leland said. "I can't kill my best friend. I can't kill Dylan."

"What?" Jennifer roared in disbelief.

***

In the far north of Oremanta, in the Valley of Crimson—an area inhabited by tri-horned beasts, deadly snakes, and red hyenas—a hooded man entered a cave and shook the rain off his cloak. The man lit a candle within the dark cave and followed a descending path. On a metal throne at the far end of the cave, in a spacious underground place, a king sat with crossed legs. Lava waves collided in the volcano pit behind the king and sent burning chunks flying into the air. The cloaked man blew out the candle and bowed to the king. Hamlet, the Black Owl, stood beside the king's throne.

"You took too long," the king said. "Come here. Get closer."

The cloaked man bowed again, then inched closer to the king. He took off his cloak and then threw it at the Black Owl.

"It's wet and dirty," the man said. "Make sure it gets clean."

"Yes, my lord," the Black Owl replied.

"Hold on," the man ordered the Black Owl. "I know what you did. Why have you strayed from the plan?"

"I had to, my lord. The Rebels changed their plans. At the start, they wanted to attack from three sides, but that was an ambush. The three divided armies reunited into one, except for Frank Hopegone, who came alone from the south gate, and every gate was secured with guards. I couldn't open the gate without killing them off."

"Did anyone notice you?" the man asked.

"No, my lord. Not even Frank knew that I allowed him in. With that, we succeeded in creating confusion and maximizing casualties."

"Good," the man said. "Now go and clean the cloak."

"Yes, my lord," replied the Black Owl submissively.

The man kneeled for the king and then asked, "May I check it, your majesty?"

The king chuckled, then nodded.

The man walked past the volcano pit, through a doorway, and into a large room filled with the corpses of humans and beasts. An evil grin forced itself upon the man's face. He slammed the door closed and returned to the king.

"Tell me," the king said, "what do you think?"

"We're close, your majesty," the man said. "Both Rebels and Castlers lost much in this war. We're the strongest in Oremanta now. Our plan is working. With the corpses we've obtained from this war and the corpses we've amassed over the years, we're closer than ever."

"You know very well I don't like mistakes," the king informed, shifting his eyes to the volcano and then back at the man. "Be careful."

"I know that very well, your majesty," the man replied. He took off his eyeglasses and then said with disgust, "I've gotten so used to these things. Earthlings are stupid." He threw his eyeglasses on the ground and then crushed them with his muddy boots.

"I haven't laughed for a pretty long time," the king said, his legs still crossed. "Tell me. What did Earthlings call you?"

"Dylan, your majesty."

ACKNOWLEDGMENTS

This story has fragments of things that happened to me, and around me, in the five years I spent writing it, melting surreptitiously into the corners of the world of Oremanta and the characters inside it. Writing this story hasn't been less tough than being a medical student (but at least it was more enjoyable). And they both shared one thing in common—lots and lots of coffee.

This is to my mother, who gave me a box full of old novels and introduced me to the world of words when I was only seven. I will never forget how much you support me. This is to my father, and my siblings, Lulu, Nora, and Mohammed, who, at times, were more excited about the book than I ever was.

I would like to thank my badass editors: J. McCoy (who read the first manuscript, a thing you don't ever want to read) and B. Atwood. They taught me the rules of writing—to show and not to tell, to avoid head jumping, and the different types of third person POV, among many other things.

Special thanks to all my beta readers (M.Collins, S.Terry, A.Toug, T.Madi, Mr.Midhat, S.Almutairi) for sticking with me for so long, even when I thought this book would *never* get published. You guys rock.

To Dane, the gifted artist who created my cover— thank you for your patience.

Huge thanks in advance to everyone who is going to read NOSTALGIC RAIN and dive into its world—you are my fuel.

They say having a baby is the best feeling in the world. I'm really having the best feeling in the world. But it's not over yet. I've just stepped into a new territory in life. And I have more to deliver, so let's just see what the future will bring.

One more thing: If you enjoy this story, kindly leave a review on Amazon and/or Goodreads.

Follow me on twitter at:

@NostalgicRainGA

@Altabtabaii

Visit www.NostalgicRain.com for updates.

Regards, A.S. Altabtabai